FIVE MINUTES FROM CHAOS

A hilarious satire of academia, love, and modern life

A Novel by

William Missouri DOWNS

Black Rose Writing | Texas

The author grants the final approval for this literary material.

First printing

ISBN: 978-1-68513-473-0
PUBLISHED BY BLACK ROSE WRITING
www.blackrosewriting.com

Printed in the United States of America
Suggested Retail Price (SRP) $21.95

Five Minutes from Chaos is printed in Minion Pro

*As a planet-friendly publisher, Black Rose Writing does its best to eliminate unnecessary waste to reduce paper usage and energy costs, while never compromising the reading experience. As a result, the final word count vs. page count may not meet common expectations.

Praise for

Five Minutes from Chaos

"This novel made me realize that I was wrong; God isn't dead, he just lacks a sense of humor."
–Friedrich Nietzsche

"This novel is a wonderful lesson on how to live in the age of post-happiness. I wish it had been published a hundred years ago before I wrote all that depressing crap."
–Franz Kafka

"Having problems with the chaos of modern life? I did. If only *Catch 22*, *White Noise,* and *Five Minutes from Chaos* had existed in my day; I wouldn't have been so damned depressed."
–Emily Dickinson

For Lucy

Special Thanks To

Tyler Fall
Patricia McLaughlin
Sean Stone
Lisa Konoplisky
Tony Dobrowolski
Lew Hunter
Richard Walter
Lanford Wilson
&
Milan Stitt

Five Minutes From Chaos

Augie Omega

(Part One)

1

"It's all unraveling, rage is everywhere, and the apocalypse is live streaming!" jumping girl said as she leaned out, tempting gravity. "We all live five minutes from chaos!"

"You think you got problems," I said, standing beside her on the bookshelf-wide ledge, "I'm a philosophy professor."

"Oh my God, you do know the humanities are dying?" she said. "I thought my life was dumb. Yours is much worse!"

Sirens blared six stories below as the rubbernecking mob swarmed the police barricades. Nearby, the campus fire department struggled with a still-puckered jump cushion. They couldn't inflate it because an illegally parked cherry red BMW convertible blocked their way.

"Want to know the truth about life today?" jumper whispered.

"Sure, not doing anything."

"We don't live in the postmodern age."

"No?"

"We live in the age of post-happiness."

Minutes before, I was doing what I did every Saturday night, rummaging in the orchard of books on the top floor of the deserted library, when I heard the post-game football crowd chanting, "We want Felice!" Then the elevator opened, and she entered my quiet, bookish life. Barely twenty, she wore a cheerleading uniform with a short, pleated skirt and ribbons in her long, curlicue hair. A silver stud pierced her slightly crooked nose. Her intense peacock blue eyes locked on me for half a sec before she mic-dropped her T-shirt cannon and coolly said, "I will no longer tolerate absurdity." Then she opened the window and crawled out. Without thinking, I followed. My plan? I'd overcome vertigo, save her, and impress the tenure committee. But once on the high ledge, I couldn't move - my knees had become as soft as warm Vaseline, my brain stem numb.

"Know what I need right now?" she said.

"To work on your coping skills?"

"The Bible. My favorite quote is, 'When you stare into the abyss, the abyss stares back at you.'"

"I hate to correct you at a time like this," I said as I gripped the bricks behind me with my sweaty fingernails, "but that's not the Bible. That's Nietzsche."

"No, Nietzsche is the one who said, 'You are what you eat.'"

"No, that was Julia Child. Nietzsche said, 'God is dead, and we've killed him.'"

"You do know this is about me right now?" she insisted. "I'm the jumper, so if I say it's the Bible, dammit, it's the Bible!"

Ping! We both flinched.

"Yours or mine?"

"Mine," I said.

"Answer it."

I fumbled for my cracked iPhone. It was a text:

> Dr. Neb,
>
> It's come to my attention that you are currently present at the unfortunate post-game incident regarding Felice Wolinski, sophomore communications major, head cheerleader, and president of Kappa Delta.
>
> Please note, you're allowed to help anxiety-challenged students only if you've taken the university's five-part deep-dive stress abatement training webinar.
>
> Please provide evidence you've done so.

> Be Happy,
>
> Dr. Jerry Loudie
> Campus Mental Health Engagement Officer
> Mental Health Solutions Center

Below, in the frenzied crowd, the rest of the cheerleading squad used their pom-poms to direct the stalled post-game traffic. Then the marching band paraded in—one hundred and fifty strong, their hat-topping ostrich plumes dancing with the sousaphones' silvery bells. With three tweets, the school's fight song "Go Wild Hogs Win" fired up. They must've thought it was a publicity stunt.

"What set you off?" I said, attempting to buy time. "Test anxiety? Grade troubles?"

My question sparked a nerve, and she cried. "My problems began in preschool. I was part of a delayed gratification marshmallow test."

"Is that the one where they tell you that you can have one marshmallow now or two if you wait five minutes?"

"This white-coated researcher placed a creamy confectionery within my reach, started a clock, and left."

"Did you make it five minutes?"

"He never came back."

"What do you mean?"

"He must've got distracted or had an important phone call because he forgot about me," she sniffed. "Three hours later, the night janitor came in to turn off the lights and found me. By then, I was cold, lonely, and the marshmallow dry."

"Tell ya what, let's climb back in the window, go over to the Stop & Shop, and I'll buy you a nice big bag of marshmallows."

"I still remember the researcher's name–Augie Omega."

"Augie what?"

"Omega!"

Just then, the Channel Six news copter hit us with its buffering wash as it arched over the library's gothic pillars, banked, and blinded us with its spotlight. Oh, this was going to be good. What's the point of heroic masculinity if there are no witnesses? I know, terrible thought, but deep down, we all want to believe something more significant than our puny selves is watching us, like the almighty creator of the universe, or better yet, the chair of the tenure review committee.

Jumper's breath staggered as her eyes fixed on the bell tower across the leafy quad, "That's the problem," her voice went soft, "bell towers used to be works of art, but today you can't look at one without wondering if…" her voice trailed off.

"If?"

"If there's a gunman inside. Admit it, when you see a bell tower, you don't see beauty or architecture but a sniper's nest."

"Rather disturbing."

"But you've thought it."

"Well, I suppose."

"That's because we live in the age of post-happiness, and it changes us at a metabolic level."

"You know, there's a self-checkout Mental Health Solutions kiosk in the Student Union," I said. "Why don't we go there and see if we can find a pamphlet that might be apropos of the situation."

"I don't need a damn pamphlet. I need God!" she shouted. "Where the hell is God?"

"Hello, I'm here!" a voice echoed. And for a moment, I thought perhaps it was God.

"Yes!" I shouted, looking up, trying to locate the voice. "Where are you?"

"Down here!"

Below, in the carnival of gawking faces and streetlights, I found a uniformed bear of a man waving from the roof of a squad car. I couldn't make out his face, only the megaphone. "My name is Lieutenant Joe Patroni, and I'm with the campus police. I am a T.C.I.O., a Trained Crisis Incident Officer. My certification number is 49250489. How are we doing tonight?"

"Not good," I shouted back.

"First, I need to get acquainted with the situation. Are you both jumping or just one?"

"Just the cheerleader."

"Are you a trained T.C.I.O., and if so, what is your certification number?"

"I'm not certified!"

"Do you have any experience with mental health crisis management?"

"None whatsoever."

"Then why are you doing this?"

"To get tenure, I mean, being a good Samaritan."

"Do you know what triggered her?"

"Not sure. We were discussing Nietzsche."

"It's not recommended that you bring up Nietzsche at a time like this! If you had T.C.I.O. training, you'd know that!"

Ping!

"Yours or mine?" jumping girl said.

"Mine."

"Answer it. Now!"

It was an email.

> Dear Students, Faculty, and Staff,
>
> If you're suffering from depression, joylessness, inadequacy, anxiety, emptiness, or despair because of tonight's season-opening loss to BYU, please know that tomorrow, near the foosball tables in the student union, Campus Mental Health volunteers will be handing out free squeeze balls from noon to two.
>
> Limit one. While quantities last.
>
> Be Happy,
>
> Dr. Jerry Loudie
> Senior Campus Mental Health Engagement Officer
> Mental Health Solutions Center

PS: This offer does not apply to faculty.

"Sir, this is an inappropriate time to check your messages," boomed the bullhorn.

"Sorry, she asked me to do it. I'm not really into my phone."

"Are you in a relationship?"

"Who?"

"You and the bi-polar cheerleader?"

"What? No," I shouted. "We just met five minutes ago."

"What can you tell me about her? Need specifics."

"Ah… Well… She likes marshmallows, and she believes we live in the age of post-happiness."

"And is the fact that the dorm cafeteria ran out of marshmallows this afternoon what triggered her?"

"From what I can figure!"

"If we get her some marshmallows, will she come down?"

"Perhaps."

"To be effective, I need information. What happened?"

"Well, I was in the library reading a book by Viktor Frankl!" I hollered.

"Who?"

"Viktor Frankl. He's a philosopher who survived the Holocaust."

"Sir, if we don't want you bringing up Nietzsche at a time like this, how do you think we feel about the Holocaust?"

"I'm just saying I was in the stacks, and I found Frankl's book, *Man's Search for Meaning*, when she walked in, opened the window, stepped out, and I panicked."

"Why?"

"I don't know. Maybe because my mother never told me she loved me, and my father left when I was seven."

"Not you! Her! Why did *she* go out the window?"

"Oh, other than the marshmallow thing, she didn't say!"

"Young lady!" the bullhorn cracked. "It's the season opener. Thousands of people are here. Students, parents, alums, and let's not forget, prospective students. For them, this, and our 54 to 0 loss to BYU, is not a good introduction to college life!"

"Read this," jumper murmured as she tossed me a crumpled wad of paper."

"She'd like to make a statement," and I unfolded the tight note and read to the throngs below, "'Life is nothing more than the dissonant lyrics of despair, the bankrupt chronicles of disillusionment, and unfulfilled delayed gratification!'"

"Is she a philosophy major?" boomed the megaphone.

"No, I think she's communications!" I shouted back.

"Oh God, that's much worse," the bullhorn said to some assistant, forgetting to take his finger off the mic. "Give me a second. The school's lawyers just arrived!"

During the pause, I studied jumping girl. How could such deep sadness come so soon in life? Then it hit me. Her crooked nose, it was the butterfly effect. It was the reason the handsome quarterback dumped her, leaving her with feelings of inadequacy, which is why she pledged Kappa Delta rather than Kappa Kappa Gamma.

"Good news!" the bullhorn barked, "We just got word that the Stop & Shop is sending over several large bags of Jet-Puffed marshmallows! Which would she prefer, colored minis or white jumbos?"

"I don't give a shit," jumping girl whispered.

"She doesn't give a shit," I shouted.

"When they arrive, how should we get them up to you?"

"I'll meet you at the window!"

"She's barricaded the doors and turned off the elevators!"

"In that case, could you throw them up?"

"Six stories? Too far!"

"How about a slingshot?"

"Good idea. Show of hands! Who in the crowd has a slingshot?"

Ping!

"Mine or yours?"

"Yours."

Without a care for survival, she retrieved her iPhone from her bra strap and thumbed. Then, her crooked nostrils flared with delight as she recklessly bounced on her tippy toes, "Success! Two hundred thousand are watching my podcast! I'm going live." Selfie-ing herself, she began a well-rehearsed presentation. "Fellow students here on campus and all around this screwed-up world, zero hour has arrived! It's time you know college football is nothing more than a historic leftover pulled from the rubble of the Roman games! And fans are shallow barbarians trying to alleviate their chronic boredom!"

Boos from the crowd. Most students were now watching her on their phones while the firefighters inflated the jump cushion beside the BMW convertible. More desperate shouts and pointing. Firefighters love to point.

"Our educational institutions are Ponzi schemes that create graduates who are disappointed, dour, docile, and wasted!"

"Yeah, wasted!" some frat bros yelled from the crowd, "Go, girl!"

"We are short-lived, gig-economy droids who are desperately trying to assemble some flat-packed IKEA with impossible-to-follow instructions while anxiously praying to some vast unknown-unknown! No wonder the Bible says, 'Why should any young person be made to study for a future when no one is doing enough to save that future?'"

"I hate to interrupt," I interrupted, "but that's not the Bible. That's Greta Thunberg."

"Greta who?"

"Thunberg, the climate activist."

"No, it's not. It's God. I found it in my Bible."

"Look, I know what I'm talking about. I use that quote in my Existentialism 101 class."

"Shut up! I'm live streaming!" she shrieked, which made her nose bow even more to the left. What the hell was wrong with me? Why was I so fixated on her nose? It wasn't like a Picasso nose. It was just a touch off. I'll bet her mother made her look slightly to the right in her childhood portraits to compensate.

"I've lost my country! My politics! The college fight songs I once proudly sang are now no more inspiring than silly commercial jingles! We're trapped in a Nietzschean hellish tragedy, pushing a rock up and down for no reason!"

"Sorry to interrupt again, but that would be 'Sisyphean hellish tragedy,' not 'Nietzschean.' That is if you're referring to Zeus punishing Sisyphus by making him roll a boulder up a hill for eternity."

"What the hell is wrong with you?"

"I might be a tad A.D.D."

"Shut Up! Shut Up! Shut Up!" Silence. She caught her breath. "And so, it's time. I must leave this earth to prove I will no longer tolerate absurdism. Ready! Set!"

"Wait!" I yelled. She jumped, not off the ledge but in her skin, launching her pink bedazzled iPhone. It arced in the white shaft of the helicopter's spotlight, buoyant for a sec before it plummeted like an actor in a Spiderman musical. In convulsive silence, we waited for the inevitable. Then, crack, as it smithereened on the roof of the fire truck.

"What have you done?" she screeched. "You ruined me!"

"It's only an iPhone. There are lots of others."

"I had this great line I was going to say on the way down. Crap! I'm jumping anyway!"

"Please Don't!"

"Why not?"

"Cause, cause, cause…" I had nothing.

"Give me one good reason!"

"Good news," the bullhorn announced, "the marshmallows have arrived!" which brought a cheer from the crowd. Then abruptly, it hit me - the answer was right in my hand - Viktor Frankl's book, which I was still holding. In it, he wrote you can't evoke happiness, you have to do something to cause it, just as when you want to make someone laugh, you've got to tell a joke. To relieve her sadness, I had to be funny.

"These two psychiatrists are driving back into the city after Thanksgiving," I said.

"What the hell are you doing?"

"Telling a joke."

"Why?"

"You said we live in the post-happiness age. I'm going to prove you wrong."

Boing! A marshmallow bounded up from below, barely reaching the window ledge before being pulled back by gravity.

"Are the psychiatrists in your joke Jewish?" she said.

"Perhaps. Don't know."

"Are you Jewish?"

"No."

"Only Jews are allowed to tell jokes about Jews."

"Okay, these two non-Jewish psychiatrists are driving back into the city."

"Why do they have to be psychiatrists? Psychiatry is a noble profession."

"I have no doubt you know that, but it's a Freud joke, so the rules of comedy state it has to be about psychiatrists."

Boing! A second marshmallow arched at knee level before losing orbit and falling back to earth.

"Nor should any joke make fun of ethnicity or gender."

"Yes, I know. I only tell woke jokes."

"Nor should they make fun of disability or sexual orientation!"

"These two non-specific psychiatrists - they could be any race, religion, or ethnicity—"

"Or physicality or sexual orientation?"

"That too - are driving back into the city when—

"Automobiles cause carbon dioxide, which ruins the stratosphere."

"Are driving in an electric vehicle—"

"E.V.s cause greenhouse emissions during their manufacturing."

"These two non-specifics are taking public transportation when one turns to the other and says, "I made a terrible Freudian slip at my mother's house."

Boing! The next marshmallow hit my knee, but I wasn't quick enough to catch it.

"Is this joke going to trigger me?"

"No more than you already are."

"I don't like being triggered."

"Please hear me out. One psychiatrist turns to the other and says,

'During dinner, I meant to say, Mom, would you be so kind as to pass me your delicious *hot cross buns*?'"

"Sounds like a sick sexual reference."

"It does, but it isn't. It's a joke about a man who hates his mother."

Boing! The next small white missile danced across the ledge before jumping into space.

"Mothers are underappreciated. You shouldn't make fun of them!"

"It's just a harmless joke."

"Jokes are used to camouflage prejudice and categorize people!"

"This one doesn't."

"Comedy is about the powerful making fun of the weak!"

"Some jokes do, not this one!"

"Laughter is inhumane because someone is always the butt of the joke!"

"Oh, for God's sake!" I blurted. "It's not like I'm going to make fun of your crooked nose!"

The blank space above is intentional, for no words in any language could express how much I wish I hadn't said that. The philosopher Thomas Hobbes thought humor was a method to tear down and mock. Freud believed it was the release of deeply hidden sexual tensions that bypass internal censors. Immanuel Kant thought we used humor to point out contradiction and absurdity. In my case, Kant got it right. I could see my reckless blunder stumble over the blank page between us. Then it breached her soul. I got out, "I meant to say…" And I tried to come up with a word that rhymed with nose. Elbows. Juxtapose. But all I said was, "You're wrong. There's no sniper in the bell tower. It's been locked for decades!"

"Young lady," the bullhorn echoed from below, "the university lawyers want you to know that if this is a publicity stunt, you could be liable for costs!"

"What the hell am I promoting?" she yelled down to the police.

"Jet-Puffed marshmallows."

Her eyes narrowed, and she calmly said, "Find Augie Omega. Stop him before he screws up the whole world." And she took one last look at the bell tower and added, "Once you know life is absurd, all you see is absurdities." She leaned out too far. "Once you look, you can't unlook."

Then, pom-poms wide, she telescoped headfirst towards the partially inflated target. The crowd gasped. I leaned right, attempting to steer her plummet toward the bullseye. And she was going to make it. But then some subtle aerodynamic force veered her gently to the left, towards the soft white marshmallow top of the BMW convertible.

Up to that point in my life, it was my fate to spend my nights in scholarly quarantine and my days lecturing about Plato and Aristotle to nineteen-year-olds who only had a vague sense of who the Beatles were. But then Felice Wolinski, sophomore communications major, walked into my cloistered life, and I realized I, like her, like you, live just five minutes from chaos.

2

To deal with the homecoming tragedy, the administration activated the 24-hour "emotional hygiene" hotline. A "scream tent" was placed in front of the classroom building, and the Mental Health Solutions Center started taking reservations for puppy play dates and kitten cuddle time. In addition, the administration announced that the coin-operated womb-chairs in the student union would be free for the next twenty-four hours. And for the first time, traumatized students were allowed to tape eulogies to the orange steel I-beam modern art sculpture entitled "Reflections of Echoes" that stood in front of the old Arts and Science bell tower. A sign hung from the haphazard maze of girders warned grievers to use only painter's tape to attach their obits because Scotch brand would harm the finish.

Monday morning, I canceled class and took a bus to Clint's Custom Car Care, where the pit mechanic looked at the collapsed roof of my cherry red BMW convertible, gave me a chew-filled cankerous smile and said in vocal fry, "What you got there is an Augie Omega."

"Excuse me?"

"An Augie Omega. You never heard that expression?"

"No."

"In other words, one screwed up human made disaster," he said as he held up a cigarette, his hand tattooed with Jesus holding a cigarette. Behind him, a crusty radio scratched out Fox News.

"My car is completely totaled, right?" I asked.

"Not at all. All's you need is a new driver seat, steering wheel, gear shift, carpeting, convertible top, and a few parts in the instrument panel. According to your insurance, that don't count as totaled."

Ping!

> Dr. Neb,
>
> I just received word that a student has filed an anonymous complaint against you for telling a joke last week in class. As you know, jokes violate University Regulation #384-1.
>
> Best,
>
> Dean Frank Gacy, PhD
> Arts & Sciences

"Want your fancy car fixed or not?"

"So sorry, I gotta answer this," I said as I shot back a response. The problem was, I didn't have the slightest clue of which of my occasional in-class witticisms triggered the complaint. All I knew was that in the current anti-comedy climate on college campuses, this was not a battle someone dwelling in the steerage of the tenure caste system could win. So, I quickly thumb-typed a Maoist confessional, showing I was open to reeducation.

> Dean Gacy,
>
> I sincerely apologize for my sexist, offensive, juvenile, and/or inappropriate joke. I completely acknowledge that my attempt at humor contained egregious levels of misogynistic ignorance and/or Western exceptionalism.
>
> I will attend any training webinars you recommend and will interrogate my masculinity. I hope we can make this a teachable moment.
>
> Sincerely,

> Charlie
>
> Dr. Charles Neb
> Assistant Professor
> Philosophy Department

"Wait," the mechanic said, "is this the BMW I saw on Channel Six News?"

"Ah… Yeah."

"And the cheerleader went right through the roof. Holy smokes."

Ping!

> Dr. Neb,
>
> Until an Academic Ascertainment (A.A.) hearing can be scheduled, you are relieved of teaching duties. Your students will be reassigned to different sections.
>
> This is a significant charge and may well result in your dismissal.
>
> Best,
>
> Dean Frank Gacy, PhD
> Arts & Sciences

"What the hell is an Academic Ascertainment hearing?" I wondered out loud.

"You okay?" The mechanic must've seen the life force slipping from me. "Need water, a Budweiser?"

"No, I'm fine," I lied.

"So, what are we doing about your convertible?"

"I really don't want it," I said, trying to stay focused.

"Then sell it."

"Who would buy it?"

"I will."

"What would you do with it?

"Fix it, resell it."

"But there are philosophical and moral issues here."

"How so?"

"Shouldn't you tell the new owner about the car's dubious history? And yet, if you do, wouldn't the knowledge spoil their top-down enjoyment? Maybe by not telling them, you'd be doing them a favor. Hypothetical: What if we could empirically prove God *doesn't* exist? That we are, in fact, completely alone in a cold, dark, threadbare universe. What good would it do? Wouldn't it be best not to know? Not to look?"

"Wanna sell it or not?"

"It's only a month old. If I sell it, I'll lose my shirt."

Ping! I checked my phone.

> Dr. Neb,
>
> If you tender your resignation forthwith, you will receive two months' pay without benefits. I highly recommend you accept this generous offer.
>
> Best,
>
> Dean Frank Gacy, PhD
> Arts & Sciences

"Holy shit," I said as I quickly typed an answer—my thumbs stumbling over the keys.

> Dean Gacy,
>
> Would you be so kind as to tell me what joke I told? I would like to learn from my mistake.

Sincerely,

Charlie

Dr. Charles Neb
Assistant Professor
Philosophy Department

PS I just made a sizable PayPal donation to the campus
chapter of #metoo

"You know spending lots of time on your phone causes skepticism and
eye cancer," the mechanic said as I tensely waited for my iPhone to ping. "I
took those damn phones away from my kids because they forgot how to
talk."

Ping!

Dr. Neb,

I have no idea what the joke was. It doesn't matter.

The scheduling committee has set your Academic
Ascertainment (A.A.) hearing for a week from Monday at
8am—Old A&S. Room #151.

Best,

Dean Frank Gacy, PhD
Arts & Sciences

PS If I were you, I'd take the University's 32-part,
professionally produced, educational webinar

"Objectification & You" before the hearing.

PPS There is no campus chapter of #metoo.

I felt the floor slip away. I staggered and tried to breathe, but my lungs were stuck to my ribs. Seeing this, the mechanic said, "What happened? Someone die?"

"Yes. Me."

Ping!

Campus-Wide Scarlet & Brown Alert,

The Wild Springs Fire is now 20 miles from campus. There is no need for concern. Fire crews are containing it.

The smoke you smell is actually coming from a fire in British Columbia mixing with smoke from Siberia.

Safety First,

Lieutenant Joe Patroni
University Police

PS If you are suffering from eco-anxiety, eco-phobia, eco-rage, or just feelings of planetary gloom, please know the Mental Health Solutions Center has installed a new self-checkout kiosk in the lobby of the Rupert Murdoch Life Sciences Building.

Back on campus, I sat on "Reflections of Echoes." As I sucked on a double shot of cheap tequila mixed in a bottle of Pedialyte, my mind swirled with questions: What joke did I tell that caused the anonymous complaint? Who is Augie Omega? How could cheerleader Felice Wolinski, Sophomore communications major, get the quotes from the Bible so wrong? How do you find comedy in the age of post-happiness? But most importantly, once you know that life is absurd, can you see it any other way? Once you look, can you unlook?

The bell tower rang noon, and it knocked me back to childhood and my first experience with absurdism, Tchaikovsky's *The Nutcracker*. I was seven, and my father, at least the one I thought was my father, unexpectedly showed for Christmas. I heard a thunderous Harley enter the row house mobile home park and knew it was him. He claimed he'd landed a job at NASA and was taking us away from this "Midwest armpit" to sunny Florida. After an hour of arguing with my mother, followed by make-up sex, he came from the bedroom, zipping his shaggy chest into his chunky rawhide jacket that smelled of burned oil. He was only forty, but cheap gin, Marlboros, and an endless diet of Taco Bell had swollen his liver and grayed his gruff horseshoe mustache. He put my spindly seven-year-old self on his knee, popped open a beer, and said, "Tell me a joke."

"How does my Daddy treat me like a God?" I said. "Because he ignores me except when he needs something." He laughed so hard I thought his corrugated skin would pop a rivet. Then he broke into tears. It took little for my biker father to cry. Rom-coms were a trigger, the final scene of Charlie Chaplin's *City Lights* another. At his core, he was a clueless romantic who believed that just around the next bend, he'd find virtuous maidens, infinite blue skies, and sacred texts with straightforward answers to every question humans could ask. He was inconsolable when he told me about the day NASA lost contact with Pioneer 10, the first human-made object to leave the Solar System. Weeping, he said, it was headed in the direction of a star named Aldebaran and that it'd make it there in two million years, give or take.

To make up for his being "missin' in action," he took me to a production of *The Nutcracker*. We were the only ones who pulled up on an Easy Rider chopper with a black "POW" flag. Outside the theatre, the well-groomed patrons flaunted their disdain for his skull tattoos, chaps, and "Ride Hard or Die" jacket. In defiance, he placed his authentic World War One German biker helmet on my soft head and drunkenly penciled a Charlie Chaplin mustache on my upper lip with a black Sharpie. As the ticket taker pulled back in disgust, my dad whispered, "Don't mind him, boy. He's just jealous of our freedom."

At the end of act one, as the saltshaker snowflakes peppered the stage and the starry-eyed prince swept the blissful ballerina off her tippytoes, my father began to cry–deep, fat, biker tears. They turned into loud sobs as the prince gently cupped the ballerina's wafer-thin waist, and she swirled into a picture-perfect arabesque. As the audience shhhed my father, on stage, the prince edged his graceful hand away as if he had just placed the final ace atop a long-legged house of cards. The slightest wisp would've toppled her. Yet she held. Three seconds. Four. At that moment, I knew I wanted to grow up to be a dancer, or an actor, or an astronaut, or maybe an actor/dancer who was a part-time astronaut. Any profession that would allow me to kill the spirit of gravity.

But then I thought a ballerina parked on her big toe upon a glazed bed of slippery white plastic was just a disaster waiting to happen. Maybe not tonight or tomorrow, but at some point, somewhere, there was going to be a Sugar-Plum-Fairy-Space Shuttle-type debacle. I became aware of my father's quivering, cuticles-chewed hands as he leaned over and whispered, his breath cut with Jägermeister and Parkinson's, "I'm sorry to tell you, boy, but your mother and I are no longer at the same emotional bandwidth. Our love is just a waste of cosmic space, so I'm leaving tonight and not comin' back. I'm telling you this here because I want you to know there's still beauty in the world."

Just then, an immense clump of fake snow fell from the flies and whacked the ballerina in her silver, sequined eyes. Temporarily blinded, her gyros wobbled, and she crossed the narrow gap between graceful and awkward. The prince tried to catch her but missed, and she slipped and bumbled over the snow-covered stage. For a moment, it looked as if she'd recover, and if she'd had three inches more stage to work with, she would've, but instead, she careened headfirst into the orchestra pit. The violins and cellos squeaked to a stop. A hushed gasp escaped from the audience as they blinked in disbelief. Then the Wooden Soldiers rushed to the edge, and from their shock, we knew it wasn't good.

"Is there a doctor in the house?" the Mouse King squeaked.

From the darkness, a woman shouted, "I'm a doctor!" And this smartly dressed patron of the arts darted down the aisle and leaped the railing that corralled the orchestra. Lacking dance training, she mistimed her jump and crashed headfirst into the trumpet section. A second cry came from the pit. "Is there another doctor? We need two!" And then a voice as thin as new ice rose from the strings section, "My legs, I can't feel my legs." It was the ballerina. I bolted towards the stage. My biker dad shouted, "Don't look!"

There are those who look and those who don't. The ones who don't are smarter because they know once you look, you can never unlook. There's no way a seven-year-old can unsee a sweaty ballerina's ruined leg bent back under her cracked hip, her eyes cut with shaved plastic, surrounded by a stunned blizzard of tuxedoed tie-and-tail musicians. And once you hear, you cannot unhear the ungraceful whimper, "My career. My career."

I looked down on her from the railing, she up from the floor scattered with fallen instruments and sheet music. What a sight I must've been, this scrap of a kid sporting a Charlie Chaplin mustache and an oversized World War One helmet with a spike on top. And then the most mind-blowing thing happened. Through her misery and tears, she laughed. It started as a low ironic chuckle which grew into an honest absurd guffaw.

"She's in shock!" shouted an oboe player.

At that second, gripping the railing, I knew I'd found my soulmate. Sure, there was an age difference, but we could work it out. Over twenty years later, as I sat on the college quad, I was still in love with her, still picturing our future together. Upon her release from the hospital, I'd wheelchair her to her weekly physical therapy sessions. After, we'd go home and make pasta with shiitake mushrooms and crushed garlic. Then sip organic wine, laugh about the absurdity of the world, go to bed, and under the sheets have a long intellectual conversation about the Danish philosopher Kierkegaard. It was Kierkegaard who wrote that contradiction is what makes us laugh. And humans are a massive contradiction, for we can build a spacecraft that can leave the Solar System, yet we suffer, as Edward Gibbon said, from the "crimes, follies, and misfortunes" of fake snow.

"Will you marry me?" my seven-year-old self wept from the railing. She squinted as if to see and not hear my words. And then, she smiled like a shattered angel and said, "Yes, little boy, I'd love to marry you." I swear, all these years later, I wasn't dreaming. She said yes.

My dad swooped me off the rail, and as the theatre's aisles filled with gurneys and medics, he hustled me through a side door, and we choppered off. With my tiny arms glued to his thick leather neck and a cold rush of air drying my tears, we thundered to Big Dipper Ice Cream, where he bought me a banana split made of very berry cherry, gung-ho cookie dough, and topnotch butterscotch. And we sat in the shivering cold on a sagging picnic table in the empty parking lot under a star-cluster of lonely neon that stood against the night like a miniature temple. Even though my hands and tongue were frozen, I took my time eating. After a pause that lasted all the way to the banana, he said, "I want you to do something for me, boy."

"Sure, daddy, anything."

"I live my life without a job, phone, or home, so while I'm away, I want you to send me postcards with jokes. That way, I'll know you're doing okay."

"How will I know where to send them?"

"I'll post you a card telling you where my next stop will be. I'll include latitude and longitude, so you'll know exactly where in the world I am. You send it there in care of general delivery. You got that?"

"Yes."

"And on my card, I'll tell you what it's like wherever the hell I am. Deal?"

"Deal."

He put his sunbaked arm on my shoulder, pulled me close, took a big pink lick of his bubblegum dream ice cream and said, "There's something you need to know, boy. Most of us enter this world screamin' and kickin' as if we know from the start it's going to be a crap-fest. But you were different. Instead of being startled by existence, you were born laughing. You came into this world laughin' your fool head off. It freaked out the doctors. And your mother. And me. It was as if God told you the funniest joke ever just before you came out." And he looked up at the cone of winter stars and drifted, "Wonder what the punch line was."

Then he dropped me back at my mother's mobile home and gave me my Christmas gift: a shabby, Salvation Army-bought copy of Carl Sagan's *The*

Pale Blue Dot. An astronomy book inspired by the photo the spaceship Voyager took of the Earth before it left the solar system. In the picture, taken four billion miles away, Earth is a tiny 0.12 pixels point of light. Inside the book's cover, he'd written, "Once you see a ballerina fall, you'll always see falling ballerinas. So don't look."

"But I already looked," I said.

"Then you gotta kill the spirit of gravity with a good joke," he said just before he choppered off. And I never saw him again.

Ever since that night, I've been unable to lose myself completely in a performance, or a church service, or a poem. During Beethoven's 9th, as the chorus sings about the unity of all humankind, I'll inevitably check my phone at least five times to ensure it's off. When I try to lose myself in the splendid beauty of a flowering forest, I always know exactly how to get back to the car. And no matter what argument is given for the existence of God, I know by heart a dozen equally convincing counterarguments.

My father's postcards arrived pretty regularly after that. On each, he told me about the part of the country he was in, including latitude and longitude. And I wrote back no matter how lonely or how often I scratched at my wrists with safety pins.

> To Charlie Neb Senior,
> General Delivery
> Sturgis Motorcycle Rally, South Dakota
>
> What do Alexander the Great, and Winnie the Pooh have in common? The same middle name.
>
> Little Charlie

But after a year, his postcards became sporadic–Chattanooga (35.0458° N, 85.3094° W), Nashville (36.1627° N, 86.7816° W), Niagara Falls (43.0962° N, 79.0377° W). The last one I got had a picture of a cow on the front. On the back, he wrote he was lost near the town of Omega Kansas (000.000° N, 000.000° W), "Boy, if you want to know what crossing Kansas is like, take this postcard, go out, sit in the car and stare at it for eight hours." After that, his trail went dry.

All these years later, when I'm feeling low, I'll sometimes buy a postcard, write a silly joke on the back, and send it to whatever random town I think he might be in. Ping! My phone brought me back to the campus quad and my double shot of tequila mixed in Pedialyte.

> Dear Faculty and Staff,
>
> I'm proud to announce that my daughter is the lead dancer in the Theatre and Dance Department's all-modern dance version of Samuel Beckett's *Waiting for Godot*.
>
> I hope to see all of you at tonight's opening!
>
> Best,
>
> Dean Frank Gacy, PhD
> Arts & Sciences
>
> PS Before you ask, no, I do not have comp tickets.

The clouds in my soul lifted. This was my opportunity. Hypothetical: What if during intermission, I sidle up to the dean, schmooze him, compliment his daughter's dancing, and show him that I was just a defective human being who had been a bit depressed of late because we're facing massive global warming, dwindling resources, genocidal wars, pathogens emerging from the melting permafrost, and another presidential election, i.e., the age of post happiness. If he had an ounce of humanity, he'd have to empathize. Perhaps I'd tell him a charming joke about academia, and we'd share a knowing laugh. And then, pleased with my delightful wit, he'd say, "All charges are dismissed." It had to work. It was my only hope.

3

The Theatre and Dance Department had a reputation for its long day's journey into night productions, and since the dean's daughter often participated, it was politically prudent to attend. But as I took my seat, the dean was nowhere to be found. So, I sent him a text.

> Dean Gacy,
>
> I'm writing to say I fully support your executive order removing August Strindberg (and other dead white male writers) from the Honor Program's summer reading list and replacing them all with the musical *Hamilton*.
>
> Sincerely,
>
> Charlie
>
> Dr. Charles Neb
> Assistant Professor
> Philosophy Department
>
> PS Interesting side story. I once spit on Strindberg's grave. Perhaps we could talk about it during intermission.

Send. A "ping" echoed among the chattering audience. But before I could locate it, the jolly English professor beside me stuck an elbow deep in my ribs and said, "This your first *Waiting For Godot*?" Only he pronounced Godot "Go-Dot." His rosy Santa face smiled, anticipating an engaging academic chitchat. I knew he was an English professor because they're so desperately lonely they'll start a conversation with anyone.

"Yes. My first. But I read it in college."

"You know it was written by the great absurdist playwright Samuel Beckett?"

"Yes."

"This!" he proudly broadcast so everyone could hear, "is my seventeenth *Waiting for Go-Dot!* I've seen it in New York, Vienna, and Düsseldorf, to name a few. Although I've never witnessed a modern dance version." Then he boomed with great panache as if we were pals even though we'd just met, "Dr. Skippy is a genius. I think so, don't you?"

"Who is Skippy?" I said, trying to be polite while still scanning the audience for the dean.

"You don't know who Dr. Skippy is?" That's what English professors do: They probe until they find something you don't know, and then that's all they talk about. "Why, he's the distinguished chair of Theatre and Dance. Not only is he a brilliant Beckettian scholar, but he wrote the ultimate scholarly book on the subject, *Waiting for Go-Dot. A Critical Line-by-Line Explorative Analysis.* In its four volumes, he set a record of 40 lines of commentary for every two lines of the play's text."

"Sounds like his commentary is more important than the dialogue."

"Oh, it is!" he proudly announced. "It is!" Then he added, "Dr. Skippy is one of those rarefied dynamos who has a dog-whistle sensitivity to the synergy of text. He also choreographed tonight's production."

"Oh God, no. Theatre scholars should never be allowed near a theatre." Shit, did I say that out loud?

"Well, I completely disagree," he boomed as he removed his round glasses and cleaned them with a pre-lubricated wipe. "Beckettian intellectuals are the only ones who can possibly unpack the nuances and deconstruct the absurd layers found in Beckett's multidimensional *meta-theatrical moments.*"

Oh, how I dislike words like "unpack" and "deconstruct" that literary paleontologists use. If you unpack a novel, you kill it, just as when you explain a joke, it's no longer funny. As Santa deconstructed Professor Skippy's deconstruction of Go-Dot, I thumbed my phone.

Dean Gacy,

PS While I'm at it, we should also defund the Department of Theatre and Dance's annual StrindFest.

Sincerely,

Charlie

Dr. Charles Neb
Assistant Professor
Philosophy Department

Send. Ping! Got him! He was sitting three rows ahead and slightly to the right. I watched as he read the bright red dance program. Now all I needed was an icebreaker, a fantastic intermission conversation starter. Perhaps I could bring up defunding the April Fool's edition of the student newspaper, an idea championed by all administrators. Then I panicked. I'd forgotten to pin the pink ribbon onto my lapel, which showed I was open-minded enough to know it was World Violence Awareness Month.

"And, of course, you do understand theatre of the absurd," Santa pontificated.

"Sure, I guess."

"Samuel Beckett was attempting to instill a sense of metaphysical anguish upon the audience at the meaninglessness of the human condition."

"Right," I said as I searched my pockets.

"But in this unique production, Dr. Skippy wants to trigger a critical response in the spectator through *verfremdungseffekt*. Also known as the 'alienation effect.' In other words, he'll use unique staging effects to remind the audience they're in a theatre and can think for themselves as they are filled with metaphysical anguish. The entire English department has been lit up for weeks in anticipation of what Dr. Skippy will do."

Found it! I'd already pinned it on my lapel next to the light blue ribbon representing everything from juvenile arthritis to water safety, so I figured I was safe on all fronts.

"Beckett and Dr. Skippy are geniuses! And I don't use that word lightly," he said as he opened the playbill. "Oh dear, some genius misspelled *'verfremdungseffekt'* in the program note," he boomed to the surrounding professors. Some overly delighted academic shot back, "I noticed that too," and they shared a knowing chortle. Then Santa took me back into his confidence. "Samuel Beckett also wanted to show that not only was human-to-human communication futile but also totally impossible!"

"Thank you, you communicated that quite well," I said as I opened the program in an attempt to appear too busy to talk. My eyes stopped. I couldn't believe it. In the production's crew list, in tiny print, was "Master Electrician: Augie Omega."

Just then, the house lights dimmed, and Dr. Skippy stepped from the wings into a pool of light. He was a broad man with a narrow chin he tried to hide with a patchy gray beard. He looked like a beat poet. Delighted with himself, he started into his curtain speech, "Hello, everyone in the gender universe. Welcome to our all-dance production of *Waiting for Go-Dot*. But before we begin, I must say a word about the recent tragic homecoming event. Felice Wolinski, sophomore communications major, was not only head cheerleader but also a stagehand in our all-dance production of Sartre's *No Exit*." He pronounced it 'Sar-trah.' "And so, the theatre students and I would like to celebrate her brief life. To help us, we invite Dean Gacy to our humble stage to lead us in a moment of silence." As the dean made his way through the audience, a leotarded dancer entered from the wings with a long-stemmed candle borrowed from the prop department and a match. "Fire regulations state we're not allowed to have open flames in this building, but I think we can break this rule once," Skippy said as he lit the wick.

There were no stairs, so the dean had to crawl awkwardly onto the stage, which gave the five-hundred-plus audience an expansive view of his big round butt and loose-fitting diabetic socks. Once on stage, he hoisted himself upright, brushed off his dusty knees, and joined Dr. Skippy center stage.

"Thank you all for coming," Dean Gacy said, not finding his light, so the spot's shadow halved his face. "We are gathered here on the traditional territory of the Mohawk, Cayuga, Cherokee, Navajo, Seneca, and Choctaw people in what is today called the United States of America." It was the first time I'd seen Dean Gacy up close since my orientation six years earlier. He wore a long tweed jacket and a black turtleneck that cupped his calcified jowls. Rumor had it that he wore high-necked sweaters to hide a thyroid condition or maybe a tattoo. For a moment, his bureaucratic eyes caught me in the crowd. I offered an amiable nod, letting him know I was a harmless team player and dance lover. He was unimpressed.

"Please bow your heads," he announced. "Unless your religion doesn't allow you to do so or if you have a physical impairment that prevents you. Also, lowering your head does not mean you're performing an act of submission, unless you want to perform an act of submission. If you wish, you may say a prayer during this moment of silence, but you're not required to do so, nor does my broaching the subject in any way suggest the university endorses or opposes prayer. Also, know that the following moment of silence does not imply an assumption of belief unless you want it to imply an assumption of belief. If you do say a prayer, please whisper, as this is a moment of silence. But also know that by asking you to whisper, I'm not attempting to censor you in any way. This moment of silence is a nonsectarian act that can be interpreted as sectarian. If you wish to hold hands or hug the person beside you, do so only after you have asked permission and after you have received a positive confirmation that is witnessed by at least one person. We shall now begin a moment of silence."

As I looked around the theatre full of bowed heads, all I could think was, I'm an academic stowaway, a decoy in a sea of real professors. I've always been jealous of those who genuinely want to profess. The types who throw tenure parties, volunteer to head committees, and record exhaustive bullet lists in little monographed Moleskine notebooks during faculty meetings. The type who has the confidence to walk up to the dean after an idiot-proof moment of silence and, without a touch of irony, say, "That really spoke to me."

After five seconds of quiet, the dean mumbled, "Thank you." Then he worked his way to the corner of the stage and tried to get down the same way he got up, but his legs were too short. So, he sat and, as we all waited, crab-walked his butt to the edge of the stage. Then he stretched both legs down, pulling his trousers upward where they tightly gathered at his crotch - the stretched polyester giving the audience an exact outline of his impressive balls and floppy drive. Two student ushers offered help, but he refused, saying, "I've got it, I've got it." Finally, he placed his tippy toes on firm ground, the wedgy released, and he wiggled his way through the aisle. As he passed, a gaggle of professors fluttered like butterflies around him, offering congratulations on a job well done. I took the opportunity to thumb my phone one last time before shutting down.

> Dean Gacy,
>
> PPS Nice job with the moment of silence. It really spoke to me. 😊
>
> Sincerely,
>
> Charlie
>
> Dr. Charles Neb
> Assistant Professor
> Philosophy Department

After the dean took his seat, Skippy announced from the stage, "Now people listen up. *Waiting for Go-Dot* contains references to death, suicide, slavery, boredom, nihilism, and futility. But this production also has quite a few delightful dance numbers, so it all balances out."

Moments later, the lights dimmed, and the curtain rose on a bench, a leafless burnt tree, and a post-nuclear dystopian hellscape. Scratching atonal music blared as the dean's daughter entered as a toe-tapping Estragon. During the performance, on an enormous screen behind the dancers, videos of various A-bomb tests (Marshall Islands, Trinity, Bikini Atoll) played in a continuous loop. I always wanted to be a dancer, ballet, not modern. All bad modern dance uses interchangeable choreography and only the music is slightly different. Lights up. Walk. Run. Leap right. Jump. Wave. Jump. Crouch. Kick. Leap left. Jump. Hands-Up. Hands-Down. Run. Run. Jump. Jump. Lights down. Go home. Open beer. Take sleeping pills. Jazz hands. Do you know what jazz hands are? They're the choreographer admitting they've run out of ideas.

Once, after a dance concert, this B12-deficient dance professor asked if I was "cognizant" of her theme. I said, "Yes, you're trying to say that even after years of vigorous training, we can only jump about three feet in the air (five for Baryshnikov on a good day) before the laws of the universe that control everything from falling apples to the planetary orbit of Neptune stubbornly re-establish dominance. That no matter what we do, when we go up, there can be only one outcome—down. And this Sisyphean fact has haunted humans since the first homo-erectus suffered lower back pain." She said, "No, my theme was 'Spring.'"

Fifteen minutes in, the dean was all smiles, and I was about to pop a second Zoloft when the curtain crashed down, and a dancer ran from the wings and yelled, "Ladies and Gentlemen, an electrical fire's broken out! The alarms aren't working! We ask you to leave immediately," which brought a nervous snicker from the audience. "I'm serious. There's a fire!" pleaded the young dancer, which made the professors laugh. It was a knowing laugh, as if they were in on some inside joke.

"We should go," I said to Saint Nick.

"Oh no, trust me, it's part of the performance."

"I think she's serious."

"No, she's not. It's theatre of the absurd. I told you Dr. Skippy was a staging genius."

"Ladies and gentlemen, I mean it! We have a fire backstage! Leave! Now!" the dancer shouted. The English professors around me slapped each other's knees and hooted with scholarly delight.

"Dr. Skippy is playing us," said Santa as he winked and nudged.

"You sure?"

"Are you feeling metaphysical anguish?"

"Yeah, a little is creeping in."

"And alienated?"

"Very much so."

"Are you aware that you are in a theatre?"

"Yes, it's relatively clear to me."

"And are you thinking for yourself?"

"Mostly, I'm thinking about not burning to death."

"That's *verfremdungseffekt!*"

The audience was now in complete hysterics. Then I saw Dean Gacy was laughing the hardest, and I thought perhaps it *was* part of the performance. Just then, Dr. Skippy skipped down the aisle. His girth made it challenging for him to get on the stage because his belly had swollen from years of passively sitting in his office, inflating his resume, and telling stories about how Meryl Streep saw him play Puck in Poughkeepsie.

"People, this is no joke!" he snapped. "The costume shop is in flames! It's spreading quickly! Save yourselves!" This resulted in a standing ovation. And it wasn't your typical ovation inflation that professors usually give bad modern dance productions. It was the real thing.

"Do you see what he did?" Santa shouted over the applause.

"Who?"

"Dr. Skippy! The candle he held during the moment of silence."

"What about it?"

"It was part of the performance!" And he hunkered against me, shielding me from the mob's wild enthusiasm, and shouted, "What frightens you most about the human condition?"

"That we're stuck in a vast and empty eternity."

"Bingo! We might be able to nudge the orbit of a comet hurtling toward us or someday extend human life to two hundred years, but overall, the indifferent universe is going to do what it's going to do. Does that stop Sisyphus from pushing his rock?"

"I guess not, but I'm sure Sisyphus would run if the rock were on fire."

"All of us, like Sisyphus, are living an absurdist comedy while we await Go-Dot!"

I know I sometimes come off rather pessimistic about dance, and for good reason, the ballerina falling into the orchestra pit thing, but at that moment, I understood what the philosopher Albert Camus meant when he wrote, "One must imagine Sisyphus happy." I'd lectured about it many times but never entirely took to heart that the struggle towards the top of the hill, even if it was absurd, was also meaningful for Sisyphus.

As I stood and joined the frenzied ovation, I became fully cognizant of the metaphysical anguish that ruled over my misplaced life and I vowed to overthrow my stale Sisyphean logic and install optimism into my soul. Never again during Beethoven's 9th would I check to see if my phone was still on, for I'd leave it at home along with my doubts. From now on when I was in a flowering forest, I'd enjoy the splendid beauty and not think about where my car was. And dammit, I would consider the existence of God without counterarguments. Because of Dr. Skippy's unique staging, I'd successfully unpacked Beckett and deconstructed *Waiting for Go-Dot*! But more, when I approached Dean Gacy at intermission, I'd have the perfect conversation icebreaker! Verfremdungseffekt!

4

The estimated damage to the theatre was $29 million, mainly because the stage and costume shop were total losses. English professors were hospitalized in greater numbers because they were the last to admit they were wrong. A week later, after forming a "Grand Challenges Affinity Committee" to confront the situation, Acting Dean Popkov announced there'd be a candle-lighting ceremony so faculty, staff, and students could pray (or not pray, it was their choice) that Dean Gacy would regain consciousness. Apparently, tweed is highly combustible.

The student paper announced that the theatre fire was not caused by Dr. Skippy's candle but by an electrical problem. I tried to locate Master Electrician Augie Omega but was told he was no longer employed by the university and had left no forwarding address or phone number.

Ping!

Dear Dr. Neb,

It has come to our attention that in Beginning Existentialism 101, you gave three students early warning grades of "C" or lower. If a student gets a deficient grade, you are required to take responsibility for your actions by sending us the answers to the following questions:

1. Did you attempt to reach out to the student? On what dates?

2. Did you allow the student to make up or redo all assignments? On what dates?

3. Did you contact the Office of Student Achievement? On what dates?

4. Who did you meet with at the Office of Student Achievement? What was their advice?

5. Did you take their advice? If not, why not?

6. On what dates?

7. What was the student's response to your efforts to help them? On what dates?

8. Did you set up private tutoring sessions with the student? On what dates?

9. How did you fail when the student was unable to respond to your private tutoring?

10. How will you make this class work for the student?

Remember, retention is not the student's responsibility, but yours.

Good luck with your existentialism class.

Dr. Darrell Dahl
Office of Student Achievement

Two days later, the scream tent was removed, the 24-hour "emotional hygiene" hotline disconnected, the support pets kenneled, and the grounds staff set out to touch up "Reflections of Echoes" with orange paint patches that didn't quite match the original. And I took a mental health day to drive my loaner three hundred miles into the boonies to the poorly attended funeral of Felice Wolinski, sophomore communications major.

Ping!

> Dear Everyone,
>
> To accommodate student diversity, Dining Services has installed pork-free microwaves in the cafeterias and the student union food court.
>
> We urge you not to place pork products in or near the designated pork-free microwaves, as we are unable to afford their replacement if they are desecrated.
>
> Eat well,
>
> Dr. Albert Fish
> Vice President for Inclusive Excellence

I paused outside Faith Light, a forgotten clapboard church flanked by a field of piglets, milk cows, and "no hunting" signs. Beside it, a teetering oak had just begun swapping its greens for a haze of muted lemon butter. This would be my first time in church since my thrice-divorced mother sent me to Virgin Mary Grade School so they could "teach me some stupid morals."

Ping!

> Dear All,
>
> Dr. Fish's email got me thinking. We should also take into consideration all the religious POVs of our students. I'm therefore proposing we change our school mascot. A Wild Hog is a form of pig and is potentially offensive to Muslims,

Hindus, Buddhists, Jews, and Rastafarians.

Look at this as an opportunity.

Have A Great Day,

Assistant Dean Bobby Popkov, PhD

*"Never lose sight of the fact that the most important yardstick
to your success is how you treat other people."* - Barbara Bush

On my second day at Catholic school, the nuns held a God trivia quiz. The first question was: "Why is there somethingness rather than nothingness?" I knew the answer the pixie of a nun wanted. She even put three lines in the answer box (_ _ _) to make sure none of us would experience free will. But is "God" an answer? If you say a tree falls in the forest because of "gravity," does that mean an eight-year-old understands Newton's Laws? And that goes for rosary beads, baptism, atonement, and papal infallibility.

Ping!

Dear Assistant Dean Popkov and Faculty,

What if we changed the mascot to a gopher? I've checked,
no religion is offended by gophers.

Just a suggestion,

Dr. Randolph Miller
Religious Studies
Assistant Accreditation Advisor
Active Team Player

The second question was: "God is (_ _ _ _)." Instead of writing the correct answer, "love," I wrote "deaf," and not because of some profound philosophical deism-like deduction, I was eight, my first philosophy class was a decade away. I just reckoned if Carl Sagan was right and the universe was billions and billions of years old, that meant God's at least that old, if not older, so there's a good chance he's senile, and because he's a man, not a good listener.

Ping!

> Dear Assistant Dean Popkov and faculty,
>
> Far too many mascots are based on animals. We should stay away from wildlife in general.
>
> Is there a vegan option?
>
> Sincerely,
>
> Dr. Elizabeth Boone Helm
> Department Chair
> Dietetics, Sports Nutrition & Public Health

The last question on the Bible test was, "If you kill yourself, God will send you straight to (_ _ _ _)." I faked illness, left the severities of the nuns early, went back to my mother's single wide trailer home, and asked her if it was true. Was God so cold-blooded that he'd send me to eternal damnation forever and ever if I killed myself? She answered, "Only if you mess up my carpet." Even at eight, I was predisposed to ontological anxiety and early-onset mortality awareness.

My mother ordered me to get my ass back to school, where I asked the nuns, "If God made us in his image, and he is perfect, then why do you teach us to be ashamed of our bodies?" That day, the nuns denied me a "Holy Jellybean" and sent me home early. As a side note, I was later permanently banned from Virgin Mary Grade School because I kept referring to the holy trinity as "me, myself, and I." And on my eighteenth birthday, I was permanently banned from my mother's trailer home because it was my eighteenth birthday.

Ping!

> Dear Assistant Dean Popkov and Faculty,
>
> We need a mascot that's nonbinary. It's challenging to tell the sex of amphibians. My daughter had a frog for five years and never knew its sex.
>
> So, how about the Fighting Frogs?
>
> Sincerely,
>
> Dr. Dorothea Puente
> Department Head
> Gender Studies

I silenced my phone as I entered the stained-glass glow of Faith Light. The service had begun, so I tiptoed over the creaking floor and hunkered in the last pew. There's something pacific about organ music in a candled sanctuary that makes me want to believe there's an omnipotent powerbroker up there. But having been a regular reader of the New York Times op-ed page since I was fourteen, that's not been a viable option.

From his elevated pulpit, the near-sighted preacher-man unlatched his king-sized Bible, carefully opened to a bookmarked passage, coughed, and dramatically paused to consider the closed casket, which was topped with a set of scarlet & brown pom-poms. To one side, a wonky spray of mums had a ribbon that read, "From your sisters at Kappa Delta." On the other, a wobbly easel held a poster-sized photo of Felice Wolinski, sophomore communications major, looking slightly to the right. Draped over it was a bright white lei of Jet-Puffed marshmallows.

Then, preacher-man cast his eyes over the puny ensemble of mourners and waited as two old ladies in the front had coughing fits. After they finished, he nodded to the diva at the organ, and the somber chords ceased. The stillness of the churchly catacomb held us. He pushed a button on the pulpit, and a recorded sound of a dove's call filled the sanctuary. "As our Lord-God says in the Bible," preacher man began his well-tuned words, "'We are crawling between heaven and earth desperately trying to pluck some absolutes from a forsaken universe!'"

Hold on, I thought, that's not the Bible. That's the Swedish playwright/poet Strindberg. I knew because I once took a literary bicycle tour of Stockholm centered on the prominent non-linear misogynistic writers of the twentieth century. The feminist NYU prof who led the tour ended it at Begravningsplatsen cemetery, where she offered us a full refund if we were willing to spit on Strindberg's grave. Then we all went to see the musical *Hamilton*.

"As it says in *Joshua*," he stopped, hacked, cleared his throat, and continued, "Death itself doesn't frighten me. It's the jump I'm afraid of."

Sitting in the back near the abandoned collection baskets, I thought that's also not the Bible. That's Simone de Beauvoir. I know because I once had an on-again-off-again, non-exclusive relationship with a French woman and her younger sister, both of whom dumped me on the same day because I shaved too closely. No wonder Felice Wolinski, sophomore communications major, was so screwed up. Her church was a misquoting mess. And what was all the coughing about? When one stopped hacking, another started.

"In *Deuteronomy*, we find," Preacher man said, "'Where am I? What is the meaning of the world? Who tricked me into this whole thing and leaves me standing here? How did I get into the world? Why was I not asked about it? Why was I not informed of the rules and regulations? Why should I be involved? If I am compelled to be involved, where is the manager? How can I make a complaint?'"

As the faithful coughed and nodded, my hand shot up. I know you're not technically supposed to ask questions during funerals, but that quote was from the theologian and existentialist Kierkegaard. I know because my dissertation was titled "An Analysis of Kierkegaard, Comedy, and Contradiction as it Relates to the Philosophy of Schopenhauer and the

Chinese Cultural Revolution." The preacher pretended not to see my waving hand.

After a half hour of misplaced quotes from Maya Angelou, James Baldwin, Anne Frank, and much more wheezing and coughing, preacher man pushed a pulpit button, and the trumpets of heaven sounded as six members of the university's cheerleading squad marched in and lifted the coffin on their shoulders. Then the tiny congregation, buoyant in their faith and singing off-key, followed the cheerleaders out to the church's backyard cemetery. There, surrounded by rattling poplars and drab headstones topped with granite angels, the cheerleading squad performed one last mournful graveside pom-pom cheer:

Sea to holy sea

We will always miss thee

We'll miss you on our caller I.D.

And when we graduate with our bachelor's degree

From the bottom of our hearts, we guarantee

That we will be thinking of the absentee

F.E.L.I.C.E.

Dear sweet Felice Wolinski

Sophomore communications major

Then a waiting heavy-lift Caterpillar dieseled the coffin and the pom-poms into the fragrant dirt filled with fishing worms and root knobs. As the last weeping mourners wandered off to their consoling teas and brunches, I nosed up to the grave's lip and peeked down into the silt at the reasonably priced casket.

"Just so you know, funerals don't have question-and-answer sessions." I looked up to find the misquoting minister glaring at me with such contempt I thought for a moment he'd reach across the grave and slap me.

"Yeah, but those quotes weren't from the Bible."

"Young man, have you read your Bible?"

"Yes," I said. "Almost all of it, almost all the way through."

"Then you know what I read comes directly from the pious lips of the Almighty!"

"Are we talking about the same Bible?" I said. "I'm referring to the one with, like, a virgin birth and walking on water."

"One and the same."

"Then some rogue editor made unauthorized changes."

"If that happened, God surely would've smitten them!"

"Then maybe God's playing a joke on you."

"God doesn't have a sense of humor."

"You sure about that?"

"Yes, because he lives in a world too perfect for comedy." He coughed, cleared his throat, and started away.

I called after, "Would you mind if I snuck a peek at that Bible of yours?"

He turned, and his damning eyes scanned me, hoping for a rare sign of belief. Detecting none, he held the good book close and pitied my insignificant soul. "At Faith Light," he said, "we have but one Bible and only the most honorable may touch it."

"The entire congregation shares a single Bible?"

"Once you find the truth, your soul is full, and nothing else will fit."

"But you've heard of things like the printing press and xeroxing?"

"Here is a quote for you," and he opened his Bible and read, "There is but one good, and that is God. Everything else is good when it looks to Him and bad when it turns from Him—"

"I hate to interrupt," I interrupted, "but that's not the Bible. That's C. S. Lewis."

"You're wrong. It's a direct quote from Jesus, the man himself!"

"Look, I know what I'm talking about. When I was ten, after reading all seven volumes of the *Chronicles of Narnia*, I was rushed to the hospital with a severe allergic reaction to didacticism."

He wheezed, wiped a bit of spittle from the corner of his mouth with a well-used holy hanky, and dismissed me with, "You are the essence of loss and loneliness. May God have mercy on you."

As he walked away, I said, "Have you ever heard of a man named Augie Omega?" He stutter-stepped and turned like a gunslinger, ready to take offense at the slightest challenge.

"How do you know that name?"

"Felice Wolinski, sophomore communications major, told me about him. I've been looking for him, but there's nothing on the web, no address, no phone number."

"Stay away from that man. He's trouble."

"You know him?"

"We hired Mr. Omega to fumigate the church," he said as he drifted into the past.

"Augie Omega is a bug exterminator?" I said, confused.

"He covered the church in a huge tent but said it'd be okay if I used the sanctuary for morning services as he wouldn't begin fumigating until afternoon. I had just asked God to anoint the flock when this unholy hissing started. People began coughing and gasping as the church filled with a white toxic haze. The holy choral singers began vomiting. A slap fight broke out as the congregation was forced to claw their way over each other to get out. In the apocalyptic panic that followed, over two dozen were injured, many hospitalized with lung issues, and one—" He stopped. This wasn't easy. "One questioned her faith."

"Let me guess, the one who questioned was Felice Wolinski, sophomore communications major." He looked down. The answer was yes. Just then, the tiny bell in the church steeple rang, and we both looked up, he with a faint issue of hope. I with concern. "When you look at a bell tower," I said, "do you ever wonder if there's a gunman inside?"

His eyes slowly fell on me, and he said, "I believe that when the end times come, and cataclysmic disasters take hold of the earth, in the middle of that epic battle between the forces of God and Satan, you will find Mr. Omega enjoying every minute of it." Then he turned and tottered off. I stood there for a moment. Then I turned on my phone.

Ping!

Dear Faculty,

It's easy to identify a frog's gender. Follow these simple steps:

<u>Size</u> - Females are typically larger and slightly heavier than males. This makes it easier for the male to mount them during mating.

<u>Vocal Sac</u> - Males have a pronounced vocal sac. Females have a baggy sac.

<u>Ears</u> - Male frogs tend to have ears larger than their eyes. Female frogs have ears and eyes that are the same size.

<u>Thumbs</u> - Male frogs often have hook-shaped adornments on their hands used to grip females during reproduction. Do not look for these while the frogs are mating.

I hope this helped.

Dr. James Canarock
Department of Acarology and Herpetology

PS I would be happy to be a consultant in designing the new mascot if we take the frog route.

Back in my rental, I plotted how I might get my hands on Faith Light's misquoting Bible. My hunch was that there was a connection between it, the researcher/ electrician/bug exterminator Augie Omega, and our age of post-happiness. But first, I had to go to room #151 in old A&S and win my Academic Ascertainment hearing. To succeed, I needed to take the university's professionally produced educational webinar "Objectification & You," which I was positive would be most helpful.

5

"What you gotta know is that we're all equal. Anything less is totally feeble. Times are a-changin' we ain't medieval," were the Rap lyrics sung by animated multiethnic cartoon owls that started and ended every episode of "Objectification & You," produced by Achieve Corporation of New York. I spent the next few days preparing for my hearing by binging and re-binging all 32 episodes from "Adjunct Professors Deserve Respect" to "Xenophobia & You" while consuming thermoses full of Mad Dog 20/20 mixed with shots of Pepto Bismol. Soon I was singing along, "There's never been a cause to be deceitful, cause if you do, know it's illegal!"

"Welcome back," the botoxed actor smiled from my tiny laptop. "Today's lesson is titled, *Jokes: No Laughing Matter - Intent, Impact, Synergy.*"

I've always thought it would be neat to be an actor but felt sorry for webinar actors. You know the ones who appear in industrial training videos. I'm happy they're working, but at some point, while shooting *Twenty-Seven Telephone Etiquette Tips That Can Make Or Break Your Company*, they must question the meaning of existence. I believe it was the Roman emperor Marcus Aurelius who wrote in *Meditations*, "This is why you went into debt getting an MFA in acting? So you could train idiots to answer phones? And don't give me that bullshit about how your purpose is to be an actor, or worse, God wants you to be an actor. Either God exists or doesn't. If he doesn't, then he can't want you to be anything. If God exists, then given all the world's pain, chaos, and suffering, he can't be your motivation for being an actor!" But before you use that quote, check it because I might've been drunk when I wrote this.

"Here's a situation you might've encountered," the webinar actor grinned from my laptop screen. "One day, Betty and Harry are in the company breakroom when . . .," the music swelled, and the screen faded to a simple white cube of a room with a coffeemaker and two actors phoning it in. I'll bet the stage manager was standing just off-camera, armed with a team of psychiatrists and a bowl of Prozac.

"Hi, Harry."

"Hello, Betty."

"Coffee?"

"Thank you."

"Did you get my text?"

"Oh, that was you?"

"Don't you think that popular comedian I mentioned was funny?"

"I did not!"

Then the screen froze, and the webinar host stepped in front and beamed. "How should Betty react? Here are your options." And the screen lit up with:

➢ Maintain workplace cohesion by not reacting.
➢ File a Title IX complaint.
➢ Try to top Harry with an even funnier text.
➢ Inform Harry we need to empower people by creating a respectful workplace environment.

I scored a perfect 100 and downloaded my "Certificate of Completion," which the web host said was "suitable for framing." The next day, armed with my framed certificate, I walked into old Arts and Sciences, a once-great land grant cathedral now reduced to the sagging hemline of indifference. They were going to tear down old A&S when they built new A&S, but the provost decided more committee rooms were needed, so they kept old A&S until they could con the legislature into funding an even newer new A&S. However, when they finished constructing the new A&S, the administrative oligarchs realized they had failed to consider the need for additional custodians due to the addition of 95,000 square feet of atriums, balconies, and water features. This posed a problem, as the university was currently under a two-year hiring freeze. So, the president reassigned the custodians in old A&S to new A&S, leaving the few scholarly oxen left behind in the old building to clean, mop, and take out their own trash. As a result, its decorative granite latticework and imitation medieval architecture were always dusty.

Ping!

> Dear Faculty,
>
> Thought for today.
>
> Your classes should not be a "weed-out class" or to "set the bar." Instead, you are here to promote the student's well-being because carefree students say nice things, which keeps our US News ranking high.
>
> Teaching is good.
>
> Betty D. Debowski
> Executive Assistant Chancellor of the Subcommittee for Learning Relations and Strategic Inclusive Planning

"Oh, Charlie! Happy to see you!" It was Dr. Jerry Loudie, the psychology department professor who was also head of the Mental Health Solutions Center. He was always trapping me in the hall like a desperate Hollywood screenwriter and pitching me the ergonomic benefits of standing desks. I had briefly considered one but figured the chipping lead-based paint in my old A&S office would kill me long before my sedentary lifestyle. He was a quill of a man who, no matter the weather, always dressed as if he were about to play Wimbledon. Even in winter, he wore wrist sweatbands and copper-lined socks.

"Heading to your A.A. hearing?" he said.

"Yeah."

"Just so you know, having an A.A. doesn't necessarily mean the end of your academic life."

"No?"

"I had an A.A. hearing once."

"What did you do wrong?"

"I was talking with another professor. A nothing special conversation, just chatting, when I offhandedly mentioned I liked the novelistic structure of Woody Allen's films. The professor bristled and condemned me for condoning a quote, 'neurotic sexual predator who rips off Fellini.' Then I made a total mess of it by defending myself. I said that even a neurotic-Fellini-mimic-predator can, on occasion, make a funny movie. I would've been okay, but I was talking to an English professor."

"Oh god no."

"All hell broke loose. But! I won my case."

"How?"

"First, by admitting I was wrong."

"I've done that. Several times."

"Second, roadside beautification."

"Excuse me?"

"I gave back to my community."

"You mean, like, by picking up trash on the side of the road?"

"My friend, you must not just talk the talk but also walk along the side of the road picking up trash."

"Why?"

"It shows you're willing to be a team player. Matter of fact, this Saturday, a bunch of us profs are going to roll up our sleeves on Highway 47. Care to join us?"

"Oh, gosh, this Saturday, I don't know."

"All you gotta do is avoid trucker bombs - plastic Coke bottles, jars of Gatorade, anything filled with yellowish liquid. If exposed to too much sun, they can ferment and explode without warning."

"Let me give it some thought. I'll get back to you."

"In her annual State of the University Address, President Boucher did say we professors needed to up our game by becoming part of the fabric of the community. We put up a huge sign that says, 'We Professors Care.' Get lots of honks."

"Can't think of anything better to do with my Saturday, but—"

"When I put my feet up after a hard weekend of roadside beautification, I feel edified," he said, so upbeat I suspected he was a motivational speaker on the side. People who are that optimistic have got to have a torture chamber in their basement where they skin cats and cook children.

"Sounds great. Really does," and I nodded as if I was seriously considering the offer.

"Think about it, and if the answer is yes, I'll catch you bright and early Saturday at mile marker 14. Bye-bye." Sartre was wrong. Hell isn't other people, it's other professors.

Ping!

> Dear Faculty,
>
> This Friday, there will be a moment of silence and a candle-lighting ceremony to wish Dean Gacy a speedy recovery. It will be held in the lobby of the Bitcoin.com Student Union. 1 pm.
>
> This is an opportunity to show the dean how much we really care.
>
> Have a great day,
>
> Acting Dean, Bobby Popkov, PhD
>
> *"Hope is the thing with feathers that perches in the soul and sings the tune without the words and never stops at all."* – Emily Dickinson

The sheet of paper thumb tacked on the door of old A&S room 151 read, "A.A." It was written on letterhead from "Omega Corporation." Suspicious,

I slowly opened the door. I was the first to arrive, so I clicked on the buzzing fluorescents, revealing a neglected hearing room from the 1950s House Committee on Un-American Activities. A yellowed American flag had hung itself in the corner. Faded portraits of bygone deans lined the walls, black and white photos until the 1970s, all men until the 1990s, all Caucasians until the 2000s. I wiped down a seat and waited for my future. President Boucher had decreed that all meetings should begin with the faculty chanting the administration's newest battle cry, "Retention! Retention! Retention!" I'd resolved to show my complete allegiance by being the loudest.

Ping!

> Faculty and Staff,
>
> Open flames are not allowed in the student union or any place on campus, so I'm canceling the candle-lighting ceremony for Dean Gacy.
>
> Julio Gonzalez
> University Fire Chief

Far above the rafters of old A&S, the bell tower tolled 8am. There were no actual iron bells in the tower, only tin loudspeakers, but it sounded genuine enough. The eight serious death bongs were followed by an upbeat ring-a-ding-ding recording of a Beyoncé melody. By the time the pop diva ceased, it was 8:06. The room still sat empty. But I had expected this because nothing happens quickly in academia.

Bit by tapping bit, the arthritic wall clock plodded its way to 8:10. As I waited with the clickity-click of the radiators, I couldn't help but think that telling a joke was a ridiculous charge. They accused Socrates of "corrupting the youth," which looks good on your resume. During Stalin's purges, the Russian poet Joseph Brodsky was charged with "malicious parasitism." You may not remember his poems, but how can you forget "malicious parasitism." That charge alone was enough to confirm his immortality. But telling a joke? Hell, what did I know? Maybe someday, it, too, would be a badge of honor. Perhaps I'd become a modern-day Spartacus. I could imagine the hushed conversations in the faculty bathrooms:

"Did you hear about Charlie Neb? He was fired for telling a joke."

"He stood up for free speech!"

"He will be remembered."

"Like Spartacus."

The Pleistocene age ticked by before the clock hit 8:15. Still no one. Then at 8:16, distant voices. My heart pounded as their echoes closed in on the frosted door. But just as their shadows landed, they turned, and their heels clicked away.

Ping!

> Campus Wide Scarlet & Brown Alert,
>
> Due to safety concerns, the candle-lighting ceremony for Dean Gacy has been moved to the campus fire station.
>
> Have A Great Day,
>
> Acting Dean Bobby Popkov, PhD
>
> *"A positive statement propels hope toward a better future, it builds up your faith and that of others, and it promotes change."*
> – Jan Dargatz

At 8:20, I gently tiptoed towards the hope that they canceled the hearing or, better yet, forgot about it. I mean, the dean was in a coma, and the administration was busy dealing with the fallout from the Felice Wolinski, sophomore communications major, homecoming tragedy. It was the feeling you get when you board an international flight and they're about to close the main cabin door and the middle seat is still empty. You bombard the flight attendants with invisible thought rays, willing them to close the damn door.

And they do! And you stretch, knowing, at least for the next eight hours, you have a personal relationship with God because he, like you, occasionally needs to man spread.

Ping!

> Faculty and Staff,
>
> As open flames are not allowed _anywhere_ on campus, and since the campus fire station is located _on campus,_ that means open flames are not allowed there either.
>
> The candle-lighting ceremony for Dean Gacy is <u>canceled</u>!
>
> Julio Gonzalez
> University Fire Chief

At 8:25, the door to the main cabin closed, and for the first time in days, I relaxed. My students had been reassigned, and yet I was still being paid. I told some stupid joke I couldn't remember, yet I still had health insurance. And to top it off, the theatre had burned, so I wouldn't have to watch the dean's daughter act in this year's Strindfest!

Ping!

> Campus Wide Scarlet & Brown Alert,
>
> The venue for Dean Gacy's candle-lighting ceremony has once again changed.
>
> It will now be held in the Union Carbide Chemistry Building, Lab 3B. As candles are not allowed, please bring your Bunsen burners.
>
> Have A Great Day,

Acting Dean Bobby Popkov, PhD

"Courage is like love; it must have hope for nourishment."
– Napoleon Bonaparte

Far above, the bell tower bonged eight-thirty, and I don't know what compelled me, but I began to dance. At first, I wiggled in my chair with delight, but then I stood and mocked bad modern dance. Leap. Jump. Wave. Jump. Crouch. And I sang, "What you gotta know is we're all equal!" Wave. Jump. Walk. "Anything less is totally feeble!" Kick. Leap. Hands-Up. Hands-Down. "Times are a-changin' we ain't medieval!" Run, Run. Jump. Jump. "There's never been a cause to be deceitful!' Turn. Jump. Skip. "Because if you do, know it's illegal!"

Then, out of breath, I laughed as I wrote in the dust that covered the antediluvian wood desk, "I am a Nietzschean Superman!" And I smelled my fingers, drawing the dust into my nose like sweet happy candy. All the weight of my free-floating dread went buoyant. Nietzsche said, "We should consider every day lost on which we have not danced at least once. And we should call every truth false, which was not accompanied by at least one laugh." So, I laughed, danced, and jumped. Now I'd be free to spend my days searching for the elusive Augie Omega! Leap. Hands-up. Hands-down. Turn. Jump. Jump. It was time to steal a misquoting Bible! Leap. Jump. Turn. What I had was better than tenure. I was the best thing a professor can be in a modern university. Invisible!

Jazz hands!

6

But first, I had to go to a small office just below the bell tower and hand in my yearly GOALS report (Goal Oriented Attainment List for Success), which contained four bullet points stating what I intended to accomplish during the upcoming academic year. None of the professors bothered to put any effort into these GOALS because they knew that once turned in, they would disappear into deep space, and no one would ever refer to them again. Yet, if I didn't turn them in, someone might challenge my newfound invisibility.

Each bullet had to start with the preposition "to," followed by a verb and then a "modality shift." The key to writing the list was to include enough Edu-speak so that no one had any idea what the hell your goals were. Thus, when you failed to achieve them, no one could hold you accountable. The key to writing the list effectively was to incorporate enough Edu-speak, as it is a language that has never been successfully translated and its native speakers have no understanding of what they are actually saying. For example, my previous year's list was:

➤ To exercise metrical indicators of completion
➤ To identify/implement workflow engagement plans
➤ To rally my curricular benchmarks
➤ To holistically approach cross-content frontiers

But this time, relishing my new invisibility, I went for the gold.

➤ To throw away the Jim Beam hidden in my desk
➤ To stop going to work completely

➢ To come to grips with the fact that the purpose of American higher education is to provide multimillion-dollar gladiatorial entertainment to alums while feeding subservient worker bees to the multinational corporations that control what's left of our sagging democracy
➢ To avenge the death of Felice Wolinski, sophomore communications major. And to find Augie Omega.

"We had to replace a few parts in the instrument panel, so it cost a little more," said the pit mechanic as he revealed my rebuilt cherry red BMW. As I sat in the replacement seat and held the new steering wheel, I thought maybe Felice Wolinski, sophomore communications major, was right: Life is just the "dissonant lyrics of despair and the bankrupt chronicles of disillusionment." So, she died right where I was sitting. That didn't mean I shouldn't drop-top and enjoy the ride.

Ping!

> Dear Professorial Community,
>
> Pre-mid-term teaching evaluations are due next week.
>
> Please remind your students that if they answer the online multi-choice questions about your teaching performance, the university will send them a digital coupon that can be used to download their favorite video games, including Tetris or Pokémon.
>
> Dr. Li Haoshi
> Office of Student Achievement

Three hundred top-down miles later, I was back in front of Faith Light. My plan? Casually walk in, take the Bible, walk out, go to a copy shop, make a copy, and return the Bible before anyone knew it was missing. I know what you're thinking: What goes around comes around. But deep in your heart, if you're honest with yourself, you know this oft-repeated dictum is just a poorly told joke. There's no evidence that what goes around comes around. For example, here's a bullet list for you–The greatest natural disasters in the last 500 years:

- 1519 – Plague - 25 million dead
- 1556 - Shaanxi Earthquake - 830,000 dead
- 1633 – Another Plague - 20 million dead
- 1786 – Dadu River Landslide – 100,000 dead
- 1839 - India Cyclone - 300,000 dead
- 1860 – Yet Another Plague - 12 million dead
- 1887 - Yellow River Flood – 1 to 2 million dead
- 1918 – Flu pandemic - 30 to 50 million dead
- 1920 - Haiyun Earthquake - 240,000 dead
- 1931 - Yellow River Flood - 1 to 4,000,000 dead
- 1967 - Tangshan Earthquake - 245,000 dead
- 1970 - Bhola Cyclone - 500,000 to 1,000,000 dead
- 2004 - Indian Ocean Earthquake/Tsunami - 230,000 dead
- 2020 – Covid Pandemic - Millions dead and counting

What happened? Did the creator of the universe cunningly arrange it so that all these millions were in the right place at the right time so they could be simultaneously punished for their sins? So that what goes around comes around? If that were the case, Sam Sherbeck, my grade school playground enemy, who, to the delight of all the boys in catechism class, put dog crap in my backpack while I was praying, wouldn't have become the CEO of a major tech firm and be living in an 8,000 square foot house in Paradise Valley. Instead, he would've died in a massive septic tank explosion along with two million other fifth-grade bullies.

Ping!

Dear Faculty,

Great News! I've run it up the chain, and the provost has decided that those of you who have the wonderful opportunity to serve on the all-day tenure review committee will now not only get boxed lunches delivered during your meetings but also cookies!

You're welcome,

Acting Dean Bobby Popkov, PhD

"If you want to know what a man's like, take a good look at how he treats his inferiors, not his equals." — J.K. Rowling

The front door of Faith Light squeaked, and once again, the dusty glow of the stained-glass took hold of me, causing a twang of jealousy for those who could, despite the evidence, believe in something. I had timed my midafternoon heist perfectly. The sanctuary was empty. The floor creaked as I glided up the velvet runner to the pulpit and found what I was looking for, dog-eared and filled with colorful book tabs, *The Newly Revised Standard Living Family Bible Second Edition with helpful sidebars* published by HolyHub Press. At full tilt, I scanned the small print front matter filled with copyright notices and legal warnings, followed by a long list of HolyHub directors, associate directors, and sales managers. And at the bottom of the page, in tiny, almost unreadable print, "Edited by Augie Omega."

"Holy shit," I muttered. Suddenly, my mission changed. I wasn't going to just make a copy. I had to steal it, for I had to save other people from Felice Wolinski, sophomore communications major's fate. A side door popped open, and I dropped behind the pulpit as two disassociated voices entered the sanctuary. I pulled my legs to my chest and stopped breathing as they drew close.

"Hey."

"Yeah?"

"Know who owns the fancy schmancy convertible parked in the pastor's spot?" said the squeaky-clean voice of what must've been the church office assistant.

"It might be the I.T. guy. He's coming over to reboot the smart-pulpit," said the voice of the uncorrupted custodian.

"No, he did that this morning."

"Should I call and get it towed?"

"Oh no, we gotta love the sinner. Remember what it says in *Jeremiah* Chapter 4, verse 7, 'Life is what happens when you're busy making other plans.'" For those keeping count, that's not Jeremiah, it's John Lennon. I knew because I once faked a severe allergic reaction to get out of the audience participation part of a Yoko Ono art installation.

"Shall we find this lost soul?"

"Yes, let's enlighten him."

The voices moved on, and a door clunked. Coast clear, I grabbed the Bible and took two running steps before my feet flew out from under me, and I crashed headfirst to the floor. Blinded by a thumping headache, I couldn't figure out what had happened. Then I saw it. The Bible was chained to the toppled smart-pulpit. Desperate, I yanked the manacle. It wouldn't give. Then I saw it, in the wings, beyond the congregation's sightlines, mounted on the wall, encased in breakable glass, what every religion needs when faith and prayer fail: a fire extinguisher and ax. Until that moment, I'd lived in self-nothingness. I was no better than moss, fungus, or cauliflower. Jean-Paul Sartre said there's no reality except in action. "The coward makes himself cowardly. The hero makes himself heroic." Impelled by Jean-Paul's words, I broke the glass and grabbed the ax. A fire alarm blasted.

What Sartre failed to mention was that taking action requires talent. Being a pure academic, I'd never wielded an ax before, so my whacks cut misguided gashes in the carpet. Alarms whooped as I wildly slammed the blade into the thick chain, knocking over a row of tapered candles. A freak blow sent a chalice flying. Thwack! Thwack! My blows became drastic as time ran out. Then, as I wound up for the ultimate strike, the ax flew from my hands, spun straight up to heaven, and lodged itself in the crotch of a smiling Jesus painted on the ceiling. Desperate, I gave the good book one last Hulk-like yank, and it popped free. Chain trailing, I stumbled to the fire exit, hit the crash bar, made my convertible, tossed in the misquoting Bible, and, like 007, jumped in without opening the door. Ten squealing seconds later, I was gone.

Sartre also said we must take responsibility for our actions, but that would have to wait. For the time being, I had, in some small way, avenged the death of Felice Wolinski, sophomore communications major. If only for a moment, I was more than my algorithmic self. Jean-Paul and James Bond would've been proud, I thought, as I sped past the grain elevators toward freedom. Three happy hours later, I was almost back on campus.

Ping!

> Dr. Neb,
>
> As you know, you failed to show up for your Academic Ascertainment (A.A.) hearing. If you're going to miss such a critical meeting, it's essential you reschedule at least two days in advance.
>
> Please immediately convey the reason for your non-attendance.
>
> Have A Great Day,
>
> Acting Dean Bobby Popkov, PhD
>
> *"A whole stack of memories never equal one little hope."*
> – Charles M. Schulz

Cruise control set at eighty, steering with my knees, I thumbed my phone.

> Acting Dean Popkov,
>
> I was told the meeting was in room 151 in old A&S. No one showed.
>
> Sincerely,

> Charlie Neb

Desperate, I turned off the cruise and glided as I waited for a response. We all hope the universe - what Isaiah Berlin called the "grim causal treadmill" - is intelligent. That there's some Oscar-winning screenwriter up there connecting the dots, but you know, in your sober moments, the great drama lacks a just author and a noble end.

Ping!

> Dr. Neb,
>
> The meeting was <u>not</u> in <u>Old</u> Arts & Sciences but <u>New</u> Arts & Sciences.
>
> <u>Room 151 of old A&S is currently closed for A.A. (Asbestos Abatement)</u>. The notice about the closure was prominently displayed on the door.
>
> Have A Great Day,
>
> Acting Dean Popkov, PhD
>
> *"Healthy citizens are the greatest asset any country can have." – Winston Churchill*
>
> PS Please tell me you did not enter room 151 in Old Arts and Science or touch anything within.

I quickly asked Siri. She answered, "Mesothelioma is a type of cancer that happens when one inhales asbestos. There is no cure. Death rate: 100%." Ping!

> Dr. Neb,

Your A.A. hearing has been reset for next Tuesday. Noon. Room #151 of <u>New</u> Arts and Sciences. Let me repeat: <u>New</u> A&S!

Have A Great Day,

Acting Dean Popkov, PhD

PS University Rule 3549-C - The university's Terms of Use warranty and disclaimer states that anyone entering campus must read all posted signs. In NO event shall the university, representatives of the university, or administrators be liable for any direct, indirect, punitive, incidental, special, or consequential damages to property or life arising out of or connected with the use or misuse of its buildings, rooms, walkways, stadiums, Musical Arts Center, conservatories, dining facilities, administrative offices, Middle Earth research centers, Greek row, theatres, meeting rooms, libraries, observatories, computer science rooms, dormitories, restrooms or land. By entering campus, you agree to take due diligence and understand and agree that there are levels of risk, and, to the extent permitted by law, you expressly and voluntarily assume the risk of death or other personal injury sustained while on campus whether or not caused by negligence including but not limited to equipment malfunction. Additionally, you agree to indemnify, defend, and hold the university harmless from any third-party claims arising from any use or misuse of our products. The university shall not be liable for any damages, or any other loss, whether direct, indirect, consequential, incidental, or any further sub-licensee under any sub-license agreements arising from any defect, error, fault, or failure to perform with respect even if the university has been advised of the possibility of such defect, error, fault, or negligence.

That's when I saw the strobing lights. It was a cop. For a second, I thought I'd make a run for it, but instead, I hit the brakes and pulled up in the roadside trucker trash. The cop took his sweet time walking his Bolshevik floppiness to my door.

"Good afternoon, officer," I innocently smiled.

"Did'ya know you was weaving?"

"I was?"

"You almost took out a hitchhiker a quarter mile back. In my book, distracted driving is no different from drunk driving."

"I sincerely apologize."

"License and registration."

Trying to hide my shaking hands, I dug through my glove compartment and fished out my crumpled registration between a rock-hard Mars bar and a long-dead flashlight.

"What's this?" the cop said as he inspected the bit of dried fruit stuck to my registration. He peeled it off and held it up for a close look. "Is this a piece of rotten apricot? You a health food nut?"

"Ah. Sure, why not," I said. Then I saw that the apricot he delicately held between his index and thumb was not an apricot. It was a nostril! A nostril attached to Felice Wolinski, sophomore communications major's mummified, pierced, crooked nose.

"May I?" the cop said as he indicated he wanted to toss it.

"But, officer, wouldn't that be littering?" I said as I peed my pants a little.

"It's organic."

And he tossed the "apricot" over the hood and into the forgotten debris of the embankment.

"Now, son," he said as he tipped his hat back, "tell me what I should do. I got an idiot driving like a moron, but unlike most yahoos in this screwed-up world, he was distracted by his Bible." That's when I remembered the thick tome beside me in the bucket seat. My mind was so taken by Siri saying, "Mesothelioma most often affects the lungs, but rarer types can affect the testicles," that I'd forgotten I was on a religious crusade. "You could've caused significant loss of life," he continued. "Normally, I'd do a breathalyzer and run your ass into jail no matter the results, but you were reading the good book. Do you see the perplexing conundrum I'm facing?"

"Yes, officer, I know exactly what you mean." I had no idea what he meant.

"Do me a favor, son. Read your favorite passage."

Hiding the chain attached to the Bible, I said, "Oh, sure. I'll just open my trusty, well-worn Holy Book to one of my many pre-marked pages." I'm not sure how many times I cleared my throat, but it was at least five before I found a yellow highlighted passage and read, "And Jesus said, 'Postmodern irony and cynicism become an end in itself, a measure of hip sophistication and literary savvy.'"

"If I'm not mistaken," said the cop, "that's from the Sermon on the Mount."

"You are correct," I said. For those playing Bible Bingo, X-out David Foster Wallace on your game card. I knew it was Wallace because I also failed to finish reading *Infinite Jest*.

"Please, more."

So, I continued reading, "'Few dared to try to talk about ways of working toward redeeming what's wrong, because they'll look sentimental and naïve to all the weary ironists. Irony has gone from liberating to enslaving.'"

"Isn't that edifying?" He beamed.

"Yes, sir, good writing."

"Who would've thunk that Jesus, two thousand years ago, anticipated modern pessimism," he said as he looked up at a flyover of barking geese. And I was rather impressed that he took his time taking in the timbre of their honks. Then he looked down at me suspiciously and added, "Don't you feel sorry for them pessimists?"

"Oh, yeah, those people. Sad. Never associate with them," I lied.

"I heard somewhere that the greatest pessimist in the world is a guy named Augie Omega. Ever heard of him?"

"Yes."

"That poor schmuck has no heaven to look forward to, no reward for his suffering, no punishment for his foes. For him, all the world's wrongs will never be set right. He'll just cling to cynicism and irony - two colorless, odorless gasses that seep into our joints and do nothing to elevate the chaos of life. Don't you agree?"

"Sure do. Irony sucks," I said, doing my best at kissing ass while still scanning the side of the road for Felice Wolinski, sophomore communications major's nose.

He took my sticky registration and walked back to his patrol car. As I waited for him to discover that a BMW matching mine had been spotted fleeing from a church, I thought back to the days before the odorless gasses of cynicism and irony seeped into my joints. I needed a miracle. Then Mary came to me. Not that Mary, but Mary Goodheart, my first girlfriend. I'd never be in this mess if I had only listened to her.

We were sixteen and sitting in the back pew of an empty church when we kissed for the first time. She had sun-blond hair. I, a hopeless crush and a crewcut. Between caresses, she whispered, "Father, son, and hoooooly ghost." Taken by the spirit, I fell to my knees and proclaimed my undying love for her and God. She took my face in her butter-soft hands and whispered, "Isn't it wonderful to know God has a plan? After graduation, we'll marry and buy a house, and you'll give up that foolish dream of becoming an actor and get a proper job. And I'll stay home and care for our six children - three boys and three girls. None of whom ever question their gender identity or their faith in God. And every Sunday and Wednesday, we'll go to church and thank The Lord for a perfect life. And after death takes us, we'll awaken, and our bodies will be flawless, and everyone will be the approximate age of Jesus at the time of his crucifixion, right around thirty-something, and we'll be slender and pretty. And there will be no conflict, war, or chaos. And the words "cynicism, irony, and doubt" will disappear from the lexicon. And every morning will be sunny and a comfortable seventy-eight degrees with just enough humidity to keep our skin soft and supple without the need for lotion. And we'll spend our afternoons playing pickleball, and everyone will be on the winning team. And every evening, we'll watch amusing rom-coms written by Oscar-winning screenwriters. And we will finally be free of all this ceaseless, relentless flux, because we will have mooring and stability, which will go on forever and ever and ever and ever." And we kissed. "Amen."

That night, I went to throw away my copy of Carl Sagan's *The Pale Blue Dot*, but at the alley trash can, I stopped, opened it to a random page, and read, "Our planet is a lonely speck in the great enveloping cosmic dark. In our obscurity, in all this vastness, there is no hint that help will come from elsewhere to save us from ourselves." After a sleepless night, I met Mary at her locker and told her I'd changed my mind. I couldn't believe this massive universe was understandable using only dogma, rituals, and faith. "I don't mean to come off as a prick when it comes to religion," I told her. "The truth is, I crave what you've got. I covet your confidence. But once you see a ballerina fall, you always see falling ballerinas."

"Who in their right mind would choose washed-out calamity over comfort?" she cried. Then the bell rang, and she told me she'd pray for me during gym class. Her last words to me were, "Charlie, it's time to stop being yourself and start being normal." Years later, I learned she married a Kroger grocery store manager and lived happily ever after on a cul-de-sac in Cleveland.

Ping!

Dear Students, Faculty, and Staff,

I'm delighted to announce that the president has approved

funding for a new Dean of Loneliness to help manage campus trauma and optimize quality of life in high-risk areas like the dorms and the English Department.

Be Happy,

Dr. Jerry Loudie
Senior Campus Mental Health Engagement Officer
Mental Health Solutions Center

The cop came back, and I readied my wrists for handcuffs. "No arrests or warrants," he said. "So, I'm going to let you go."

Stunned, I managed to get out, "Bless you, sir."

"If."

"If?"

"You tell me, what's that thing on the back of your car?"

"Thing?"

"The emblem."

"Emblem?"

"The fish with legs that says, 'Darwin.'"

What the hell was I thinking putting a Darwin fish on my car? Why stick anything back there that might piss off a cop? Did I really think the Yahoo behind me in traffic was saying, "Look, a Darwin fish, that means the cynic in front of us believes the diversity of life on earth is a product of modifications that have occurred through natural selection over hundreds of millions of years?"

The officer waited for my answer. "That, sir, ah…" and I prayed for inspiration.

"Yes?"

And my prayer worked, "That's the name of the dealership where I bought the car."

"Darwin BMW?" the cop said.

"Yes." I confidently answered.

"Okay. Everything seems in order," he said as he handed back my license and registration, "and because you're not a pessimist, I'm going to overlook your transgressions."

"Bless you," I said as I scanned the side of the road for the apricot.

"Now get the hell out of here."

"But, officer, if you don't mind, I'd like to sit here and think about my transgressions." I was hoping he'd leave so I could retrieve the nose.

"No. Go. Now. Before I change my mind."

I dropped my Beemer in gear, and his flashing lights faded in my rearview. Hypothetical: what if Mary Goodheart was right, and all we have to do is behave ourselves, and we get to spend eternity playing pickleball and watching rom-coms. What if it was that simple? And that boring. I put the thought aside, hit the gas, raced the geese, and won.

7

According to the "Ask a Doctor Why" website, the latency period for mesothelioma was 10 to 50 years, which didn't explain why I was already showing symptoms: chest pain, shortness of breath, a pronounced cough, and painful testicles.

Ping!

> Mr. Neb,
>
> Thrilled to hear you will join us tomorrow for the roadside trash-athon. Yes, we will be working mile markers 14 to 15. Why do you ask?
>
> Bring lots of heavy-duty 40-gallon bags, rubber gloves, steel-toed shoes, and a sense of humor.
>
> Peace Out,
> Dr. Jerry Loudie

"Welcome to HolyHub Publishers," said the genial, prerecorded voice from my phone. "Please listen to this entire message, as our menu has recently changed. If this is a medical emergency, hang up and dial 911. We are experiencing unusually high call volumes. You might get faster service on the HolyHub mobile God App. For marketing and sales, press one. For our fax number, press two."

Zero, zero, zero, zero - Sometimes, you can get the operator if you keep hitting zero. "That's not a valid choice. Nor is Islam, Buddhism, or abortion. For information about our annual telethon for paraplegic tots, press three. To be added to our mailing list, press four. For our helpful express direct prayer line to God, press five." Nine, nine, nine, nine. If it's not zero, then it's nine. "That is not a valid choice. Nor is Hinduism, Krishna, or Socialism. Please press seven to speak to one of our client service representatives."

Seven? Why the hell seven? Beep – seven.

"This call, like life, is monitored by God for quality assurance." After a few moments of angelic music, "Good morning, HolyHub Publishing, Mary Goodheart speaking, how may I direct your call."

"Mary?" I was shocked. "Ah… You didn't, by any chance, attend Central High School?"

"I did. Who's this?"

"Charlie Neb."

"Who?"

"We dated our sophomore year." Dead air. "Hello?"

"Charlie, the skeptic," she said with that same "father, son, and hoooooly ghost" voice, but it was now made even sexier by a three-pack-a-day habit.

"I heard you married," I said.

"I did, but, ah, it didn't exactly work out."

"Sorry to hear that. Kids?

"No."

"Still Catholic?"

"Evangelical."

"Still blond?"

"Brunette."

"Still play pickleball?"

"Why are you calling?"

"Do you publish *The Newly Revised Standard Living Family Bible with helpful sidebars*?"

"We most certainly do," she said, delighted. "Oh, Charlie, have you finally overcome your cynicism?"

"No, I'm looking for Augie Omega."

For a moment, I thought she'd hung up. Then, her voice turned measured. "He no longer works here."

"Do you know where I might find him?"

"Have you tried the pits of hell?"

"Excuse me?"

"If I were looking for Mr. Omega, I'd try the deepest, darkest corner of hell. Way down near the bottom where God keeps pornographers and people who subscribe to Atlantic Magazine."

"So, you have no idea where he might be."

"He was dismissed years ago."

"I found a copy of the Bible he edited."

"No, you didn't. They were shredded."

"Yes, I'm holding it."

"No, you're not."

"And there's a small country church using it."

"I'm hanging up. Have a blessed day."

"Wait! Is there anything you can tell me that might help me find him?"

"Last I heard, he was working at a cryobank."

"You mean like a sperm donation place?"

"We do not use the word 'sperm' in this office."

"Anything else?"

"He was a deceitful devil who misquoted our holy Father, defaced the sales manager's Cadillac, deflowered the publisher's 17-year-old daughter, and introduced my husband to a massage therapist who he left me for. Why on earth would you want to talk to that horrible human being?"

"I want to ask him about the meaning of life," I said.

"Goodbye."

"No, wait! Ah, this might not be the best time to ask, but are you doing anything tonight?" To win her over, I threw in, "I drive a BMW."

"Men who drive BMWs are compensating for genital inadequacy, argumentative, hated by God, overly worried about door dings and total assholes," she said. "Mr. Omega drove a BMW." Click. The line went dead.

The following day, I traded my Beemer for a proper professorial Subaru econobox. Did I tell the dealer about the car's dubious history? I did not. Could I justify this decision philosophically? Yes. It was a simple syllogism.

All men who drive BMWs are total assholes. I drive a BMW. Therefore, all BMWs have human remains in them. Okay, that makes little sense, but it worked for me when I sold it.

Ping!

> Campus Wide Scarlet & Brown Alert,
>
> I'm happy to announce that this Friday at the University Walmart Auditorium, the administration will treat you to the wit of Jackie Diamond. You've seen him on the *Tonight Show* and *Big Brother*.
>
> 8pm. Tickets are free!
>
> Enjoy!
>
> Margrett Applewhite, Entertainment Director
>
> PS In compliance with University Regulation #384-1, Mr. Diamond has signed a contract promising that nothing he says will be offensive or hurtful to anyone.
>
> PPS Faculty do not get free tickets.

I pulled up at mile marker 14 to find Dr. Loudie waving a large sign that read, "We Professors Care." The tangled grass of the roadside was stuccoed with bottles, needles, drug pipes, bumpers, spent energy drinks, tires, diapers, pregnancy tests, roadkill, and, hopefully, one nose. Seeing my new gray econobox, Loudie said, "Where's your pretty BMW?"

"Sold it."

"Why?"

"I, ah, needed a change," I said, ducking the subject.

Just then, a honking Chevy zoomed by, and Dr. Loudie waved the sign and screamed like a tour guide, which I suspected he once was. Then he yelled to the dozen or so professors, "Hey all! This is Charlie Neb! Introduce yourselves!"

"Dr. Baker, he/him/his."

"Dr. Freeman, she/her/hers."

"Dr. Flaneur, he/him/his."

"Dr. Renaud, They/them/theirs."

There were more, but the wind blocked their shouts. I noticed a commonality with the professors, a through-line, but I couldn't quite place it. "If your tummy gets hungry or you need a drink," yelled Dr. Loudie over a buffeting gust, "you'll find fermented seed crisps, pineapple-jalapeño juice, and micro-plastic-pellet-free cucumber sandwiches in the back of my Subaru." Then it hit me, the through-line - they were all from the humanities.

"Where are the STEM professors?" I asked.

"Oh, they never show up for roadside beautification."

"Why not?"

"They don't have to. Their jobs are safe," and he handed me a peeling orange reflective vest and stabbing stick. And I began my perverted Easter egg hunt for an apricot.

Ping!

Dear Mr. Neb,

We are pleased to inform you that you've passed your physical exam, genetic analysis, background family medical history check, height evaluation, and sperm movement test.

Any time you would like to donate, we're sitting on ready.

Toodles,

Sara Thumper
Client Services
Maze, The Affordable Cryobank

> PS I was impressed that you, unlike most men, did not lie about your height. You are indeed six-foot-one-inch tall.

An hour later, I had filled five 40-gallon bags when Dr. Flaneur, the creative writing professor, straggled up. He was a mammoth, waxen man with a yellowing cigarette beard and a five-gallon gut that limited him to drawstring sweatpants. During his four decades at the university, he'd published three thin volumes of haikus, which had sold twenty-one copies, eleven, and eight, respectively, but it was enough for him to earn full professor. He often bragged about how he'd used the same syllabus for 32 years, breaking the previous record that had stood since the Truman administration. He was known for playing Tibetan singing bowls and burning frankincense during advising sessions, which had sickened several students.

"Heard about your upcoming A.A. hearing," he said as he huddled his tummy against me.

"It's nothing. Just a minor misunderstanding."

"I've got the secret," he said as he looked around to ensure no one was eavesdropping. "Similes!"

"You mean as in similes and metaphors?"

"They don't cover similes in the university's Diversity and Inclusion webinar. Pass this test and you'll do fine. I'll give you a sentence, and you rewrite it using the correct simile. Ready?"

"I don't understand."

"Drunk with power, he crashed into the room like a female driver. Go ahead. Rewrite," and he waited for my answer.

"Ah... Drunk with power, he crashed into the room like a... madman?" I said, somewhat confused.

"Incorrect. That'd be flagged by the Mental Health Solution Center. Try again."

"Ah... Drunk with power, he crashed into the room like a... bowling ball?"

"Also, incorrect. There's a bowler's club on campus. They have feelings too. Once more."

"Drunk with power, he crashed into the room - period?"

"Correct! Avoid similes! And if you write a haiku about a character drinking coffee, never ever describe the shade of the coffee. Trust me, I speak from experience." And with a slap on my back, he unlatched his tum-tum from my ribs and walked off to stab a bleached Pop-Tart wrapper.

Ping!

> Dear Mr. Neb,
>
> PS I forgot - We ask you to abstain from eating soy products, walnuts, or ejaculating for at least three days before your donation.
>
> Toodles,
>
> Sara Thumper
> Client Services
> Maze, The Affordable Cryobank

Just then, Dr. Merkin drew up, pulling a massive trash bag strapped to her back. She'd been at the university longer than anyone. Some say she was older than old A&S. "The desire to find unalterable objective truths and the eternal order behind the chaos of appearances is your ultimate struggle," she said as she untwisted her scoliosis and stuck her pearl-gray eyebrows into the breeze to make sure no one was listening.

"Okay," I hesitated, entirely confused at her starting in the middle of a conversation.

She pointed a gnarled finger at me, "This is you."

"It is?"

"Yes, because of your upcoming A.A. hearing. But I can help. Do you want my help?"

"Sure, I guess."

She narrowed in on me with her trigger-happy eyes, "At the top of old

Arts and Sciences, in the bell tower, there's a secret room."

"Uh…what's in this room?"

"No one knows. It's been locked for decades. But a rumor's been circulating since the 1970s." She stopped and waited as a professor walked past carrying a dead fish. When the coast was clear, she continued, "That in this secret room, you'll find the answer."

"And what's the question?"

"Who is Augie Omega?"

Most people believed that Dr. Merkin was senile because the linguistics department had been canceled 12 years ago. Yet, she kept coming to work to give impromptu lectures in the food court of the student union, which often degraded into irrational rants. It was said that she had an office somewhere on campus, but no one knew where.

"How do I get into this secret room?"

"There is but one key."

"And who has it?"

"No one knows. It's your quest to find it. Steal it if you must. Then go to the top of the bell tower, unlock the door, and you will find enlightenment!"

"Dr. Merkin."

"Don't call me that!"

"Why not?"

"Because I've disavowed my Ph.D. I UPSed my diploma back to Harvard with a letter informing them where they can shove it!"

"What should I call you?"

"She Who Runs On The Mountain."

"Ah, 'She Who Runs On The Mountain,' you know they canceled the linguistics department twelve years ago."

"I know."

"Then why do you keep coming to work?"

"To find the key to the secret room," she said. Then she wobbled off to help a professor with a skanky mattress.

Wild honking from a speeding Mercedes SUV with blacked-out windows - the PhDs cheered as Dr. Loudie waved the sign. I hadn't seen this many humanities professors so excited since the Faculty Senate quietly voted to remove the words "to meet the state's workforce needs" from the Arts and Sciences mission statement. The provost put them back two days later, but for 48 hours, it was reported that English professors were so delighted they actually said "Good morning" to each other.

"She's early today!"

"Mission accomplished!"

"Cheers and Beers?"

"I think they open at ten," the profs shouted as they dropped their trash bags, peeled off their rubber gloves, and started up the embankment to their reasonably priced Subarus and aging Saabs."

"What's going on?" I said.

"That was the president," Dr. Loudie beamed.

"In the SUV?"

"She saw us. We're done."

"But what about the trash?"

"What about it?" he said.

"I thought we were here to beautify things."

"You're not serious."

"Yes," I said. "I'd like to stay and get the job done."

From the causeway, he looked down on me with the spent eyes of a teacher who had just finished listening to an undergrad read her 20-page metrical composition about her uterus. "How long have you been at the university?"

"Six years."

"Sweating tenure, are we?" He sighed and gave me one of those "you just don't get it" smiles. Then he and the very human humanities professors drove off in a convoy of standardized assessment, university-community partnerships, breakout sessions, outcome-based teaching, and poorly attended service courses.

Ping!

> Dr. Neb,
>
> If you or a loved one has been diagnosed with

> mesothelioma, you may be entitled to financial compensation.
>
> Call the Copeland, Osteen, and Swaggart Law Firm hotline.
>
> We win, so you don't have to!
>
> Your Legal Team

Nine hours later, the sky had turned burnt caramel, the air nippy. I'd filled dozens of 40-gallon bags but not found the "fruit" of my labor. As the lonely lights of the whizzing cars grazed over the embankment, I looked up to find the phosphorescent sky glittering with semiprecious specks of ice. Not enough for a quorum of winter but enough for me, standing stock still, to fly through the net of stars. It was the end of Act One of *Nutcracker*, so I attempted an arabesque. Perhaps, I thought, Mary Goodheart was right, there is a God.

Just then, from the early evening sky, came a single, fully developed flake, not a crystal, but the real thing, the mother ship, the glimmering godflake. It twirled down like the white moth of the Holy Ghost descending at Pentecost, and I stepped up, away from my wayward life, and opened my mouth to take holy communion. As it landed on my warm tongue, I felt the concussive pop of the Lord.

I had stepped on a trucker bomb. I looked down to find my knees splattered with fermented big rig pee. I wiped the exploded drops from my face. And then my diaphragm wiggled, and I expelled a rhythmic belch of air gliding over my vocal cords, producing a single hardy "Ha!" Honk! I jumped. Behind me, on the gravel shoulder, sat the president's black Mercedes SUV chugging like a locomotive. Its lights flashed and the passenger door popped open. "Get in," said the dark figure behind the wheel.

8

I climbed up to a level of executive compensation no assistant professor has ever known. I was entering the idling engine room of academia. The deep state that ruled the crust of the university. The creamy leather of the SUV must've come from a patrician's villa. The chrome instruments glistened with an orange ambiance that threw candy corn-tinted darkness onto the soft outline of the president of the university.

"Good evening, President Boucher," I said with a healthy dose of ass-kissing humility.

Her impeccable black hair and airbrushed makeup hid the fact that she was well into her 60s while trying to hold on to her early 50s. "Any news on Dean Gacy?" she asked. Her cigarette voice reminded me of Lauren Bacall.

"Still in a coma."

Then she looked out at my pile of junk-packed forty-gallon trash bags and said, "What the hell are you doing out here by yourself?"

"Roadside beautification," I said, trying to hide my trepidation.

She coughed, "What for?"

"You said you wanted us, professors, to, ah, be part of the *fabric* of the community."

"I did?"

"Yes. In your State of the University address."

"Huh, you'd think I'd remember that. Where the hell are your cohorts?"

"They left."

"When?"

Self-preservation is the only rule at universities. There's no such thing as a real friend in academia. You might have a beer with a colleague or chitchat the chancellor, but everyone knows they'll sell each other for Machiavellian cannon fodder if the opportunity presents itself. It's just the rules of the game, and you play or perish.

"They left this morning, right after you passed," I said.

"I always suspected they were doing that." She wickedly chuckled. "Those cornballs have been working this stretch of road for three years, and it still looks like downtown New Delhi."

"President Boucher, I want you to know I, personally, am dedicated to optimal professor-community fabric-ness," I awkwardly said. I figured a little suck-up session couldn't hurt. She reached down to the cupholder, grabbed a half-finished party cocktail, and kissed the plastic with her thin lips.

"Drink?"

"No, but thank you."

"Mini cigar?"

"I don't smoke."

"Micro-dose?"

And she opened a gold case the size of two thumbs packed with small pills. From her eyes, I knew the meeting would end if I turned down this last offer.

"What are they?"

"Fluvoxamine, Isocarboxazid, or maybe Tranylcypromine, not sure. All I know is that they're psychiatric penicillin. My husband tells me the side effects are dry mouth, dizziness, insomnia, weight gain, high blood pressure, and increased sexual desire."

"Thank you," I said, but I didn't mean it as I picked out one white tablet. As she popped hers and chased it with a splash, I flicked mine into the backseat. Then her eyes went distant as she looked out at the roaring big rigs lit up like Christmas trees. She was a skeleton of a person who had divorced herself from attachments like God or personal salvation long ago. She seemed to be waiting for the pill to take effect, lost in her hankering sadness for nearly a minute before she cleared her smoke-damaged vocal cords with a guttural hack.

"Do you believe in heaven?" she said, almost to herself.

"Have doubts."

"What about country?"

"This country?"

"Yes."

"I guess it's hard to believe in anything today."

"And love?"

"What about it?"

"Do you believe in it?"

"Ah. Well. Sure. I guess," I said as things got weird.

"Which is more important, love or physical attraction?"

"Well, they're both important," I said, wondering where the hell this was going.

"Which would you rather have, hot-blooded sex with a gorgeous, giggling idiot or passionate lovemaking with a physically imperfect genius who is competent, self-made, and fully capable of dissecting the latest economic numbers while smoking a post-coital cigar?" she said, all in one breath.

"Well, ah, both have advantages and disadvantages," I stumbled through an answer. "Maybe I could do the gorgeous, giggling idiot on Mondays, Wednesdays, and Fridays and the physically imperfect accountant on Tuesdays and Thursdays. Weekends I'd rest."

Her eyes squinted as if she were trying to decipher the deeply hidden meaning behind an obscure German opera. I saw her mentally putting tab "A" into slot "B." "Wait," she said as it dawned on her, "was that an attempt at humor?"

"Yes."

And she stared at me for the longest time before she said dead serious, "Am I supposed to do something?"

"Yes. Laugh if you find it funny."

"Right," is all she said, but she didn't laugh. Again, she looked out at the trucks. "My first husband ran off with a gorgeous giggling idiot," she mumbled while holding the cigar and the drink against her cheek. Her drink-cigar dexterity was truly impressive, but it did place the glowing stick so close to her perfect-hold hairspray I thought she might ignite. "So, I married an unsexy man with a bad temper and a large nose."

"Nose?"

"Yes, his nose is like a sail. My husband is French," then she added, "*Pourquoi les hommes français ont de si gros nez?*"

"Don't follow."

"I said, why do French men have such large noses?"

And there was an odd pause before I realized that was not the set-up to a joke, but an honest question. "Ah, I don't know, but they do seem to have, ah, exceptional olfactory capacities," I said, thinking that was a dumb way to say it.

"Every time I see his nose," she continued, "I can't help but think that life is just a seismic shrug without meaning or purpose. Know what I mean?"

"Yes, I'm an assistant professor."

"Answer me this," she exhaled smoke through a professional embouchure, "You happy?"

"With my nose?"

"In general. Don't just answer. First, think."

And I pretended to think for a moment. I wanted a powerful comeback, but all I managed was, "No, I'm not, but I spend a lot of time trying to avoid unhappiness, which is a kind of happiness."

"That's because we live in the age of post-happiness."

I sat up. The last person to tell me that was Felice Wolinski, sophomore communications major. "Where did you hear that?"

"At the pool party this afternoon, some donor was babbling about how happiness today was, at best, precarious. A sport of chance is how he put it," she said as her eyes went back to the roaring big rigs. "He said that as we get older, the few bits of happiness we know dry up. Love leaves, wit departs, and we lose desires. Life is filled with misery and pain, and if we escape these, boredom lies in wait for us at every corner."

"I don't know who that donor guy was, but he was quoting the philosopher Schopenhauer."

"Oh, for God's sake," she said, each word dripping with disappointment, "you're a philosophy professor." And I immediately regretted my words, for I'd broken a cardinal rule at all universities: never remind the president that the Philosophy Department still exists. I thought, what the hell, it didn't matter. Even if I won my A.A. hearing, the humanities were dead, and my academic career sunk. Within three years, I'd be driving an Uber or working in a cubicle, my only hope to avoid default on my massive student loans resting on my upcoming audition for Jeopardy.

She sucked up a lung full of smoke and glared at me before she said, "Did you know there are caterpillars who feed on only one particular leaf of one particular tree, and when that tree dies, they starve rather than eat the leaves of another? Even though the other trees would afford them proper nutrition."

"Interesting," I said, trying to find it interesting.

The cigar in her hand was now pressed so deep in her cheek the glow was only a thin inch from her acrylic updo. "These caterpillars must know somewhere deep in their souls they are artifacts," she said. "So, they spend their dying days trying to convince administrators of the relevance of their shrinking patch of turf while avoiding the truth."

"Which is?

"They'd be unemployable if they went to another leaf."

"I'm confused. Are we still talking about Schopenhauer?"

"I'm talking about the humanities." And then it happened. A tiny ember from her petite cigar landed on her heavily spritzed hair, where it smoldered. "And philosophy professors are the worst," she said, as if the word "philosophy" were the filthiest in the English language. "You're all tail-chasing cabbage heads that don't make an iota of difference. Look around you! The trees are dying! Everything is dying! I'm dying. You're dying." The spark was now a tiny grass fire. How do you tell your boss her head's on fire? She'd constructed a fine little dithyramb, but I couldn't interrupt. She was on a roll. "No, I'm wrong. English Professors are worse than philosophy. They invent nothing, make no meaningful discoveries, and create in others no practical skills. They are now so unimportant that even a talentless Hollywood hack who follows tired formulas has more influence over our society than they do!"

I couldn't delay. The flame was now climbing up the rock-hard face of her temple hair. It was about to touch the propane tank of her 1960s sweep.

"President Boucher, I hate to interrupt."

"Do you ever feel disoriented by modern life?"

"Most of the time."

"Me too."

"Your hair's on fire."

She didn't hear me. "There's little left for you powerless, disoriented caterpillars to do but go down with the ship," she continued. "All you will do is debunk, unpack, and deconstruct right up to the moment of impact."

"I agree, especially about unpacking and deconstruction, but we really need to talk about your hair."

"What about it?"

"It's on fire!"

"How so?"

"It's in flames!"

Just then, an explosive surge consumed her wig, and sparks flew as she ripped it off and whacked it against the instrument panel. The Molotov refused to give, so I grabbed her cocktail and doused it, which had little effect. She powered down her window and threw the burning acrylic into the darkness, where it stopped, dropped, and rolled. Wigless, her smoldering real-life frog hair had been teased and hot curled in prep for so many faculty functions that it hardly existed. I coughed because of the acrylic smoke. She was unaffected. Then the fire of her alcohol-fueled tirade withered, and she became a shell of herself as she flashed back to some distant moment long before she joined academia, long before she married a man with a large nose. For a moment, I thought she'd forgotten I was there, but then she whispered, "You feeling it?"

"Anxiety? Tons."

"No, the joy of knowing that you and I see life as it truly is, an absurd farce."

"Oh, sure, that too."

She opened her pill case and popped one more. Whatever it was, it worked, for a blueish calmness came to her. Then she looked at me, her face speckled with ash from her burned wig. Her stillborn CEO eyes told me nothing could rumple her, not even the end of the world. And I was suddenly hit by the desire to hold her. I hovered my hand over hers.

"May I?"

"Please." I tentatively placed my fingers on hers and gently caressed the rib-like tendons on the back of her sun-damaged hand. She sniffed and gave me a tearful smile. "*J'aime ton nez.*"

"I know "*nez*" is nose, but other than that. . . "

"I like your nose," she said.

"Okay," I said, thinking that was a weird subject change.

"It's not too large or small. Fits your face."

"Ah . . .thank you?"

"Would you like to come to my place for a nightcap?" she said, but with a face that remained closed, unreadable. I sat there like an idiot clown for a moment, not knowing what to say. But then I thought. Why not? It's simple: go to her mansion, have a cocktail, if the opportunity presents itself, make love to her (hopefully, she had more than one wig), and then tell her about the upcoming A.A. hearing. In the afterglow of passion, she'd call the acting dean and order him to drop all charges. Perhaps then I could ask her about the missing key to the room in the bell tower. Hell, maybe if my game were on, I'd even get a pay raise - I mean, I hadn't eaten soy products, walnuts, or ejaculated for three days.

"I'd have to, ah, stop by my place to change pants."

"Excuse me?" she said as she looked down at my slippery, urine-soaked knees. "Is that stink you?"

"Yes."

"What is it?"

"Fermented trucker pee," I said. "And while I'm at it, I should shower."

"Sounds like a plan," she said. "While you shower, I'll drop off my grandkids." She nodded to the back. And I turned, shocked to find her grandchildren in the dark, smoke-filled backseat - evil-looking 10-year-old boy-twins and an officious 19-year-old college girl, her eyes black and blue and her nose still heavily bandaged from a recent nose job. All three consumed by the modern friction-free remedy for boredom-their phones. The white tablet I had pitched into the backseat was perched in the 19-year-old's hair. "Hi," I said, but they never separated from their earbuds. They weren't even aware Grandma had come to a stop and almost self-immolated. I looked back to the president. Her soul was losing orbit, the booze cutting her concentration. I had to do something to get her back on track. It was time to seal the deal, and I knew precisely how.

"Did you hear the one about the turtle who walks into a bar with a parrot on his shoulder—" I said.

"What are you doing?" She squinted at me.

"Telling a joke."

"Why?"

"Because I think you need a laugh."

"Oh My God!" came a screech from the rhinoplasty teen in the back. "He's trying to be funny!"

"Yes," I said. "But it's okay. It's a joke about turtles. They're the last marginalized community you can make fun of without consequences."

"Grandma, he's Charlie Neb!"

"Who?"

"The sicko professor I told you about. The jerk who told a joke in my friend Becky's beginning philosophy class."

"This true?" the president said.

"Yes, but I only tell woke jokes."

"You should see the terrible things the students are saying about him," the brat squealed as she held out her glowing iPhone to a social media warpage. The president scrolled through the lengthy list. Then she looked at me without hope. "Consider yourself suspended without pay."

"Does that mean no nightcap?"

"Get out."

Defeated, I opened the door and slipped past the ten-way power seat on my way down to the newly tarred blacktop. From the back seat, the righteous little Philistines judged me. From the front, Grandma looked down on me like a solemn pharisee and reached for the door.

"I'm on a quest to find Augie Omega," I quickly said as she slammed it and powered off, throwing pebbles. But she only made it 30 feet when her massive behemoth came to a shocking halt. I don't know what compelled me to mention Augie Omega. It was a last-ditch effort to save my job. She idled for a thinking moment. Then, the bright white reverse lights blinded me as she crept back. The passenger window powered down.

"Did you say Augie Omega?" I could see an atom-sized crack in her armor. She took a deep breath and drifted. "Some say he was a philosophy professor who went mad. Others say he's the ultimate stand-up comedian who travels the world performing outrageous acts to prove we live in the age of post-absurdism."

"Which is?"

"When you can't tell the difference between real life and a parody of real life, you're living in post-absurdism."

"Why are you talking to that ass-wipe, Grandma?" the teen complained."

"Shut up and put your headset on! Now!" the president barked, and the backseat biddy rolled her eyes and returned to her fake social life. Then, the President took me into her confidence. "Come to the mansion in an hour. I'll tell you everything I know about Augie Omega. Bring a nice wine. And flowers. No one's brought me flowers in a long time."

"What about your husband?"

"He's at a psychiatric association conference in Seattle. Won't be back until midnight." Then she hit the pedal and powered off, leaving me alone with the night, the sharp cold, the semi-trucks careening by, and the still smoldering wig. I had an hour to shower, shave, and sign up for WhatsApp, Instagram, WeChat, and X.

9

> **Coolgirl**
>
> OMG – Professor Neb told a joke today in class!
>
> 💬 1   🔁 2   ♡ 1   ⬆

> **Eulalie**
>
> He thinks he's so privileged that he's got the right to say something.
>
> 💬 3   🔁 3   ♡ 2   ⬆

> **Bull Shots**
>
> Personally, I don't feel like he intended any harm. It was just a harmless joke.
>
> 💬 4   🔁 5   ♡ 3   ⬆

> **Unicorn Queen**
>
> Intent is not as important as perceived impact. All comedy comes at the expense of someone. Thusly, comedy creates victims.
>
> 💬 9   🔁 27   ♡ 6   ⬆

> **Becky0682**
>
> We need to go mega-viral on Dr. Neb's ass!
>
> 💬 12   🔁 55   ♡ 9   ⬆

Busowner22

Was it a dirty joke?

19   71   20

CatLady

No, I would've remembered that.

20   72   22

CoffeeAddict

Sexist?

22   73   25

GoVictoria

No.

23   74   29

CoffeeAddict22

Racist?

24   75   32

GoVictoria

Not at all

25   77   35

Buzowner

It was a joke. That's all that matters!

26   79   36

CatLady

Dr. Neb was present when Felice Wolinski, sophomore communications major, offed herself. #Endtoxicmaleheroism

27   84   42

IGotAnItch

Did she get her marshmallows?

35   94   43

ActivelyActive

Why are we required to take a humanities class? Humans are screwed. We should all try to be less human. #humanitysucks

44   95   45

QueenLand77

The humanities are an artifact - I studied about them in my anthropology class.

67   103   47

DomesticDadad

Cancel his ass. We need to make his life harder to find than an episode of the Cosby Show.

72   325   48

Sowhatever

I read that during World War Two, the Japanese wouldn't let STEM majors be kamikaze pilots because they needed them for the war effort, so all kamikaze pilots were humanities majors.

73   458   49

TomPumpkinSpice

I heard that was true about suicide bombers in Iraq too. They are all, like, poets and artists. #humanitiessuck

94   743   50

Ilovegod

Let's go Biblical on Dr. Neb! Can we get him expelled?

199   1094   91

Wormhole

He is a self-interested white heterosexual privileged male who uses comedy to trick everyone in order to maintain power.

256   1563   94

GasAttack

Doesn't he teach like a lot of dead white male philosophers. He's so out of touch! We should contact The Alumni Association!

302   2045   100

Anteater

I heard Plato and Aristotle were pedophiles. What does that say about Dr. Charlie Neb?

399   2954   109

Gas-electric 24

The joker bears all responsibility for the impact of their words. #microaggression #hostileenvironment #senseofbelongingviolated #collectivetrauma #psychologicalsafetydesecrated

433   3672   123

Cupcake5599

Everything offends someone. So, best to say nothing. Communication is overrated.

543   4593   132

BatesRotaryFile

Jokes reinforce the "other" mindset which is at the core of imperialism and colonialism! A joke is nothing more than a grab for power. An attack on the vulnerable! I read somewhere that most dictators have a great sense of humor.

654   5421   145

SugarPlum

When I hear something funny, I always ask, 1) Would anyone find this offensive? 2) Do I find it offensive? 3) If it does not offend someone today is there a possibility it will offend someone at some future date? Then I choose to laugh or not.

765   6592   156

Zook

Dr. Neb is wrong, reckless, reprehensible! He is a disgrace. He should be fired immediately! No excuses. Ban him from campus before he does more damage. #FireCharlieNebNow!

845   7885   311

PrincessAdorable

I saw Professor Neb on campus. OMFG! He was eating at the Pita Pit in the student union. #BoycottPitaPit

888   8569   335

Cheesemaker

We are all going to Pita Pit to protest. Bring your bullhorns!

1045   9543   645

ASAP!

We need to stage a protest against Neb! #Comedyisdead

1155   10293   721

Handsomeguy2

Great idea! Where?

1156   19294   746

Spivey

Protests are only allowed in the campus free-speech zone.

1157   20995   810

Handsomeguy2

Free-speech zone? Where it be?

1158   20996   888

Spivey

Near the Library.

1159   20997   966

Handsomeguy2

Where's the library?

1160   20998   947

Spivey

Across from Bob's Bar.

1161   20999   955

Handsomeguy2

I've never seen a free-speech zone there.

1162   21000   1045

Spivey

You got to follow the path down the alley around the back to the loading dock.

1163   21001   1299

Bigfootisreal

Comedy = War! Neb is a war criminal. So is Pita Pit! #MyFeelingsAreImportantToo. #FireCharlieNebNow!

1699   33434   1854

BeKind

All the time he was telling the joke, I was hyperventilating. I thought I was going to lose consciousness. All I can do is add this to the litany of injuries that have been done to me. We need a therapist assigned to this class. Hell, all classes!

3500   356435   8054

Spivey

What Professor Neb did was a hate crime! We should all get extra credit! #BoycottPitaPit

4572   564393   10950

Bettyawesome

Professor Neb should be written out of polite society – Assassination is too good for him. #FireCharlieNebNow!

6789   954544   17940

MableofGod

We need Professor Neb De-balled, debunked and deep fried! End The Humanities! And Boycott Pita Pit!

9696   996696   20999

Spivey

It's a post humor world! Get used to it. #BoycottDrNeb.

10567   100K   62505

MasterJedigGirl

Jokes are a masculine way of inflicting superiority. Wit is a firearm! Laughter is a form of violence! Jokes are harassment.

14300   156K   101K

JoefromSpace

Comedy is what led to Nazism during World War 2. The Holocaust would have never happened if it weren't for the movie *Cabaret*.

15678   277K   235K

Coolgirl

I heard someone say Professor Neb hangs around with Holocaust deniers.

16750   300K   245K

Spivey

At Pita Pit?

16751   303K   2554K

JoefromSpace

Let everyone know, Pita Pit is a hotbed of Holocaust deniers.
#PitaPitholocaustdeniers #BoycottPitaPit

17448   333K   332K

Danceparty

We need to boycott Pita Pit until they come clean about their
Holocaust policy. We need a powerful and brave statement from
their CEO! #BoycottPitaPit #FireCharlieNebNow!

17594   341K   356K

JennyTrip

How do you get someone on a "no fly" list? #BoycottPitaPit
#FireCharlieNebNow!

18002   369K   369K

Peachsodawithice

We need reparations. Defund Charlie Neb! #BoycottPitaPit
#FireCharlieNebNow!

19334   405K   371K

Arlene

Maybe that's what we should do during halftime shows. I mean,
the marching band is lame. Instead, professors should be given a
chance to get up on the 50-yard line and openly confess their
sins in a sort of ritual moral purification. #BoycottPitaPit

19754   418K   833K

Danceparty

Pita Pit just posted a statement on their company website. It
reads, "Pita Pit has always taken a strong stand against the
Holocaust. We hope you can join us on January 27 for
Holocaust Remembrance Day at your local Pita Pit. We will be
giving out Free Hula Teriyaki Bowls from three to four."

22300   541K   1451K

DaddyO

Woah, that's so generic. Pita Pit needs to come clean. Are they or are they not against the Holocaust?

🗨 31K   ↻ 600K   ♡ 1453K   ↑

PettyBoopsBebop

Did anyone catch Professor Neb on their smartphone? We should record all professors' lectures. Let them know their words are going public. #BoycottPitaPit #Boycottphilosophy

🗨 49K   ↻ 667K   ♡ 1459K   ↑

Treehugger

Why are we keeping this to ourselves? We need to start retweeting. Silence is not an option! Permanent ostracism for Neb! Tell the world about Professor Neb! Everyone retweet! #BoycottPitaPit #newsflash

🗨 99K   ↻ 766K   ♡ 1499K   ↑

Weeaboo

University of Texas students are onboard. Ban Professor Neb from all college campuses! #newsflash #BoycottPitaPit

🗨 164K   ↻ 797K   ♡ 1544K   ↑

GoofyFeline

UCLA students stand with you! Professor Neb has got to be stopped! #ErasedNeb #BoycottPitaPit

🗨 167K   ↻ 855K   ♡ 1601K   ↑

Shozo 5594

上海大學聽到了呼喚！Neb 教授現在在中國受到歡迎！

🗨 629K   ↻ 955K   ♡ 1633K   ↑

Ali

إنه ليس مضحكا Neb! توقف عن الأست!

💬 720K　　🔁 1044K　　♡ 1785K　　⬆

सिको बिली बाक्रा

Профессор Neb энд Монголд, хэрэв тэр энд үзүүлбэл бид түүнийг буцаах болно.

💬 770K　　🔁 1150K　　♡ 1855K　　⬆

Danceparty

There's a new message on Pita Pit's website. "Pita Pit condemns all Holocaust deniers. To ensure our employees are well informed, they will all be required to take a Holocaust deniers webinar."

💬 790K　　🔁 1452K　　♡ 1867K　　⬆

Arlene

Not good enough, we need a strong statement from the Pita Pit CEO condemning Dr. Neb and the Holocaust!

💬 884K　　🔁 1503K　　♡ 1987K　　⬆

BurgerKingRules

Pita Pit, never again! #ErasedNeb #BoycottPitaPit

💬 990K　　🔁 1694K　　♡ 2003K　　⬆

Arlene

One thing I know for sure is that Professor Neb needs to hire himself one good-ass lawyer!!!

💬 1160K　　🔁 3905K　　♡ 3109K　　⬆

10

As I showered, I thought about Nietzsche. He said we shouldn't have too much comfort, for it makes us like sand, "small, soft and round." I think Nietzsche is full of it because I'd love to plunge my displaced feet into the comfy status quo of tenure before it disappears. And it will go missing because our institutions of higher ed, like everything in this modern world, will soon be a casualty of capitalism. I'm not saying that once puffed-up professors will be left homeless, but they will have to face their worst nightmare, a four-four load.

Ping!

Campus Wide Scarlet & Brown Alert,

The administration wishes to apologize for what happened tonight. We do not condone the actions or words of comedian Jackie Diamond.

Nor does the administration share Mr. Diamond's views on K-pop bands. They are not "skinny sexualized and infantilized men who sing manufactured music that sounds the same played backward and forwards." This type of hate speech will not be tolerated on campus.

Acting Dean Bobby Popkov, PhD

"If the freedom of speech is taken away then dumb and silent we may be led, like sheep to the slaughter." – George Washington

I left my studio apartment wearing clean khakis, a sports jacket with professorial elbow patches, and my "School of Athens" philosophy tie, which depicts Raphael's famous painting of Plato and Aristotle. I figured no woman in her right mind would be attracted to a man wearing such a tie, so I'd be safe.

My first stop was Discount Liquors. The wine selection was wretched, but I managed to nab a dusty bottle of merlot called Pyrrho, which had a dancing pig on the label. Next, I walked to the Stop & Shop, where I found a rack of half-dead, severely discounted bouquets beside the marshmallows. At the register, the dopehead cashier asked, "Are you a member of our rewards program?"

"No."

"Would you like to join our rewards program?"

"I'm not into joining things."

"What's your phone number?"

"I don't give that out."

"Do you have an email you'd like to share?"

"Why would I?"

"Have you downloaded our app?"

"I just want to buy flowers."

"Would you like to round up for kids with polio?"

"Wait," I said, "isn't polio completely preventable?'

"So?"

"Some parent ignores science, doesn't get their kid vaccinated, and now I'm supposed to round up for them?" I'd always imagined myself as Socrates, wandering Athens, tying people's brains into philosophical knots by questioning what they believed and why they believed it.

"You want to round up or not? It'll cost you 37 cents." He rolled his eyes.

"Do I get a receipt for taxes?"

"Don't follow."

"We're allowed to take charitable donations off our federal income taxes, so do I get a receipt to show the IRS that I made a 37-cent donation?"

"Don't let your brain overheat, man," said the cashier.

"I'm not. I'm simply asking questions we should all ask."

"Like?"

"Why should we give our phone numbers to cashiers? What's your company going to do with my email? And if I hand over 37 cents, who is the Stop & Shop donating it to? Is it a credible charity or scientific organization? And while I'm at it, is there any objective evidence these donations are changing anything in the grand scheme of things?" Socrates probably caused a lot of delays in grocery lines, which might have been the real reason for his death sentence.

"Have you ever met someone with polio?" the cashier said.

"No."

"Then you know your 37 cents is working."

"I knew someone with polio once," said the next in line, a chubby, barely drinking-age college dude holding three twelve packs of Coors and wearing a t-shirt that read, "Love me, I'm dyslexic."

"Really?" I said, "What were the symptoms?"

"Brain damage."

"What?"

"Yeah. He fell off a horse."

"Are you talking about polo?"

"Isn't polio what you get when you're injured playing polo?"

"No, polio causes paralysis."

"So does polo. If you fall off a horse."

For Plato to weed out the few that have survived, Socrates must've endured thousands of absurd dialogues.

"Why are you doing this?" the cashier chided.

"Doing what?"

"Thinking."

"Because the unexamined life isn't worth living."

"What good is examining modern life? What's it got us?" the guy with the beers chimed.

"Lots of things," I answered.

"Like doubt," the cashier said, "and pain and worry."

"We even worry about what'll happen to us after death," said beer boy, "waste."

"Thinking makes us a pitiful animal," the cashier added, "filled with panic, dread, and shitloads of anguish. If you think about it, in this modern world, thinking has a strangely excessive price tag."

"We should be more like pigs," said beer boy, pointing at the dancing swine on my bottle of wine. "They don't overthink, and they're happy."

"How do you know pigs are happy?"

"I know, because I don't overthink it."

"The truth is, you don't know where your 37 cents is going," said the cashier. "It might be the little bit needed to cure polio, or it might go to support the general manager's methadone habit. You don't know, I don't know, beer boy certainly doesn't, and most likely, we never will."

"It's like the date you're going on tonight," beer boy chuckled, "you don't know what's going to happen."

"What makes you think I'm on a date?"

"Flowers and wine. Come on, you don't have to have a brain to figure that out."

"There are no definitive answers," the cashier said, "and no narrative. Modern life is full of blind digressions and random alleys. You will never find a clear-eyed statement about existence because it doesn't exist."

"Tonight," beer boy said, "you might end up humping or get canceled."

"So, be a pig and find tranquility and satisfaction in not knowing. Now, empty your head," and the cashier waved his fingers like a hocus-pocus magician. "Suspend thought. Do you or do you not want to round up for polio?"

"Absolutely not," I said.

"See? Easy."

"Oink oink," added the beer boy.

Ping!

> Campus Wide Scarlet & Brown Alert,
>
> Are you suffering mental anguish from the uncalled-for jokes about K-Pop music made during Jackie Diamond's standup performance? If so, you can find free Buffalo Wild Wings coupons at the self-checkout Student Union's Mental Health Solutions kiosk. Redeemable at any of their restaurants worldwide. <u>LIMIT 2</u>. (While supplies last).
>
> Be Happy,
>
> Dr. Jerry Loudie
> Campus Mental Health Engagement Officer
> Mental Health Solutions Center
>
> PS This offer does not apply to faculty.

As I crossed the street to campus, I imagined my future with the president. At faculty parties, she'd slink up to me at the punch bowl and whisper the code words, "Does Nietzsche need help trimming his mustache?" Minutes later, as the peasant professors party in the next room, the queen and I, her courtesan, would casually hook up for a quickie in the bathroom where she keeps her defibrillator. Soon my A.A. hearing would be canceled, the social media gunslingers defeated, and I'd be tenured without having to kiss ass or publish. Well, I'd still have to kiss ass, but far less than most professors. And people would talk:

"Did you hear about Charlie Neb?"

"Yes, he was neither profound of thought nor happy."

"But then he had a wild affair with the decrepit university president."

"I heard she suffered from osteoporosis, and her hair was falling out."

"But unlike the rest of us humanities professors, Charlie will never have to worry about driving an Uber for a living."

"He will be remembered."

"Because he thinks like a pig."

"Too bad he came down with polio."

"If only he had donated 37 cents."

Ping!

> Dear Faculty Advisors,
>
> It has been determined that too many students are majoring in easy "A" subjects like art and acting.
>
> The administration has therefore decided we will pay students a two-hundred-dollar bonus if they do not major in the arts. If we can pay farmers not to grow crops, we can pay students not to major in subjects that are not of value to the taxpayers.
>
> Don't Stop Believing,
>
> Joseph Whitman, MFA
> Dean of Students
>
> PS There is a rumor that some students plan to attack the campus town and student union Pita Pits. We will not tolerate such behavior.

I found my way to the student union, where between the empty foosball tables and the students waiting for the low-frequency whale-sound womb chairs, I found the Mental Health Solutions kiosk. There, I pretended to read a pamphlet on the six symptoms of "exam anxiety" while I nonchalantly nabbed a free condom from a discreet knee-level "Be safe" basket. By the way, I was suffering from all six symptoms:

1. Sweating
2. Rapid heartbeat
3. Dry mouth
4. Nausea
5. Low self-esteem
6. Argumentative nature

As I passed the burned-out bombshell of the theatre, I remembered the words of Bertrand Russell, "One of the symptoms of an approaching nervous breakdown is the belief that one's work is terribly important." Another is arguing with cashiers. Life at a university isn't important. It's a game, and if you don't watch out, you begin to think the game is reality.

Moments later, I stood outside the barricaded walls of the president's compound. Through the gridiron gate, I could see that the Venetian blinds covering the tall Victorian windows were half-cranked, allowing a sliver of light to escape the living room. "Don't linger. Someone might see you," her voice crackled from the speaker box embedded in the brick fence. Then, a buzz as the gate opened, and I walked up the long, dark, clean-swept sidewalk leading past the Japanese-style fishpond to the stately gables. Without turning on the porch light, she partially held open the king-size front door, forcing me to brush against her. "*Mettez-vous à l'aise*," she said as I entered.

The tufted leather living room wasn't designed for everyday living, but for cosmopolitan parties staged for alumni where bored student workers presented wealthy donors with trays of champagne while the Music Department provided quartet-generated elevator music. Above the granite fireplace was a painting of the Mr. and Mrs. looking relatively youthful and patronizingly untouchable. The Mr. did have a rather large '*nez*.'

"Flowers, how nice," she was soberly unimpressed. She wore a vintage bed jacket, silk pants, elegant Hollywood heels, and her second favorite wig.

"And wine," I countered, "Just like you wanted."

"What type?"

"Pyrrho's Dancing Pig. Get it? We're the fighting Wart Hogs, so I brought a wine with a pig on the label."

"How clever. Put it over there." I put the wine on the bowlegged Victorian sideboard next to a stick-thin sculpture of Don Quixote sitting on his bowed-back donkey. "No, not there. There." She pointed at the wastebasket. I threw away the bottle. "It's the thought that counts," she patronized as she closed the power blinds with a handheld wand that looked like a personal massager. As the slits closed and the outside world ebbed away, my exam anxiety peaked, and I discovered a seventh symptom the pamphlet failed to mention—overactive bladder.

"May I use your bathroom?" I said, hoping to disappear and collect my thoughts. Or perhaps jump out the window.

"Certainly, you may use the secret one." She pushed on a hidden panel in the walnut wall under the grand staircase, revealing a tiny washroom.

"Rather small," I said, poking my head into the flyspeck. It was like a confessional with a toilet.

"Do your business. I'll wait," she said.

I found the light and closed the door. Behind it, I couldn't believe it was, in fact, a defibrillator. I tried to pee, but because of the low ceiling that sloped with the staircase above, I couldn't stand up, and nothing came. I zipped. She knocked.

"Everything okay?"

"I'll be right out," I said as I flushed and turned on the water to make it sound like I was making progress. I held my head against the munchkin sized mirror and tried to remember any philosopher who might help with the ethics of the situation. In a flash, the words of Aristotle came. In *The Nicomachean Ethics*, he wrote, "I felt like a piece of trash. I felt dirty, and I felt used." Wait, that might've been Monica Lewinsky. Look it up before you quote me. Then, I saw it. A sign from God. Behind a melting Airwick air freshener, on the ledge over the airline-sized sink, sat an old bottle of Viagra. Inside, one forgotten pill clung to the side. It must've belonged to her French husband. I shook it out, looked in the mirror. The only way to have any semblance of a normal life in this post-absurdist-post-happiness world is to compartmentalize yourself, retail your soul, and dismiss any thought of relevance. "I am a pig," I said. Then I popped the crumbling pill. It stuck in my esophagus, gagging me.

"What's going on?"

"Everything's good," I choked out as I rinsed the pill with a palm of water. Still clearing my throat, I opened the tiny door. She was hovering in the living room, rolled in a haze of cigar smoke. She stepped close, too close, and looked up as if to be kissed. It was time to make my move, but instead, I punted, "Tell me about Augie Omega," I said as I walked past, playing hard to get.

"Why do you care?"

"I've been trying to find him."

This amused her considerably. "You can't find Mr. Omega."

"Because?"

"Because he doesn't want to be found. You can't even find his book."

"He's a writer?"

"He published a distinguished manuscript on absurdism."

"I've looked in the library. On the web. I found nothing about a book."

"That's because when it was published, he immediately had all the copies shredded and then burned."

"Why?"

"To prove he is the greatest absurdist writer of all time."

"The title?"

"*The Fifth Door*. It was about the doors we open to protect ourselves from the chaos of reality."

"President Boucher, I have reason to believe that if I could find Augie Omega, I could avenge the death of Felice Wolinski, sophomore communications major."

"Who?"

"The head cheerleader and president of Kappa Delta."

"Oh, the poor thing who jumped at homecoming."

"It was Wolinski who told me about Mr. Omega."

"I'm sure she did." Then she smiled and solemnly crept close, "Mr. Neb, did you know you're not bad looking? Maybe even handsome."

"No."

"I'm guessing, six foot one?"

"Yes"

"Also, nice teeth and lips," she said as she crept close.

Which creeped me out. I felt as if I were wearing someone else's underwear. "I'm so sorry," I blurted, "but I, ah, just remembered I got grading to do. Thank you, it's been informative."

She blocked my exit and coldly challenged me. "Cut the crap and sit." Like a well-heeled support dog, I obeyed, planting myself on a ball-and-claw-footed fainting couch. With a draw from her cigar, she smoked out, "Many years ago, I had a one-night stand with Mr. Omega."

"You're kidding? What's he like?"

"Small, arrogant, and well endowed. After we did it, I told him I was in love. He put on his clothes and informed me I was a silly creature who would spend my days relentlessly stumbling in a world of conflict, confusion, complexity, and ambiguity."

"Sounds like a total jerk."

"He was, but he was also right," she said as she opened the wine cabinet and took her time making her selection. "Your average Joe, according to Mr. Omega, gets no further than door number one. There, they attach themselves to some comfortable narrative that allows them to have settled views on death, God, vaccines, and taxes, anything that gives the masses the illusion that the haze of trivial distractions that make up the boring rhythm of life is not absurd." She gave me a tight lip-closed smirk showing the fissures of her too-bright lipstick and added, "That was me before I met Mr. Omega. I went to my dental cleanings, parent-teacher conferences, wedding anniversaries, but what I was really doing was cutting my losses and eliminating hope. But then, because of Mr. Omega, I looked, and once you look…"

"You can't unlook."

She used a battery-powered gismo to uncork. Then she poured and handed me a crystal glass embedded with the school's coat of arms, a wild hog holding a shield and sword. "The second door, according to Mr. Omega, is for those who have looked and concluded they're better off dead. But most find it less messy and painful to commit mini-suicide by doping themselves or binging boring Hollywood bullshit. You suicidal?" she said, as if she would take great joy in watching me do it.

"When I was a kid. Now, not so much."

"After Mr. Omega dumped me, I found the third door, epicureanism. Instead of dropping out, I disregarded the dragon at the gate and licked the honey of life the best I could, knowing that inevitability will catch up with me." Then she sensuously added, "I'm epi-curious, you?"

"No. I don't know how to have a good time."

"The fourth door is for those who have looked and cannot unlook," she said as she polished off the lavender wine with a gulp. "These weaklings spend their days in scholarly quarantine with thoughts of metaphysics, epistemology, mathematics, and the anesthetizing analysis of poems, plays, and novels. They seek relief from their nagging doubts and the vastness of the universe by writing tail-chasing dissertations in the forgetful comfort of tenure. And as the years pass, they become smaller and smaller to the point where they crumble along with their many resignations and abstentions. Then, finally, one day, they realize that their lifetime of questions hasn't moved humankind's loneliness one iota closer to truth. Sound familiar?"

"Yes."

"Thought so."

"And the fifth door?" I said, mesmerized by her dark green eyes.

"For that, you'll have to read Augie Omega's book."

"But you said he had them shredded."

"One copy exist. A thoughtful person saved it."

"And that person was?"

"Me," she smirked. "It's in the campus library–the rare book section. They'll only let you see it if you have my permission." She gave me a superior smile, which took the air out of me. Then she poured herself another glass. "Set your meddling intellect aside and join me upstairs," she said.

"Why?"

"I want to show you my collection of vintage dentistry tools," she playfully pouted.

"You collect dental instruments?"

"I've been collecting them since Mr. Omega dumped me. I have a pair of extractor pliers from the eighteenth century and an oral speculum from the sixteen hundreds. They're fascinating and absurd, like you."

She was right. I was absurd. I was trying to find answers to questions that would always be beyond human comprehension. So, what should one do when they find themselves petrified in absurdity like an insect in amber? Try to comprehend? No. It would be better to stop thinking. Become a pig. I downed my glass. "Okay," I tentatively answered. She smiled, handed me the bottle, and I followed her to the majestic staircase that arched above the tiny hidden bathroom. I watched as she strapped herself into a senior citizen power chairlift. Its modern plastic seat and steel rail were in stark contrast to the outdated room. She pushed a button on the armrest and rode the humming chair leisurely up the wall as I climbed the squeaking treads beside her as if to my beheading.

"Double knee replacement," she said, "Can't do stairs."

And a tear came to me. The storm had arrived. The boat was going down, not just for me but for us. Global warming, deforestation, extinction, and industrialized fishing in plastic-filled rising oceans. How would I spend these last moments? Was I going to worry myself to death about tenure, or was I Pyrrho's Pig?

"Don't overthink it, pig," I whispered. "Nothing can be known."

"Did you say something?"

"What? No, just, ah, saying… Nothing like a good chair lift."

"Yes, it's recommended by AARP and rated A-1 by the Better Business Bureau. I ordered it with the optional swivel seat, which I highly recommend."

"I'll try to remember that should I ever need one."

Mmmmm, squeak, mmmmm, squeak. We leisurely reached the landing, and she struggled with the chair's seatbelt.

"May I?"

"Please."

I unlatched her, and she put her arms on my shoulders, and I lifted. She was so close I could smell the salt of her skin. "Such a gentleman," she coughed as she opened her nightgown, revealing the papery skeleton of her pierced nipples and the igneous veins on her neck. Then she laced my

"School of Athens" tie through her fingers as if it were a leash. "As soon as we're finished, I'll call the library and perhaps, if you measure up, also the acting dean and cancel one A.A. hearing." Her flesh, wrapped in chicken bones, wrinkled over me. Then I felt a rush in my soul—nope, it was the Viagra kicking in. She smiled, placed her cartilage against me so close I could feel her palpitating heart, and sweetly whispered, "Do you know what my major was in college? Go ahead, guess."

"Philosophy?"

"Got it in one."

As I held her, I lost myself in the absurd world of Augie Omega. Then I unexpectedly remembered the day I left the church. "You are unworthy of communion," the priest said. "For you, the creation will never be sufficiently sweet, and your life will be loaded with cosmic insignificance. From now on, the very core of your being will be ripe for looting, and meaning shall be uncatchable."

11

Three days after I turned eighteen, I started college. My first class was 8am, Beginning Philosophy, with Dr. Albert Vladimir, an elegant man who powered around campus in a pinstriped suit and a wobbly motorized wheelchair. The first day, he arrived five minutes late and took five more to draw the shades and dim the lights. Then he projected a lonely photo of Earth, a pale blue dot, on the classroom ceiling.

"Compared to fish, plants, microbes, and other animals, we humans are a poor fit on this planet!" he shouted his first words. "It could be argued that there's no place in this universe where we are truly at home. And we never will be as long as we ask questions about existence that fish, plants, microbes, and other animals never ask. In *The Myth of Sisyphus*, Albert Camus writes, 'If I were a tree among trees, a cat among animals, this life would have a meaning, or rather this problem would not arise, for I should belong to this world. I should be this world to which I am opposed by my whole consciousness and my whole insistence upon familiarity. This ridiculous reason is what sets me in opposition to all creation!'"

I was terrorized and fascinated. Then he switched slides to an equally menacing photo of the empty universe. "The mantra of the deep-throated cosmos is humming," he declared. "If you listen, you can hear its Gregorian chant. It's saying, 'I do not hate you - I do not hate you - nor do I love you.'" Then he flipped on the lights, blinding us, and shouted, "*Love* and its bedfellow *beauty* are human creations! And that goes for *good* and *evil*! If we must add ingredients such as art, religion, and philosophy to make the creation tolerable, how can this world be created with us in mind? Or is David Hume correct, and God is but an infant deity and his creation only a 'first rude essay' which he abandoned, 'ashamed of his lame performance!'"

I put my hand up. "Professor Vladimir."

"Yes?"

"Question."

"Proceed."

"Who is David Hume?"

He glared at my innocence, then beamed and declared, "The word 'Question!' is the most brilliant word ever invented, for every great achievement in human history happened because someone questioned!" He threw his lecture notes out the window and proclaimed, "On your deathbed, if you've lived a life of the mind, your last sentence will be a question! And that question, I assure you, will go unanswered!" I was so enthralled that immediately after class, I switched my major from theatre to philosophy, which explains why I didn't lose my virginity until the spring semester of my junior year.

She was a clarinet major who worked weekends at Happy Nails in the mall. We were both at that unfinished age—We were a set of symptoms, not complete people. To express her uniqueness, she always wore a hippie headband from which dangled a braid of colorful feathers and seashells. We met at a college talent night. She played something that sounded like Gershwin, and the audience hissed me off the stage after I stuttered through four unfunny jokes. As we walked back to the dorms, she claimed to be a small "m" Marxist, and I acted as if I understood, even though I didn't have the fuzziest idea what she was talking about. Brandishing a joint, she rambled on about her favorite bands while I nervously watched for campus cops.

"Why are you so uptight?" She blew a puff.

"Didn't know I was."

"You're not enjoying the magnificence of the world. The creation is like crazy-stupid beautiful."

"What about earthquakes and Nazis?" I said.

"Earthquakes can be beautiful if you go with the flow."

"And Nazis?"

"Nazis are absolutely divine - if they're dead."

When we got to the dorms, she asked to see my room, which I thought was odd. I mean, don't they all look alike? But I went with the flow and showed her my small shelf of philosophy books, desk, and chair. In the bathroom, she laughed as she sprayed her hairy pits with my bottle of Trigger brand cologne. Then, she handed me a rubber, mounted me, and we did it under my king-sized poster of Schopenhauer.

"No one has the remotest idea why the whole tragic comedy exists, for it has no spectators, and the actors themselves undergo endless worry with little and merely negative enjoyment."

- Schopenhauer

After ten minutes of her dangling feathers slapping my face, one of her seashells lodged in my nose, and she sat up, freed it, and asked a favor. "Sure, anything," I said in the afterglow of the acrobatic virginal event I took for love.

"Look at it."

"It?"

"You know what I mean."

"You want me to look at your…"

"Yes."

"Why?"

"I've never really seen it," she said. "You guys are lucky. Yours is right there. You get to see yours all the time, but for women, it's a mystery."

"Can't you look it up on the web?"

"But I want to know how mine is uniquely beautiful."

"How about a mirror?"

"Awkward at best."

"Okay," I said, "but my descriptive powers aren't good. I got a "B-" in creative non-fiction."

"Just be honest," she said as she opened stirrup wide. I positioned myself at the end of the thin dorm room mattress, and Schopenhauer and I took a peek.

"You want me to be honest?"

"Give details."

"Well," I said, trying to use my entire underdeveloped thesaurus, "it's sort of like an open head wound."

"What?"

"Like a gaping war wound that hasn't quite healed."

"What!"

"It's like an infant deity tried and then gave up, ashamed of his lame performance."

"What the hell?!"

Seeing she was insulted, I tried to joke, "I mean, if you looked up the phrase, 'Good enough for government work,' in the dictionary, you'll find a picture of this." She kicked me in the head and grabbed her clothes. "It's not like mine is any better," I said. "Mine's a ridiculous appendage. No perfect being could have designed such an absurd attachment!"

We argued for two hours, then went to the mall, where she asked me to buy her a pair of sandals at JCPenney. Three weeks later, she met a sweet-talking English major who wrote poems about budding flowers in bloom, had a credit card with a $5,000 limit, and informed me we were over. After she left, I thought I was lovesick, but it turned out to be a severe case of mono, which kept me out of school for a semester. Since that night over a decade ago, sex for me had always been proof that this creation is, at best, a rough draft.

Ping!

> Campus Wide Scarlet & Brown Alert,
>
> It's been determined that methane, and CO2 levels on campus are reaching critical levels. As a result, this year's annual Tyson Hamburger Jamboree will be held indoors at the Sysco Professional Development Center.
>
> Peace Out,
>
> Dr. Jerry Loudie
> Newly appointed Assistant Dean

"President Boucher, do we really need handcuffs," I said, standing in my socks and boxers beside her Victorian bed. So far, it had been as romantic as a strip search.

"You're into regular old-fashioned lovemaking? So charming, but not for me," she said as she locked one of her wrists to the iron headboard. Its bars matched the vertical-striped wallpaper, adding to her whole prison motif. With her free hand, she slipped the strap of her slip off her shoulder and gave me a sexy, wrinkled smile. "I like to start with a little spanking."

"Kind of uncomfortable with that."

"But I've been a bad girl. I cut funding for the flag girls. The head of the marching band is quitting in protest."

"President Boucher, if you don't mind, there are a few things we need to talk about before we jump to spanking."

"You're right. We need a safety word. How about 'Ayn Rand?'"

"The author of *Atlas Shrugged* is your safety word?"

"My favorite quote of hers is, 'Would you rather have butter or guns? Preparedness makes us powerful. Butter merely makes us fat.'" That quote is not Ayn Rand, it's Hermann Goering, but I didn't want to correct her because she was sort of in the ballpark.

"So, while we're doing this, if I shout 'Ayn Rand,' you'll stop?"

"No, that's *my* safety word."

"What's mine?"

"You don't get one."

"But if I want to stop?"

"You can't."

"But what if?"

"Okay, your safety words are, 'To hell with tenure.'"

I slowly sat facing away from her on the California king-sized duvet. Through the bedroom window, I could see, two blocks away, the long neck of the A&S bell tower poking its summit from the crest of autumn leaves. The ground lights arced up to capture its imposing night beauty. It looked as if it were feeding on the low-hanging stars.

"This little piggy went to market. This little piggy stayed home," President Boucher sang as she paddled her ice cube fingers up my back. "This little piggy got tenure, this little piggy had none, and this little piggy cried wee wee wee—."

"President Boucher, I hate to interrupt," I interrupted. "Have you ever thought about how imperfect the creation is? Take the giraffe, for instance. Did you know that its laryngeal nerve doesn't go directly from its brain to its voice box but instead travels all the way down the neck, turns around in the chest, and goes back up, where it finally connects to the voice box."

"How uninteresting," she said as she brushed her fuzzy upper lip on my ear.

"It goes twenty feet out of its way."

"Focus," she said as she crept her tiny claws down and perched them on my nipple.

"That means that the nerve impulse takes about five one-hundredths of a second longer than it would if it were a logical, short, direct connection. Time you need when you've got to warn the herd of an approaching lion."

"Concentrate."

"Doesn't that prove God either doesn't exist or, at best, maybe some pared-down deity rushed the design? Why six days? He had masses of time to work with. Why couldn't he have taken another second or two to get the giraffe's neck right? Would it have been that big of a rewrite to say the creation took six days and two seconds?"

"Perhaps the giraffe's neck wasn't designed by God but by Augie Omega," she said. "He seems to have a knack for screwing things up."

"Or maybe Augie Omega is God." Just then, a light caught something shiny in the tiny top-floor window of the bell tower. It was just a twinkle in the dark frame, a silver shaft withdrawn instantly. "Someone is in the secret room."

"What?"

"In the bell tower."

"Couldn't be. It's locked," she playfully whispered as her hand slipped toward my groin.

"No. I saw something. Look."

She peered out the window. Whatever it was, it was gone. "It's just the moon reflecting on the glass," she said.

"What's in the tower? Why is it locked?"

"Oh, Charlie, you don't want to know. Now, kiss me, and let's forget the abyss for a moment."

"Honey, I'm home!" came a voice from downstairs. It was an older man with a slight French accent. "Seattle was a bore, so I caught an early flight."

Our eyes locked. I terrified. She tactical. "Get the key," she coldly said.

"The what?"

"To the handcuffs."

"Where?"

"Drawer," and she pointed to the vanity. I dove over and yanked so hard the drawer came from its tracks, spilling everything. Desperate, I wrestled through the paraphernalia of knickknacks: scattered combs, nail clippers, cufflinks, buttons, used mascara, and a copy of *Atlas Shrugged*.

"It's not there."

"Then it's the drawer below."

That drawer also came out of its tracks. More forgotten debris fell to the floor. "Can't find it!" A squeak came from the stairs. We both froze.

"Disappear," she whispered.

Squeak.

"Where?"

"Closet. Don't forget your clothes."

"But the handcuffs."

Squeak.

"Go!"

And I nabbed my things, nosedived into the closet, closed the door, and bunkered in the dark, claustrophobic nest of sleeves and hanging trouser legs.

"You forgot to turn on the alarm system, but I got it," her husband said as he reached the landing. Then, "*Oh, mon Dieu!*" he said, "What happened?"

"Darling, it was terrible," the president started into her lie, "I was getting ready for bed when this man entered and handcuffed me and ransacked the drawers. When he heard you, he climbed out the window!"

"The window is closed."

"Yes, he closed it behind him."

"I'll call the police," he said as he beeped his cell, "If I told you once, I've told you a thousand times, leave the alarm on, there are students and, worse, professors out there!"

"I know. I simply forgot."

"Hello, our house has been robbed. They handcuffed my wife to the bed! It's the president's mansion! Yes, I'll stay on with you." Then he said to his wife, "If he went out the window, he's most likely on the roof. Where's the gun? Oh, right, it's in the closet," and my Viagra deflated.

"No! It's in the bathroom down the hall," the president panicked.

"What the hell is it doing there?"

"When I heard the noise, I grabbed the gun. I thought he was coming in through the bathroom window. I must've left it there." Oh, she was a great liar. I heard him blow down the hall, so I eased open the closet door. From the bed, she whispered, "Don't dilly-dally." Still in my underwear and holding my clothes, I made it to the landing when I heard him coming. I sphinxed myself behind a tall display case of vintage dental instruments as he walked past into the bedroom.

"It's not there," he said. I could see him open the bedroom closet. "What's your problem? It's right here!"

"I must have put it back. I don't know, I'm so frazzled," she playacted.

His back to me, he loaded the gun, opened the window, and stuck his head out. She shot me a look from the bed saying, "Go now or die!" and I started down the stairs. Squeak. My socked foot just graced the second step. Squeak. Then it hit me, the answer. I lowered myself into the power chair and silently mmmmed down the staircase while putting on my pants, which was made more accessible by the optional swivel seat. As I disappeared below the horizon of the landing, I heard her say, "Oh darling, it was so scary. Hold me." Then, far-off police sirens.

By the time I reached the living room, I'd managed to put on my pants and jacket. The shirt and shoes would have to wait. I found the button and sent the chair back up. At the front door, a red light flashed on the home security keypad. For a moment, I thought, take a wild guess at the code. What do you bet it's 666? But before I could, ding-dong. It was the police. I ran to the secret bathroom. On my knees in darkness before the toilet, my face lit only by a half-watt filament from an angel shaped nightlight, I genuflected. Then I lowered my head and prayed for the first time since that pregnancy scare my senior year in college.

"Dear God," I mouthed, the acid of my fear eating away at the lining of my throat, "I know you might be a little upset with me for being a part-time believer, but have you read Nietzsche and Freud? They make pretty damn good arguments for your nonexistence. What I need you to know is that it would take minimal effort on your part to make me believe in you full-time. I mean, what if one day you told a joke? Or maybe if you made the world a little less of a Kafka clown carnival. Or what if Jesus, Mohammed, and Osiris held a cosmic news conference during a Guadalupe-like Super Bowl halftime extravaganza and gave their seal of approval to Mormonism? If that happened, I want you to know I'd be knocking on doors, interrupting people's dinners, and warning them against the evils of caffeine. But right now, Heavenly Father, I'm not asking for some great revelation, only a bit of clarification. A simple sign that you do, in fact, exist." I ended my celestial petition with "Amen," genuflected and waited at the sharp edge of anxiety for an answer. And waited. And waited. But all I heard was the muffled upstairs dialogue cut by police radios. *Zzzzzzz!* I jumped. It was my phone on silent.

> Dear Faculty,
>
> The Theatre and Dance Department is excited to announce that despite our recent tribulations, we're going forward with our annual StrindFest!
>
> We will stage Strindberg's (sur)realistic, absurdist *A Dream Play* in the theatre's burnt-out (wreck)age. I know Strindberg would be delighted with our unique staging choices.
>
> Sending Good Vibes,
>
> Dr. Skippy
> Theatre and Dance
> Director of the Brechtian Institute
> Vice Chair of the Strindberg Foundation
> Co-Chair of the Ionesco Center for Advanced Study

Two hours later, I was still waiting for God to pick up my call when I heard the president and her husband say "good night" to the police. Then they set the alarm and squeaked and mmmmed their way up to bed. I sat on the cold bathroom floor and waited. Bored, I searched through the cabinet and found a well-read copy of *Eat, Pray, Love*. Perhaps there was more to the president than Ayn Rand, vintage dental instruments and a faded affair with Augie Omega. Several hours later, I was lost in the novel and craving pasta when I heard the mmmmm of the chairlift above. I nuzzled the door open and peeked into the dark living room. In the shadows stood the dim outline of the president. She smiled and whispered, "Did it ever occur to you how easy it is to disrupt the order on which we've built our sanity?"

"Yeah," I whispered back, "it has."

"Rain check?"

"Am I reinstated?"

"I'll think about it."

"You know," I said, quoting the cashier at the Stop & Shop, "thinking has a strangely excessive price tag."

Amused, she turned off the house alarm, and I ran. Outside, I hopped through the Japanese fishpond, jumped the iron fence, and didn't stop till I reached the campus library. I entered five minutes before their midnight closing and caught the elevator and my breath. On my way down, I put on my shoes and shirt. Then it hit me. I didn't have my tie. Where the hell did I leave my "School of Athens" tie? The door opened on two dismissive college girls who looked at my mussed hair, untucked shirt, and untied shoes as if I were a freak. They stepped back and let me pass before they got on. As the door closed behind me, one said to the other, "Was that Dr. Neb?"

"I think so."

"He still works here?"

Ping!

> Faculty and Staff,
>
> Plays are not allowed to be produced in the burnt wreckage of the theatre or any building on campus that has sustained fire damage.
>
> The Strindfest is canceled.
>
> Julio Gonzalez
> University Fire Chief

The Fifth Door, by Augie Omega," the rare books librarian said, glaring at me as if she were a Nazi interrogator, then she added deliberately, "Interesting."

"Yes, I have the president's permission to check it out," I lied as I wiped the beads from my temple and tried to act normal.

"Who told you that you need the president's permission?"

"The president."

"Bullshit, you don't need anyone's permission," she said as she studied my unnerved eyes. "You okay?"

"Oh, I, ah, had to run here. Wanted to make it before you closed. Do you have it?"

"Strange that you should ask for that book today."

"Oh?"

"Because someone stole it yesterday."

12

He looked like a crooner on the old Lawrence Welk television show–blond, youthful, down-home, clean-cut. I thought at any moment he might break into the "Pennsylvania Polka" or "Deutschland uber Alles." His facsimile Armani suit made him look like a pretty competent lawyer, but to move up from junior partner, he'd have to lose the Star Wars tie. After the indifferent server snatched away the BBQ chicken wing lunch plates, he dropped the meaningless happy-face talk, and we got down to business.

"Where are the spies?" he whispered.

"Spies?" I asked.

"We're eating at a restaurant in campus town. You know there's gotta be enemy combatants, i.e., people who don't have your best interest at heart."

"Like?"

"Deans, administrators."

"Right," I said and turned to look.

"Don't!" he snapped.

"Then how do I know if there are enemy combatants?"

"Old law school trick - Pretend you're yawning or stretching, and as you do, nonchalantly glance around the place to ensure no one's listening. Ready? Go." And I coolly pseudo-stretched as I scanned the grubby chain restaurant for combatants–My wide panning shot started with the day-drunk frat boys two booths over and crossed the blinking sports bar flat screens to the bored servers merging ketchup bottles near the kitchen.

"Clear," I said.

"Good. So, let's start at the beginning. How did your testicles come in contact with asbestos?"

"Oh, no, that was just something I read on the Mayo Clinic website."

"What part of your body *did* come in contact?"

"Lungs."

"You inhaled asbestos?"

"Yes."

"You *are* aware that asbestos causes a form of lung cancer called mesothelioma."

"Extremely aware."

"And there is no cure."

"Thanks for reminding me."

Sensing a fat payday, he clicked his rococo retractable pen and made an extended legal notation in his notepad. During the pause, my mind wandered as it always does:

There once was a man who was breathless
Because he ate too much asbestos
So, he hired a lawyer
Sued his employer
And died in a brand-new Lexus

He unclicked his pen and gave me a long, sober look before asking, "What were you doing when you inhaled?

"Dancing."

"Am I correct to assume this activity meant you were breathing heavily? Which means the asbestos most likely really got up in there. Would you say it *really* got way up in there?

"Yeah. Way up."

"So, death is a distinct possibility."

"Isn't that true for all of us?"

"I mean premature."

"Yes."

"Painful and premature."

"Is pain important?"

"You gotta be a victim today if you want to go anywhere."

Click—more silent notes.

What if the truth about death was so awful no one could cope with it? For example, what if the all-powerful ruler of the universe needed souls as nourishment, so it created millions of earth-factory soul farms? And after death, we're painfully and laboriously harvested the same way we humans cut up beef and bunnies? You must admit, it makes about as much sense as catechism, confession, and immaculate conception.

Unclick.

"And where were you when you inhaled?" he asked.

"Old Arts and Sciences Room 151."

"Wasn't there a sign on the door warning you that asbestos abatement was taking place?"

"There was, but it was ambiguous."

"And why were you in room 151?"

"The dean sent me there by mistake. I have his email as evidence."

"Good, we'll subpoena him."

"You can't. He's in a coma."

"Because of mesothelioma?"

"No, he was injured in a theatre fire."

"Caused by?"

"Samuel Beckett."

"Can we subpoena him?"

"No, he's dead."

"Because of mesothelioma?"

"I doubt it."

Click. More notes.

If my earth-soul-farm hypothesis was valid, you might ask why people die at various ages. Why doesn't the master of the universe harvest all souls simultaneously, as we do corn and carrots? Well, it turns out the Creator has a broad palate. Sometimes dinner calls for a zesty young veal-like soul. Other times, the master prefers old nursing home souls much as we hanker for the punch of finely aged Feta.

"Are you currently having breathing problems?"

"Yes, but I think they're psychological."

"Do you anticipate having breathing problems before we go to trial?"

"How would I know?"

"Once again," he insisted, "do you anticipate having breathing problems? Hint-hint."

"Oh, sure," I said, throwing in a bogus cough.

"Work on it. Think guttural."

Click. More notes.

What could we do if the earth was just a soul farm? I suppose we could rebel. But the all-powerful would quickly quell any such revolts. We could resolve to make the world an Epicurean cocaine-induced orgy, but we'd never be unshackled from our fate.

Unclick.

"Why were you in room 151?"

"I was there for an A.A. hearing."

"A.A.?"

"Academic Ascertainment. The university is trying to sack me. I'm suspended without pay."

"And you want to use this mesothelioma lawsuit as leverage to save your job."

"Yes."

"Mr. Neb, that's the most despicable thing I've ever heard." But then he gave me a juicy smile. "I like it!" Click. More notes.

We could appeal our fate with rosaries, relics, menorahs, prayer wheels, animal sacrifices, the trinity, and virginity. But let's face it, we've been trying that for thousands of years with no credible results. So, what if, instead of churches, tabernacles, mosques, and temples, we built pulpits atop mountains where, rather than sacrifice virgins, we'd tell our best jokes to God. There would be amateur nights and ladies-only Tuesdays, all designed to answer the most crucial question religious leaders fail to ask - is there a joke so funny even God would laugh?

Unclick.

"Why is the university firing you?"

"I told a joke in front of my class."

"What was the joke?"

"I don't remember."

"How are you supporting yourself?"

"I drive an Uber and donate sperm."

"At the same time?"

"No."

"Oh, good. What's your rating?"

"My sperm quantity index is 98.4."

"I mean as an Uber driver."

"Oh, ah, haven't checked of late."

"Let's get you lots of money, so you don't have to drive or donate," he said as he presented me with a contract. "Just sign here and here and initial there." And I lawyered up. "If we win, my firm takes half your settlement. If you lose, which won't happen, you give us your house."

"I rent."

"We have payment plans." Click. More notes.

And what happens if my comedy pulpit idea fails to make God laugh? Then what? Nearing death, Oscar Wilde said to his close friend Robert Ross, "When the last trumpet sounds, and we are couched in our porphyry tombs, I shall turn and whisper to you, 'Robbie, Robbie, let us pretend we do not hear it.'" Ah, there's the true purpose of every philosophy, work of art, and religion—they help us pretend not to hear "it."

Unclick.

"There's only one thing left to do," he said with a warm smile.

"Retainer? I'm a little short right now."

"No, prayer. We can't win without God's assistance," and he lowered his head and went into full Tammy Faye evangelist prayer mode.

"Ah, sorry to interrupt," I interrupted. "I'm a little confused. You're asking for God's help with a free speech-asbestos lawsuit."

"Mr. Neb, you do know that you contacted a faith-based law firm?" My stunned silence was enough for him to know I didn't know. "Heavens, it's happened again," he said. "Some hateful soul keeps hacking our website and switching our phone number with the liberal firm down the block. What type of sick mind would do such a thing?"

"Does the name Augie Omega sound familiar?"

"Augie Omega," he said, picking a sesame seed from the tip of his tongue and trying to place the name, "Augie Omega. Wasn't he the head engineer at Chernobyl?"

"What?"

"Don't quote me, but it seems I heard that name associated with some Chernobyl-like disaster. Maybe it was the Titanic or the Space Shuttle. No, I think it was a problem at a Cryobank. Don't remember. Anyway," he said, "we're a conservative values law firm that specializes in mesothelioma and the war on Christmas," and then he added with deep concern for my soul, "Please tell me you're not one of them."

"Them?

"Doubters."

"Me? No," I said, but my answer was phony.

"Then let us pray," he insisted, and he lowered his head in silent supplication. Ping! Having no objective evidence prayer worked last time, I decided I'd multitask by placing my phone in my lap and checking my email while I prayed.

Campus Wide Scarlet & Brown Alert

The police are looking for a man who made off with hundreds of Buffalo Wild Wings coupons from the self-serve Mental Health Solutions kiosk in the student union. The suspect was wearing khakis and a sports jacket with elbow patches. And a tie with a picture of old white men on it. If you see this individual, contact the police.

In addition, the police also need your help finding a man who broke into the presidential mansion. Please contact us immediately if you have any information about this heinous act.

Lieutenant Joe Patroni
University Police

"Amen," he said as he breathed in the love of Christ and took back his pen. "I'll get my team on this right away. And, oh, by the way, I'll be attending your A.A. hearing. Nothing puts the fear of God into administrators more than the presence of a lawyer." For the first time, I felt I might win. "All we need is . . .?" he said and indicated I was to fill in the blank.

"Ah, faith?" I guessed.

"That's right. It's the ace up our sleeve, just like Luke Skywalker."

"You mean like Star Wars?"

"Dr. Neb, what happens in the final climactic scene of that great movie?"

"Something blows up?"

"Pilot after pilot uses their computer aiming devices, attempting to destroy the Death Star and dies trying. Then it's Skywalker's turn. But just as failure is at hand, Luke turns off his computers and uses his faith to launch his proton torpedoes."

"I'm almost positive it's The Force, not faith."

"And God gloriously guides Luke's torpedoes into the two-meter-wide thermal exhaust shaft, resulting in a chain reaction, and...?"

"Thousands incinerated in the vacuum of outer space?"

"A happy ending."

"But wait," I said. "Can you imagine if one of our Air Force pilots turned off their computers and aimed their F16 missiles simply by using a metaphysical energy field created by all living things?"

"He'd be a hero."

"He'd be court-marshaled."

"Dr. Neb." He laughed with a bright, extraordinary confidence. "You just watch. With The Force on our side, losing is not possible." Then he added, "I think we've lost our sense of humor in this country."

"I agree. Everything can be funny."

"Except, of course, The Lord. No one should ever, ever joke about the one true God. Am I right?" and he waited for my response. I tried not to let my thoughts show, but he saw my doubt. "Am I right," he insisted.

Hypothetical: What if a husband gave his wife flowers on Monday, took her to a romantic dinner on Tuesday, and brought her breakfast in bed on Wednesday? On Thursday, he fires up a chainsaw and chases her around the bedroom. Then Friday, he gives her a full-body Swedish massage with aromatherapy. You'd have to admit that on Saturday, when he proclaimed his undying love, it'd be kind of hard to overlook the chainsaw incident. That's how I feel about God. Our relationship with the Almighty is like a Zoom conference where the geriatric boss is talking away but has forgotten to unmute, and all us peons are waving and yelling, singing, praying, building churches, and writing requiems, all of which have the same theme, "Dammit, asshole, unmute yourself and stop chasing me around the bedroom with a chainsaw!"

"Right," I said with a stupid smile. "We should never make fun of God."

"The one true God."

"That's what I meant. All those other deities-fair game."

"Oh, if we're going to win, you also need a good asbestos cough."

"I've been working on it," I said, and I gave him a harsh test cough.

"I like the bold choice you're making, but you're obviously asking for sympathy." I tried again, and this time, I pulled back, letting just a puff of gasping air barely touch my lips. "More diaphragm, you're not acting, you're reacting. Find the cough in yourself, not yourself in the cough." So, I dug deeper. The result was a noble concussive hack with just a twig of expectorate, which I dabbed with a napkin. "Holy cow," he said. "That was so natural. It was the embodiment of the universal mesothelioma cough. Have you ever considered being an actor?"

"I wanted to, but my mother beat it out of me."

"Keep working on it. Practice makes perfect," he said as he put away his notepad. "Now, all you gotta do is see a psychiatrist, and we'll be ready to settle out of court.

"A psychiatrist? Why?"

"We need expert testimony to prove you've suffered serious emotional injury because of the university's negligence. Our company has a standard shrink we send all our clients to. His name is Dr. Boucher."

"Boucher? Wait. Not the president of the university's husband?"

"Now that I think of it, might be."

"You want me to see the president of the university's husband about a lawsuit I'm filing against the university? Isn't that a conflict of interest?"

"It won't be a problem."

"But he'll know I work for the university."

"Just tell him you work someplace else."

"Like where?"

"Tell him you're an actor. Trust me. He won't know who you are." Just then, the bored Buffalo Wild Wings server walked up with the check. "Let me get this," my lawyer said.

"No, please, let me," I said. "I've got lots of coupons."

13

The sign above the white-washed waiting room door read, "Maze Cryobank. We Aim To Please." I couldn't figure out if that was an attempt at humor. I'd been donating at every bank in the area. When I asked about Augie Omega, I always got the same answer: "We can't comment on current or former employees." But when I called Maze, the receptionist stumbled before giving the pat answer. It had to be the right place. So, I applied. Being over six feet tall and having a Ph.D. certainly helped with my sperm application. But I left off that my Ph.D. was in the humanities as they said it wouldn't be a selling point. My plan? I'd escape the collection room and wander the halls looking for Augie. Or maybe I'd break into their HR office and rifle through their files. But first I had to wait my turn in the hushed holding room with a dozen other six-foot under-employed Ph.Ds.

Ping!

Dear Faculty,

The artistic temperament breaks tradition! Dreams the (un)dreamable! Fans the flames of (trans)formation! Beyond the narrow corridors of our humanity, there's a universe of creative possibilities that transmutes the (sub)conscious and (re)awakens the theaterscape of the mind.

I'm happy to announce we will be going forward with Strindberg's (sur)realistic *A Dream Play* in the burnt-out

> wreckage of the theatre.
>
> Sending Good Vibes,
>
> Dr. Skippy
> Theatre and Dance
> Director of the Brechtian Institute
> Vice Chair of the Worldwide Strindberg Foundation
> Co-Chair of the Ionesco Center for Advanced Study
>
> Please note: this play is immersive theater, so do not wear anything that cannot be washed or dry cleaned.

"Donor number twenty-two?" said the young nurse, holding a clipboard at the door. Her humorless face scanned the room for a response.

"That's me."

"You're up."

Again, I wasn't sure if that was an attempt at humor. She extended a firm hand, and a fixed smile. Her dark hair was pinned atop her head, except for two long strands that cupped her face. Her eyes, buried behind horn-rimmed glasses, were icy black.

"I'm Nurse Cox," she said.

I'm not the type to lower myself to laughing about a woman named "Cox" working at a sperm bank, but still, I answered with a slight concussive nose laugh. Her eyes narrowed, as if to say, "If you find my name humorous, I'll rip your balls off and slingshot them into outer space, you stupid little man-child." I heeded her warning, and we trekked down a long corridor toward the collection rooms.

"Do you need to use a bathroom?" she said.

"No."

"Good, they aren't working."

As she walked, she glared at the vinyl floor. Something wasn't right. Her soul was heavy. But it wasn't just her. Everyone we passed also seemed depressed.

"Nurse Cox, I think I have a friend who works here."

"Oh?"

"Augie Omega."

Her stacked heels skipped a beat, then she cleared her throat. "I can't comment on current or former employees," she said as she opened the door to a small room with a power recliner and a remote to a 75-inch ultra-high-definition TV with an on-screen menu that read, "Amateur, Hardcore, Gonzo, Hentai, and Alt."

"Wow, big TV for such a little room," I commented.

"All we ask is you keep the volume down."

"Me or the TV?"

Every class clown who has attempted a stupid joke knows there's a fraction of a second of death between the punch and the payoff. As I waited for Cox's cheerless eyes to grin, I thought of the ancients. I read once the Greeks believed comedy, not tragedy, gave us true catharsis. If you think about it, wouldn't *Oedipus* make a much better bedroom farce? In the final scene, Oedipus and his mom would file for a no-fault divorce and provide for their hemophilic-Habsburg jaw sons, and instead of all that regret and self-harm, Oedipus and his mother would learn to laugh about their very human mistake. And then they'd have makeup sex.

Cox handed me the donation jar and a look that said, "Don't they have a minimum IQ requirement here?" and closed the door.

Ping!

> Re: Strindfest
>
> Faculty and Staff,
>
> You may "break, dream, and transmute" as much as you like, but you will not be doing it in the burnt-out wreckage of the theatre. Perimeter fencing has been installed.
>
> "Sending Good Vibes,"
>
> Julio Gonzalez
> University Fire Chief

Moments later, I peeked out the door. To the right, industrial neons lit the hallway. To the left, Nurse Cox! I jumped.

"Have you started?" she said, glaring at me.

"No, ah, was just channel surfing."

"In that case, the Director of Operations would like to see you."

"Why me?"

"I told him you were looking for Augie Omega. Take your coat. Leave the remote."

Ping!

> Dear Faculty,
>
> As the beloved Rosa Parks said, "Most of the important things in the world have been accomplished by people who have kept on trying when there seemed to be no hope at all."
>
> We in Theatre and Dance are not afraid to amplify the performance vibe exquisitely, profoundly, and fearlessly.
>
> Tickets are now on sale for our all-dance version of Strindberg's *A Dream Play.*
>
> Sending even better Good Vibes,
>
> Dr. Skippy
> Theatre and Dance
> Director of the Brechtian Institute
> Vice Chair of the Worldwide Strindberg Foundation
> Co-Chair of the Ionesco Center for Advanced Study

Seated behind his monumental desk, the middle-aged Cryobank director scanned me, trying to understand how I fit into this rotten game. Atop his shiny bald head stood a single, white, three-inch hair. Behind him, dozens of skewered photos of jovial parents and their overindulged, freeze-dried technological wonders were push-pinned on a bulletin board. On his desk sat a life-sized anatomically correct model of a bisected womb. The baby inside none too happy about the situation. Nurse Cox guarded the door.

"You a reporter?" the director said as he popped a tiny pill and downed it with a glass of liquid the color of whiskey.

"Me? No," I nervously laughed.

"Lawyer?"

"No."

"FBI?"

"Just a donor."

"Then why did you ask about Augie Omega?"

"He's an acquaintance," I lied. "I haven't seen him in years."

Using the eraser of a number two pencil, he flipped open a file with my name. It was my "sperm report." Whatever he saw was enough to allow him to inch down his guard. His tragic eyes drooped as he carefully considered his following words. "Dr. Neb," he said as if he were handing down a death sentence, "Have you noticed that we, as a people, no longer look forward but sideways?"

"Okay," I said, wondering where the hell this was going.

"I believe we all have a deep internal compass that lets us know that what we do in this life will somehow provoke tomorrow. But what if there's no long-term? What if we were the last generation and everything in the universe was moving away from us at the speed of light so that in the not-too-distant future, not only will the earth be a lifeless rock, but the starless night utterly dark?"

Why are deeply depressed people always drawn to me? What makes them take one look and think, "He's the type I can start a crazy conversation with."

"I guess that would be kinda, ah, bad," I said.

"We would lose ourselves in the future tense. It would eliminate the very soul of what it means to be human." Then he added, "Are you aware we're facing a catastrophe?"

"You mean, like global warming?"

"The fact that the Earth will be virtually uninhabitable by the end of the century is the least of our worries."

"Asteroid?"

"Dr. Neb, in the last sixty years, the sperm count of your average male has dropped 51.4 percent. In addition, penises are getting smaller. What are the latest numbers, Nurse Cox?"

"In the last twenty years, the average penis size has dropped 22.4 percent," Cox answered.

"Do you know what that means?" the Director grunted.

"Fewer Ford truck sales?" I smiled. He didn't. Nor did Cox.

"Sperm banks will be able to repopulate for a while," the Director continued in all seriousness, "but the day will come when the last frozen warrior will be spent. Then will come Spermageddon."

The air vent above his desk clicked on, and the single hair on top of his waxen head did a little flagellum dance. I tried to hold it in but couldn't—a squeezed honk escaped my nose. His eyes constricted, then they looked past me, through me. He was a soldier in a righteous fight, gazing upon the mud and fog of the morning ramparts and a coming battle that he knew was already lost. "I've always thought the purpose of life was to nudge the world a bit," he confessed as the hair frolicked. "That if I did my part, maybe someday my tiny push pins would make the future better. But how do you find meaning when you know the annihilation of the entire species is at hand?"

"Well, we all know forever doesn't exist." I squeezed my gut, trying to hold in the laugh, but the dancing hair was more than I could take. I let out a little giggle.

"I still had a modicum of hope, but then Augie Omega came to work here," the director said. "He committed the greatest sin one can commit at a sperm bank."

"Walk in on someone?"

"Mixed ejaculates. We're now dealing with over three dozen lawsuits by white parents with interracial children, Jewish parents with Muslim children, and conservative Republican parents with Democratic-Socialist children." Life is full of these moments where you think that's got to be a joke. Where you want to yell, oh, come on, you can't say that with a straight face.

"Augie Omega also brought into the building damaged ejaculates from unknown sources," Nurse Cox coolly added, "and mixed them with samples in our nitrogen storage tanks."

"How could you tell they were damaged?" I asked, while suppressing a wheeze-laugh."

And then, with the sober seriousness of a prisoner eating his last meal, the director managed, "Because we found sperm with two tails."

"One on each end," said Cox.

The director added, "They just sort of swam in circles."

And I lost it. Total meltdown. Horse laughter. I banged on his desk with crazy hilarity. I laughed so hard my diaphragm hurt.

"Dr. Neb, this is hardly funny."

Nothing makes something funnier than someone saying it isn't funny. And while laughing, I must tell you Arthur Miller's play *Death of a Salesman* would also make a better comedy. Just before curtain, there'd be a touching scene where Willy apologizes to his sons for giving them such stupid names. Biff and Happy, are you kidding me? He must've known those handles would scar them. And then Willy would talk about how there's more to life than trying to live up to the unachievable American dream - like enjoying the afternoon with your newly named sons, Ethan and Owen.

The Director stood and snapped, "Nurse Cox, escort this funny man from the building! And remove him from our donor list! He obviously needs psychotherapy!" Cox yanked me into the hall. My legs jellied from comedy, I could only comply.

Ping!

> Faculty and Staff,
>
> As the creator of the universe said, "If you put a bunch of dance majors cavorting on the watery fire-ravaged grave of a theatre, the immutable laws of the universe (including but not limited to gravitation, motion, mass, and energy) will apply.

> <u>The Strindfest is canceled</u>.
>
> Julio Gonzalez
> University Fire Chief
>
> PS Your quote is not Rosa Parks, it's Dale Carnegie.

Moments later, Cox shoved me through the clinic's back-alley door. "What the hell is wrong with you? We're facing dozens of lawsuits!" she said as she slammed my giggling ass against a dumpster. "If word gets out, we may lose our license! I could be fired!" My heel rolled over a used syringe, and I looked up to find the rainy back street was a tent city of forgotten humans. Looking at the dilapidated mess of shopping carts and sleeping bags, a tear came to Nurse Cox. Me too. Laughter and misery are not opposites. They march together, only a synapse apart. "In the three days Mr. Omega worked here, not only did he mix sperm, but he also hopelessly clogged the toilets and sold drugs from the loading dock," she said. "Then, one night, Marcellus went out to have beers with him. Five hours later, when he returned, he wasn't the same."

"Marcellus?"

"My husband. Augie convinced him to join this strange country church with a weird Bible. Then he screwed with him so badly he's now in a psych hospital."

"Three days, and he did all that?"

"Three horrible days," she said as she looked at the bombed-out homeless camp parked in the shadows without hope or salvation. "Everywhere I look now, I see Augie Omegas." Her tears pooled in her lower lids. She had long lashes and a sexy nose. It was a little on the small side, so tiny she had trouble keeping her glasses up. She looked down at the shamble of rubbish at our feet, wiped a tear, and said, "You know who Marcus Aurelius is?"

"The Roman emperor."

"He wrote, 'Observe how transient and trivial is all mortal life - yesterday a drop of semen, tomorrow a handful of spice or ashes.'" She was lonely, confused, and could quote Marcus Aurelius. She was the first person like me I'd ever met. I almost fell to my knees and proposed marriage right there, but instead, I finished the quote, "'Spend, therefore, these fleeting moments of the earth as Nature would have you spend them, and then go to your rest with good grace, as an olive falls in its season.'"

She closed her eyes and drifted. "Life is a grim joke told in extremely poor taste."

"Or maybe it's the best joke ever," I said, "told by an infinite comic genius, and we've forgotten how to laugh."

"You think God has a sense of humor?" she asked. "I don't. I can't find humor anywhere in the creation. Not even in the books that claim to be God's word. The Koran, joke-free. The Bible, from the apple to Armageddon, humorless."

"I don't know about that. I find them both good for a chuckle now and again."

She gave me a gloomy smile. Then, with her dark eyes swollen with the complexity of the human tragedy, she smirked, sniffed back her tears, met my eyes, and said, "A sperm donor, a carpenter, and Julius Caesar walk into a bar." Holy crap! She was telling a joke! "They came, they saw, they conquered." And she laughed through her tears like a schoolgirl. And I joined her. We're odd creatures—when happy, our facial muscles convulse, and our lungs puff. When sad, we drip salt. And sometimes, like now, both. But then, as quickly as the comedy came, it wandered off. "Life is just one big bowl of Augie Omegas," she said. I could picture our future together. After my third donation, I'd get up the courage to ask her out. And then, one day in the donation room, as she handed me the channel changer, the scintillating breaths of pent-up desire would be so great we'd jump each other, and inspired by the TV's menu, we'd make the best amateur-hardcore-gonzo-hentai-alt love the world has ever known.

"Gotta get back. Donors are waiting," she whispered. Then she slipped through the back door and left me with the lonely, trash-filled alley. Socrates said the true tragedian is also an artist in comedy. In other words, if you can tell a good joke, you have all it takes to live a tragedy. But the fantastic thing about comedy is that it, unlike tragedy, is always transferable. Suppose I tell you that, at long last, I've finally experienced the pins and needles of love but know she'll never feel the same way about me. You may experience sadness for me. You might even have a tragic, empathetic response based on your own familiarity with lost love, but you don't also fall in love with Nurse Cox. But with comedy, you laugh at the exact same thing I laugh at - Laughter is the closest people can get to shared experience.

I started through the trash towards my car, but then the alley door reopened, and Cox stuck her head out and said, "You might have a very mild case of pseudobulbar disorder. People who have it can't help but laugh. It can be caused by physical damage to the brain. Have you ever been hit in the head?"

"My mother often beat me with a spatula."

"That explains it."

"I'll look into it," I said, and she turned to go back in, and I blurted, "Would you like to have dinner?"

She stopped and considered me before saying, "With you? Why?"

"Because the annihilation of the entire species is at hand, and everything in the universe is moving away from us at the speed of light."

She smiled, took a deep breath, and said, "My husband's next mental competency hearing is in three days. They can't release him till then. Can we do it before he gets out?"

"Tomorrow night?"

"It's a date."

"Buffalo Wild Wings near campus? Seven?"

"I'll see you there."

"One more thing. Do you know what happened to Augie Omega?"

"I heard a rumor that he went into Campanology."

"Campanology?"

"Yes. Someone who studies bells."

"You mean like in bell towers?"

"Yes."

14

I tried to hide, but it was too late, he saw me. It was Dr. Jerry Loudie, head of the Mental Health Solutions Center. As always, he wore tennis sweatbands and copper-lined socks. "Charlie!" he bubbled like an unbroken puppy as he obstructed my path. "We missed you at roadside beautification last Saturday." I've never understood people who are so enthused. Didn't he know the rainforests were burning and the Great Barrier Reef dying? In private, he was most likely an emotional heap who couldn't drag himself out of bed without overdosing on enough Prozac to cheer up a small country. "Are we looking to get our mental geometry recalibrated?" he twinkled. We had bumped into each other miles from campus outside a psychiatrist's office.

"Sure, I guess," I said.

"Oh, Charlie, no need for embarrassment. Today, there's nothing wrong with asking for a little psychiatric tune-up. Everybody does it. Everybody!"

"Good to know. Gotta run."

He blocked me again. "Have you seen what the students are writing about you on social media?"

"Yes."

"I can't confirm this, but I've heard a rumor that the Multicultural Student Activities Board is thinking of hiring one of those billboard trucks and driving around campus with a picture of you and the words, "Fire the Joker."

"That I hadn't heard."

"Ouch ouch ouch," he said as he gave me a knowing smile and added,

"Disheartening."

"I've got it under control. Nice running into you, but—"

"Where would you say your chaos level is on a scale of one to fifteen - one being everyday living-in-America type anxiety, and fifteen being I've bought an AK-47, and I'm heading to the bell tower."

"Ah. Nine-ish?"

"I can solve your problems. All you have to do is post about your emotional issues on social media. And while you're at it, share the personal details that took you into this spiral of depression."

"I'm kind of not into sharing."

"Don't you want your students to know you have the courage to be transparent about your psychological messiness?"

"Why would I do that?"

"So you can be a victim and claim the power that goes with."

"Power?"

"Charlie, today, if a professor wants to get anywhere with his students, he has to admit that he's overwhelmed by life and that there's nothing he can do but confess it, hopefully in front of his class or any large public gathering. Thus, you gain power by showing weakness."

"How does being weak give me power?"

"Because now you'll have the privilege of being a victim. Oh, and while you're at it, throw in a statement about how you're also a member of a privileged class and how that really bugs the hell out of you." He placed his fingers against his temples and pantomimed his head exploding. "Two birds, one stone!"

"Then what?"

"Do nothing. Make zero changes."

"But why?"

"Charlie, the only way to survive at a modern university is to cancel yourself before anyone can do it for you." Then he knowingly smiled and added, "Do I have permission to touch you?"

"Where?"

"Shoulders," and he seized my rotator cuffs and gently shook me as he growled like a bear, "Grrrrrrr! Come on, Charles, get with the program!" I couldn't be sure, but I swear I heard the rattle of a pharmaceutical bottle in his pocket.

"Gotta run," I said, extracting myself from his arms. "Don't want to be late."

"Whom ya seeing?"

"Dr. Boucher."

"Oh, A.O.!"

"A.O.?"

"The president's husband! Everyone calls him by his initials, A.O. He helped me with my difficulty with relationships, my unsustainable self-image, and my problems with excessive masturbation."

"And you posted about this on social media?" I said with deep concern for the human race.

"And do you know what it got me?"

"Great student evaluations?"

"And a Top Ten Prof Award!" He beamed and winked as he mounted his electric scooter and rode off, probably to find a place to masturbate.

Ping!

To All Humanities Professors,

Your PIS (Professor Impact Statement) is due today at noon. It's critical you underscore the financial opportunities you (personally) and your department (as a whole) have given to the state. You must also highlight the significance of your service. Feel free to include graphs, charts, and maps. Also, be sure to answer the questions, "So what?" and "Who cares?"

Have A Great Day,

Acting Dean Bobby Popkov, PhD

"The purpose of life is to live it! – Eleanor Roosevelt

"Your problem is that you live in an age of profound angst," Dr. A.O. Boucher said from his king-sized psychotherapy chair. "Your life is full of injustice, stupidity, and insecurity. God is just a vague spiritualism, a muddy makeshift metaphysical hope. For you, there's no paradise for your suffering nor a last judgment to guide you towards good. In other words, you have failed to functionally adapt to the demands of this screwed-up modern world."

I sat there, dumbfounded. All I could say is, "Wow. Nailed it."

Then he smiled and threw in, "It's a minor condition, the common cold of psychiatry. It's all in my letter."

"Sounds great," I said, "but could you also toss in a line or two about mesothelioma?"

"That's in there too. My assistant is printing it now."

"You already wrote it?"

"It's a form letter."

I sat tense and pigeon-toed on a hard chair. Everything about Dr. Boucher, from his French accent to his flying armrest chair, projected the power of self-confidence. He was the gold leaf gatekeeper of a great medical-industrial complex who could solve all your psychic illnesses by prescribing a pill made by a corporation in which he most likely owned stock. All I had to do was fake my way through the next few moments, and I'd have the letter my lawyer wanted and be one step closer to settling out of court.

"So, you're suing your employer," he said.

"Yes."

"Because you were exposed to asbestos."

"That's right."

"What do you do?"

"I'm… an actor," I lied, clearing my throat to cover my edginess.

"How does an actor come in contact with asbestos?"

"Ah… It was in a prop."

"What kind of prop?"

"A fake… ah… orange." It was the first thing that popped into my head.

"I was once in a play."

"Oh?"

"Played Cyrano in college," he boasted, and I tried to act as if I didn't already know this, for the university president was right, her husband's nose was like a sail - Two stacked double 'A' batteries could easily fit inside. He tapped its broad flank while he studied me for a pensive moment. He was trying to place me. "You look familiar. Have you ever been at a party at the president of the university's house?"

"No," I said as I nervously fidgeted.

"Or maybe I saw you in a movie?"

"No."

"Stage?"

"No."

"TV commercial?"

"No."

"What type of actor are you?"

"Ah…" I stalled as I tried to come up with a fib. "I'm a webinar actor."

"You mean industrial training videos?" he said, unimpressed.

"Yeah."

"And you were filming one of these when you came in contact with an asbestos-laden orange."

"Yes. It was a training video for, ah, orange pickers."

Then he did it again. Every two minutes, like clockwork, he picked up his mug with his right hand, passed it to his left, then sniffed the coffee before he sipped. After which, he handed it back to his right and put it down. I wondered why he didn't just drink with his right hand. Why this odd, repetitive, labor-intensive coffee genuflecting?

Suddenly, harsh voices cut through the thin wall from the next office. "Go screw yourself!" a man shouted. A woman barked back, "I'm sick and tired of your bullshit!"

"Excuse me," Dr. Boucher said as he calmly walked to the wall, lightly rapped it with his hairy knuckles, and loudly but politely insisted, "Quiet, please! I'm with a patient!" Then he returned to his chair and scrutinized me. "An asbestos-laden prop orange," he said to himself.

Worried, I went to my default, a joke, "Did you hear the one about the man who worked in an asbestos factory for fifty years? He never got sick, but when he died, it took three days to cremate his body."

My pathetic attempt at humor failed. Not even a slight polite chuckle from him. Instead, he let out a tiny disdainful grunt and said, "You carry a lot of pain, don't you. Comedy comes from pain, doesn't it?"

"True, that's why so many stand-up comedians come from Somalia," I chirped, doing my best Groucho imitation. Not even a nose titter from him. Instead, he made a note on his yellow legal pad.

"Have you had an MRI recently?"

"Why would I need one?"

"There's a condition called Witzelsucht, also known as compulsive joke syndrome. It's often seen in patients with right frontal damage."

"I did have an MRI once, but not for that."

"Then why?"

"My doctor wanted to know if I suffered from claustrophobia."

He looked at me as if I had squirrels crawling on my face, then said, "You think that if you can make people laugh, you'll be popular, or at the very least, they won't attack you. But what you don't know is that those who make jokes are only announcing to the world that they are powerless, insignificant, and fundamentally insecure." He genuflected his mug - right hand, left hand, sniff, sip, back to the right. What the hell was the little sniff about? Then his eyes narrowed on me, "What truths about yourself are you trying to deflect by telling jokes?"

The argument bursting from the next office interrupted again. "Shut up, you silly fool!" the woman shouted. Then a muffled thump - Someone must've thrown a flower vase or a trumpet against the wall.

Dr. Boucher hollered at the wall, "Shut the fuck up!" Seeing my concern, he calmly smiled, took a deep breath, and psychoanalytically said, "Are you aware that you hum?"

"I do?"

"When you're not talking, you, ever so gently, hum to yourself. You didn't know this?"

"No." And for the first time, I became aware that I was quietly humming. I stopped, and a vacancy took up in my skull. It was a feeling I hadn't known since I was a child. I'd been humming for thirty years.

"It's as if your heartbeat isn't enough for you to know you exist." He snorted and then beamed as an acerbic remark came to him, and he added, as if to an adolescent, "Most people think, therefore, they exist. You hum, therefore, you exist. Do you know how you can stop humming and become emotionally healthy?"

"Sue my employer?"

"That'll change nothing."

"Then how?"

"You must grab power, and then you will know happiness. Life is about the will to power. Say it with me. Life is—

"The will to power," I echoed him.

"Once more with feeling."

"Life is the will to power!"

"Very good," he said.

Again, muffled shouts cut from the next room. A man cried out, "Omega doesn't exist!" "Yes, he does, and he's driving me crazy!" the woman answered. "He's a figment of your imagination!" "No, he's real!" "Shut your mouth and meditate!" "Screw you and your meditation!"

"So sorry," Dr. Boucher said, and again he walked to the wall, but this time, he unleashed a sudden barrage of fierce blows and screamed, "Shut up, you deeply disturbed people! Shut up!" Then he turned to me and said, "Join me."

"You want me to—"

"Yes. Show me you have power." I crossed to the wall and followed his lead as he hammered the sheetrock with his fists. "Harder!" he insisted. Our blows caused his framed diplomas to dance on their hooks. "Harder!" I attacked the wall, my knuckles becoming red and arms sore. Then suddenly, Dr. Boucher lost it, shrieking in a psychopathic rage, "Shut up, or I'll come over there, pry open your mouths, reach down your throats, and rip out several vital organs!"

Then.

Silence.

Breathing fiercely, Dr. Boucher listened, his eyes darting to me and back to the wall and then back to me. "Success!" he said, beaming. "You see? It's all about power."

"What's next door?" I said, as I caught my breath. "Another psychiatrist's office?"

"No. The Buddhist Center." He touched up his hair in a vanity mirror next to his diplomas. "They've been a pain in the ass since they moved in. Let me get you your letter." And he crossed to a side door that led to an outer office. There, he stopped. "Wait, got it!" He snapped his fingers. "You were in that movie about that man who fell in love with an older woman."

"No, really," I insisted, "I've never been in a movie. Only industrials." Then my heart stopped. I couldn't believe it. On his coat rack, beside his head, hung my "School of Athens" philosophy tie. His eyes followed mine to the tie. He looked at it for a thinking moment, then back to me.

"Like my tie?" he said.

"Yes, nice."

"Found it on my closet floor. The wife told me it was supposed to be a birthday gift. But it wasn't my birthday." Then he added, "I know I know you." And he turned and walked out. He's playing me, I thought. I had to act before he could. I hauled out my phone and dialed.

"Office of the President," the iPhone voice said.

"I need to talk to her right now."

"Who is this?"

"Dr. Charlie Neb."

"Is she expecting a call from you?"

"No."

"May I take a message?"

"Tell her I'm currently in her husband's office and I feel a confession coming on."

"Excuse me?"

"Tell her, word for word. I'll wait."

"One moment."

My blood pressure inched up. I loosened my tie to let my brain breathe. I was developing tunnel vision when my phone clicked. "Hello, Charlie?" President Boucher cheerfully said, "So nice of you to call."

"I'm in your husband's office, and the conversation is about to come around to Ayn Rand and handcuffs."

"Excuse me?"

"I'll tell him the truth about the other night unless you give me my job back."

"Why are you doing this?"

"The will to power!"

"Have you looked at your email?"

"No. Why?"

"Charlie, I reinstated you twenty minutes ago."

I checked my phone.

> Dear Acting Dean Popkov,
>
> On my authority, reinstate Dr. Charlie Neb and cancel his A.A. hearing.
>
> President Boucher
>
> CC: Charlie Neb

Stunned, I said, "Why?"

"Because, after much thought, I've determined I'm in love with you."

"Holy shit," I heard myself say.

"Were you going to blackmail me?" She laughed. "Really, Charlie, that's got to be your best joke ever."

"I'm so sorry. I'm feeling tons of anxiety."

"Charlie, shut up and listen. Get your ass out of his office immediately. He can be violent."

Click, and the line went dead. Just then, more shouts came through the wall, "I don't care that the root of suffering is attachment, you son of a bitch! I'm a human being. It's natural to want things!"

I lost it, ran over, and slammed my fists into the wall. "Shut up!" I yelled, "Shut up, you stupid Buddhists!" One of A.O.'s framed awards crashed to the floor, yet I continued pounding. "There is no nirvana, no definitive answer. All we do is spend our short time on this earth struggling with our need for basic nutrition and unfulfilled copulatory instincts!" I pummeled the wall. "Schopenhauer was right, 'only an idiot could imagine life was worth living!'" Then silence. I caught my breath, pulled myself together, and turned to see A.O. standing at the door with the letter.

"You can quote Schopenhauer. Not many webinar actors can do that. Interesting," he calmly said. Then he looked at the cracked frame lying at my feet. "You broke my Chamber of Commerce Psychiatrist of the Year award."

"Sorry, the Buddhists were at it again."

He sat at his substantial desk, took out a fountain pen, sniffed it, and signed the watermarked letter. "There you go."

"Thank you. I'll work on the humming thing," I said as I quickly took the letter and started for the door.

"Oh, by the way," he stated with a calculating smile. "How long was your dissertation?"

I stopped. My heart wobbled. My knees felt like soggy toast. "Excuse me?"

"It's a simple question. What was the word count of your dissertation?"

"Don't know what you're talking about."

"Yes, you do," his eyes tightened on me, "Dr. Neb."

The game was up. It took me a moment, but I finally said, "101,482."

"And how many people read it?"

"I don't understand."

"How many humans laid eyes upon it?"

"Four, maybe."

"Not counting yourself, that would be three," he dismissively said. "I've never understood why someone would waste years writing a dissertation on philosophy. Has there ever been a philosophical dissertation that's produced legislation or improved the morals of a society? Has a dissertation in philosophy ever curtailed drug use in children or improved general health and well-being? Can you think of, even on one occasion, when a dissertation in philosophy successfully predicted an eclipse or improved the structural integrity of a building in an earthquake zone?" My lungs froze. I couldn't even form the word "no." My lips moved, but the word failed to materialize. "Then there is only one logical conclusion. And that is that a Ph.D. in philosophy is the ultimate—."

"Joke."

Then, with a superior relish, he smiled, picked up his mug, and genuflected. "Are you aware that being a professor is no longer something to be proud of? Like comedians, professors are now at the bottom of the food chain."

I wanted so to defeat him, but all I got out was, "And are you aware every time you drink coffee, you sniff it first?"

He stopped mid-sniff, the mug perched under his long nostrils, and chuckled. "And are you aware I have home security video of you in my house, which I can edit to fit my needs, and then turn over to the police. And when I do, they will know exactly who molested my wife." He grinned. "I wonder how many PhDs in philosophy are also convicted felons?" Then he added, "I knew I'd seen you in a movie. I just didn't expect it to be my home security video."

He had diced me into a fine powder that lacked human form. "What do you want?" I said.

"First, you're not to see my wife again."

"I can do that."

"Next, I want your friendship."

"Why?" I said, quite confused.

"Do you know what friends do?"

"No."

"They run little errands for each other."

"What type of errands?"

"Don't know. We'll see. I'll text you when I need something, and you'll do it without question. Know why?"

"Because we're friends."

"Very good."

"You're not going to harm her?"

"Not if you do as I ask." When he saw my despair, he smiled and threw in, "To conclude our session, would you like a prescription? Fluvoxamine,

Isocarboxazid, Tranylcypromine. Name it, and it's yours."

"No, thank you," I whispered.

"Going it alone, are we? Brave man. Now, if you don't mind, I've got another client coming in. Also, a professor. She made the unfortunate mistake of confessing to me she'd plagiarized parts of her dissertation. She's also a friend. She washes my car every Thursday." He smiled and added, "'Only an absolute pauper with a thorough conviction of his utter insignificance, worthlessness, and complete, profound inferiority can quietly take his place in the political machine.' Know who said that?"

"Schopenhauer."

"Correct. We all want more, not even the Buddhist's self-abnegation can purge us of that, but we must accept our limitations and our place within the political machine. That, Dr. Neb, is what makes your life a tragedy. And a farce." Defeated, I walked to the door. There, I stopped and looked back. He had the smallest amount of power a person could have, yet, like most humans, he still found a way to abuse it.

"Your initials, A.O.," I said, "by any chance, do they stand for Augie Omega?"

"No. Andre Oliver. But I once took a correspondence course from Omega University."

"Augie Omega has a university?"

"Yes. He took my tuition, went bankrupt, and disappeared. But he taught me a great lesson. A lesson that you have failed to learn."

"Which is?"

"How to functionally adapt to the demands of a world filled with scarcity, misery, and exploitation."

"And how does one do that?"

"By becoming more like Augie Omega."

Sisyphus Laughing

(Part Two)

15

"Why does it take 100 million sperm to fertilize an egg?" Nurse Cox said. "Because they won't stop to ask for directions." I thought our dinner date would be spent talking about philosophers like Marcus Aurelius, but all she did was tell sperm jokes. "Why was the London sperm bank so unsuccessful? There were only two donors. One came on the bus. The other missed the tube."

Outside the restaurant's windows, a tiki torch carrying mob protested at the Pita Pit across the street. Their signs read, "Pita Pit Denies the Holocaust!" "Pita Pit supports Fascism!" and "Pita Pit Sucks!"

"I've enjoyed this," I said as we sat in one of the half-shell booths at Buffalo Wild Wings. "But could we talk about something other than sperm?"

"Like?"

"Well, we don't know much about each other."

"What do you want to know?"

"Why do you eat with a baby's spoon and fork?"

When we arrived at the restaurant, Nurse Cox pushed aside the flatware and replaced it with a tiny set of children's silverware decorated with happy pandas. "Smaller bites make life last," she said. "What else?"

"Well, ah, what do you want from the world?"

"Where to start," she said as she drew a figure eight in her ketchup with her last French fry and offhandedly mentioned, "I'm moving to Belize."

"Belize," I said. "That's a country south of Mexico?"

"Yeah. Made my final decision last week. In fact, you coming to the sperm bank kind of pushed me over the edge." Then she leaned forward and added, "I've packed a few gold coins, antibiotics, batteries, potassium iodide tablets, and a gas mask from the army surplus store."

"Why?"

"Haven't you heard? It's the last days. Everything's flying apart." She met my eyes to see if I understood the gravity of her statement. When I did, she gave me a distant smile as she drifted into her inner poet, "I'm hoping for the softest possible landing against the great unbreakable wall of reality," but then she shrugged. "Plus, I understand it's cheap to live down there."

Outside, the megaphoned leaders led the crowd's chant, "Hey-Hey Ho-Ho, Pita Pit has got to go!"

"When are you doing this?" I said, baffled.

"Friday."

"Like this Friday?"

"November 7th." She gurgled the last bit of orange from her tropical cocktail through a curly straw, unaware I was stunned by the news. "Quit my job, sold my car, and gave away my stuff to Goodwill. Whatever's left, my husband can have if he ever recovers." Then she proudly added, "I'm down to two suitcases and an oversized backpack. That's all anyone needs in the way of worldly possessions."

"But why?"

"Stefan Zweig."

"The novelist?"

"You read him?"

"Yes."

"When things got bad for him in Europe because of the Nazis," she said, "he moved to South America. So, I figure, as things are getting pretty fascist here, I'd do the same." And she smiled, drawing me into agreement, "Wouldn't it be grand to go stateless? As Zweig said, 'To be obligated to no one country and for that reason undifferentiatedly attached to all.'"

"But that would mean… ah…" I said, trying to come up with a counterargument, but I had nothing.

"We all live in exile, Charlie. It's just that some are aware of it. Besides, the whole idea of country, government, and patriotism is bogus. The only way to survive in the post-happiness age is to become consciously detached from the shitstorm that occupies the deranged public."

"But in South America, Zweig killed himself," I said, finally coming up with a counterargument.

"Really? Huh, didn't know," and she ruminated for a moment, but then she threw in, "You having dessert? Their loaded ice cream is naughty, but only 500 calories."

"No, I've lost my appetite," I said and then interrupted myself, "I think you need to give this more thought," but my words were phony.

Still playing with her French fry, she said, "Stefan Zweig wrote, 'Flee, take refuge in your innermost self, in your work, flee to where you are no more than your own being, not the citizen of a state, not a plaything of this infernal game, where alone your bit of intellect can still function rationally in a world gone mad.'"

"I know modern life seems completely absurd, but is running away the answer?"

"I'm not running away. I'm fleeing," she corrected me. "There's a difference."

"No, I think they're pretty much the same."

"Hey-Hey Ho-Ho, Pita Pit has got to go!"

She placed her cheek in her palm and smiled, tiny and ironic. "Aren't you tired of the relentless futility of life? Tired of living in the gutted world of the Corporate States of America? Tired of the monthly wars. Tired of the Macy's Thanksgiving Day parade being an advertisement for Wheaties and wetland preservation." She took a breath and drifted into her inner self. "I go to Walmart and watch what's left of America's walking wounded. As I pick up my medication, the pharmacist doesn't answer my questions. Instead, he just gives the prefabricated responses that the company's lawyers have approved. I try to escape this gerrymandered mess by going to the mountains, but on the way, I have to defend myself against massive pickup trucks and win-at-all-costs BMWs that cut me off, tailgate, and play chicken. When I get to the mountains, what do I hear? The healing sounds of nature? Not anymore. Now it's motorcycles and snowmobiles. I'm tired, Charlie, tired of school shootings, bizarre presidents, heat domes, trash on Mount Everest, and this screwed-up, debt-driven economy that could head south at any moment. Sirens keep me up at night, and backup alarms wake me every morning."

Outside, sirens blared as three firetrucks ripped down the street, chasing some awful new chaos. I had to cover my ears, but she didn't change her far-off gaze. Not even a flinch. It was as if she had forgotten the pains of modern life and was already on the plane a thousand miles out. Then she blinked and came back to me. "But do you know what bothers me the most?" The hypernormalization of it all. Know what I mean?"

"I guess. But every society has its way of doing things, its habits, tradition."

"Yes, but 'tradition always means repression.'"

"Also, a Zweig quote."

"I know," and she paused. There was more she wanted to say, but her complaint list was too long. Then she hugged herself and summed it up nicely. "What happened to kindness and courtesy?" She looked to me for an answer. But once again, for the billionth time in human history, one lost soul turned to another, hoping for a ray of insight only to find that still, again, we didn't possess it. Above, the universe kept its answers to itself. Or perhaps it was hoping we'd come up with something. She finally broke the silence, "Did you know the ancient Greeks sacrificed chickens to Asclepius, the god of medicine? And when they weren't doing that, they sacrificed cows to Athena and goats to Aphrodite. They'd wake up in the morning and think, what's on my to-do list for today? I gotta pick up some bread at the market, have a dialogue with Socrates, and I'm forgetting something. Oh, that's right, I've got to get a cow and cut its heart out to make the Gods happy. Know why they did that?"

"No."

"Because they thought it was normal." Then she studied my plate and added, "You want that last French fry?"

"It's yours." She stabbed it with her tiny fork and made more circles in her ketchup. Outside, another round of sirens as cops weaved their way through the Pita Pit protesters. "What are you going to do in Belize?"

"Follow Stefan Zweig's advice. I'll be free of vanity and pride. Free from belief, disbelief, convictions, and political parties. I'll have no habits, ambitions, or greed. I'll liberate myself from family, fanaticism, and fate. But above all, I will be free from meaning."

"Is that possible?"

"Aren't you tired of living in a world where everything is embedded with meaning? A car is no longer transportation but a personal lifestyle statement. If I post a photo of myself with rings under my eyes, my girlfriends celebrate me because I'm empowering myself 'against misogynistic standards of beauty.' Charlie, what's this preoccupation humans have with meaning?"

"Don't know."

"It's destroying our ability to enjoy life. A car is just a car, and the rings under my eyes mean nothing more than I am at the mercy of chaos. And the meaning of life is that it has no meaning."

"But how do you live if there's no meaning?

"By stringing together a whole bunch of pointless, insignificant days, then hanging a sign on it that says 'welcome home.'"

"Rather pessimistic."

"Hey-Hey Ho-Ho, Pita Pit has got to go!"

"In a world filled with Augie Omegas, isn't pessimism the only relief?" Then she considered me for a long moment before adding, "I bought two one-way tickets. I thought Marcellus would come with. But that's not going to happen."

"Marcellus, your husband."

"Yes. They tell me all he does is sit on his bed chanting, 'Augie Omega, Augie Omega.' Doctors don't hold out much hope." She took a deep breath, her gaze anchored on me, and gently added, "Got a passport?"

"Yes."

"Join me. I hear they've got beautiful beaches and jungles so thick the modern world would never catch us." I could see the slightest fear of rejection in her and the hope that she wouldn't have to make this unique journey to the edge of her known world alone.

"But we hardly know each other."

"I know you're the first man who ever laughed at nineteen sperm bank jokes in a row. My husband never laughed at one."

"But there's more to a relationship than comedy."

"We got sperm bank jokes in common. That's a good start." She popped the last fry and licked her soft lips.

"Hey-Hey Ho-Ho, Pita Pit has got to go!"

This was for real. She was asking me to drop out of the only life I'd known and run away to some bohemian life in a Caribbean country I knew nothing of. I could see our life together. Steeped in anonymity, we'd grow strawberries and eat our daily bread of shredded coconuts with tiny utensils. We'd spend our mornings making ships in bottles and selling them to tourists who lingered long enough to become jealous of our psychic peace and eternal youth. In the afternoon, we'd milk our flock of pet goats.

"Maybe we'd become lovers," she said as she unpinned her hair and let it fall, "maybe just friends who share a jungle hut." Stunned, I tried to formulate a sentence, but I was blank. "The old Roman rules of bread and circus are insufficient to keep the population in check," she said. "So, they've added worry and status. Let's throw them all away." At that moment, the word "fleeing" was the most beautiful verb I'd ever heard. Never had I been so tempted.

"Why me?"

"Because you're nothing like my husband."

"How do you know?"

"My husband spent his life wanting one thing and one thing only. A BMW convertible," she said as she shook her head in disappointment. "Can you imagine? He's got this one brief visit to Earth, all these possible days and nights, and he spends his time lusting after a gas-guzzling, overpriced, bullshit car he can't afford. Do you know the surest way *not* to enjoy a BMW?"

"No."

"Own one. Because it, too, will become hypernormalized."

Did I tell her about my own illogical BMW lust? No. Outside, the police showered the crowd with tear gas. "Hey-Hey Ho-Ho, Pita Pit has got to go!" The smell seeped into the restaurant. The server covered their noses with masks but continued to take orders and bus. She was unaffected. Her eyes were clear, bright, forgiving.

"Can I have until tomorrow to think?" I said.

"Sure. Tonight, I'll change Marcellus's ticket to you."

"But what if I don't show?"

"I think you will," and she gave me a buoyant smile. "Magic hour is 5pm, Friday, November 7th. That's check-in at the airport. Just before I board, I'm throwing away my phone, closing my Facebook account, and calling my lawyer and filing for divorce. But the very last thing I'm doing is mailing a letter to the State Department renouncing my citizenship in this madhouse. Then I'll fall off the corporate grid." She grinned and added, "What do lawyers and sperm have in common? They both have a one in two million chance of being a real person someday."

Ping!

> Dr. Neb,
>
> I must work late tonight. Bring me a steak, grilled, not pan-fried, and seared. Medium rare. And a generous dollop of béarnaise butter. Plus, a simple green salad.
>
> And, of course, I expect you to pay. Be quick. I'm famished.
>
> Your Friend,
>
> A. O.

"Sorry," I said, "I've got to answer this," and I placed my iPhone below the horizon of the tabletop, trying to hide that I was furiously typing, letting my overlord know his wish was my command. But then I felt a strange prickling energy. For a moment, I thought a microwave in the kitchen had gone haywire and was bombarding the hair on my neck with electromagnetic waves. I looked up to see what I felt wasn't coming from the kitchen, but disappointment radiating from Nurse Cox.

"You can't opt out of capitalism. Especially Laissez-faire," I said in my defense. "It's the way things are. It's the only hypernormaliztion I know."

She looked through me as if she was already in Belize, living a modest life with nothing to prove, not affected by status, not judging herself with material possessions, not embarrassed by the bare walls of her simple jungle tarpaper shack or the rust on her secondhand Chevy. Coming back to me, she gave me a forgiving smile and said, "Do you know what the problem is with consciousness?"

"That we have it?"

"No, the problem is it evaporates much too quickly. What if the average length of life was two hundred years? I read it'll soon be possible. In fact, the first person to live that long might be alive today. It might be you."

"Hey-Hey Ho-Ho, Pita Pit has got to go!"

"Won't that person be lucky?" she said. "Two hundred years to ask the important questions and try various religions, philosophies, and loves on for size. And if one weren't the answer, they'd have time to reverse course. But for the rest of us, life is absurdly quick, so panic sets in early. This lack of time forces us to make decisions long before we can run the experiment. We're all just guessing. You're guessing. I'm guessing. The Pope, when he stands before the multitudes in St. Peter's, is guessing." As the fog of tear gas invaded the room, she pushed her dishes away, propped her chin in her hands, and added, "Would you like to kiss me before time runs out?"

"You mean, like, right now?"

"Yes."

"On your lips?"

"Yes."

"Very much so."

"Just so happens, I'd like to kiss you too."

And she leaned forward over the dirty dishes, and I pressed my lips against her softness. She tasted of nachos, rum and tear gas. Her nose was cold and soft. Then our lips parted, and she glowed. "Time's almost up," she said as she rolled her childish silverware in a paper napkin, placed them in her purse, picked the maraschino from the crushed ice of her tropical drink, popped it between her lips, and playfully added, "Come with me and you'll never have to deal with Augie Omegas again." Then she got up and smiled a goodbye. "Be at the airport Friday, November 7th, 5pm."

Just then, a large billboard truck outside the restaurant's windows distracted me. On it was my picture, and the words, "Fire the Joker. Sponsored by the Multicultural Student Activities Board." Just as Nurse Cox was about to see it, I distracted her by holding up her polka-dotted mittens. "You forgot your gloves."

"Don't need them anymore," she beamed. "I hope this isn't goodbye, Charlie." It was lyric, the voice of happiness and serenity. Then, just as the billboard truck disappeared, she turned and opened the restaurant's door. The shouts from the cold street intensified. "The whole world is watching! The whole world is watching!" And she put on her gas mask and disappeared into the haze of the frenzied crowd. And I sat there alone, dreaming of a life where there was no need for philosophy or religion. No desire for heaven. No fear of hell.

Wait, do you milk goats? There'd be a steep learning curve.

16

After a night of staring at the ceiling from my studio apartment hide-a-bed, consumed by philosophical insomnia, the following morning, I crossed campus on my way to Beginning Philosophy, the large class from which the anonymous complaint had come.

Ping!

> Professor Neb,
>
> I can't entirely agree with President Boucher's decision, so I've placed you on a RAP (Review Assessment Plan).
>
> This means your students, using the RAP app on their smartphones, can rate your teaching minute-by-minute. And you can monitor your PR (Positivity Rating) from the lectern screen in real time. I will also be able to supervise your evaluative growth from my office.
>
> Think of this as a positive learning opportunity.
>
> Have A Great Day,
>
> Acting Dean Bobby Popkov, PhD
>
> *"The most courageous act is still to think for yourself. Aloud."* - Coco Chanel
>
> PS In order to restart your paychecks, we need you to take twenty hours of webinar sensitivity training, and you'll have to write three self-reflection essays.

It was my first lecture since being reinstated. I felt rusty. As I opened my backpack and took out my notes, four students stood, crossed behind me, and silently held up protest signs that read: "It's Too Late For Apologies!" "Jokes = Violence!" "Don't Lecture Us!" "You Are The Joke!"

"Trigger warnings," I started, "Today's lecture is about Nietzsche and contains subjects some may find offensive or troubling. If you cannot tolerate this, university rules state you're free to leave. Half the class walked, and I checked my RAP positivity rating on the lectern computer screen - 7%. Frankly, I was shocked it was that high. "In *The Birth of Tragedy*, Nietzsche wrote about the nauseating absurdities of existence." My rating fell to 1%. I was sure the 1% came from the dozy frat bro in the back. "But before I begin, I'd like to say I'm sorry I told a joke. I'll never make that mistake again." My rating went to 4%. "I've been experiencing tons of anxiety." My rating jumped to 10%. "I'm seeing a psychiatrist." 28%. "I'm now on a cocktail of antidepressants - Fluvoxamine, Isocarboxazid, Tranylcypromine." I was making shit up, but my rating jumped to 39%. "I had a difficult relationship with my mother. She crushed my hopes of becoming an actor." 43%. "Plus, my dating life is a mess." 48%. "Then, this morning, it occurred to me that I am a victim." 55%. "Plus, I'm a member of a privileged class, and that really bugs the hell out of me." 68%!

Ping!

> Campus Wide Scarlet & Brown Alert,
>
> The Wild Springs Fire is now ten miles from campus. If evacuations are necessary, we will inform you over TikTok.
>
> Safety First,
>
> Lieutenant Joe Patroni
> University Police

After class, I walked over to old Arts and Sciences and, like a pallbearer, climbed the steep staircase towards the bell tower. As I passed each landing, the air grew chill, the roof slanted, and the steps narrowed. On the fifth floor, I found only one vault-like door with a sign that read "Professor Chuck

Whitman Memorial Bell Tower." Under it was taped a piece of paper that read, "A.A. No admittance." Four heavy copper hinges held the windowless steel. No door handle, only a large prison lock. Around this were several dents where someone had tried to use a hammer or crowbar to pry it open.

Ping!

> Charlie,
>
> Between your classes today, meet me at the Hilton Hotel. Bring flowers and wine. I'll be in room 532.
>
> President Boucher

I sat in front of the door on the tired linoleum floor and looked up Belize on Wikipedia. "A Caribbean country on the northeastern coast of Central America. It borders Mexico to the North and Guatemala to the west and south. To the East are the beaches of the Caribbean Sea. It is the least densely populated country in Central America and the only one where English is the official language."

Ping!

> Professor Neb,
>
> I am impressed with your RAP rating of 68%. It was the highest this week of any humanities professor.
>
> As a result, you are the winner of this week's PIE (Promoting Intellectual Enjoyment) award. This entitles you to one free slice of homemade pie from Mama Martha's pie shop in the food court of the student union.
>
> Congratulations,
>
> Acting Dean Bobby Popkov, PhD
>
> *"Tough times never last, but tough people do."* – Robert H. Schuller

I was enjoying the flaky crust of my PIE award in the student union next to the boarded-up food court Pita Pit when someone shouted, "What the hell is wrong with you people?!" It was Dr. Merkin, the bizarre professor who kept coming to work twelve years after they canceled the linguistics department. She made a grand gesture to the students, but they didn't notice because their eyes were fixated on their phones. "If you need evidence that the Enlightenment is a flop, look around you!" she announced. Then she sat at my table and dug a plastic fork into a double slice of berry pie. With her dentures full of blue, she said to me, but loud enough for all to hear, "We now live in the post-romantic age where egoism and individualism has reached its climax! Thus, universities are waste dumps!" Then she turned to the students and shouted, "Are you listening?" A few students glanced up, but most didn't. To the three or four who did, she returned their stares by bouncing in her seat and shooting them bug eyes. This was nothing new for them, as they had grown up in a country that allowed mentally disturbed individuals to roam the neighborhoods and universities.

"Look at yourselves," she shouted. "All you project is ironic detachment! You think it makes you intellectually deep! But ironic detachment is a pose, not significance! Ironic detachment brings you down to the level of Vogue and GQ magazine models who get paid to project disinterest in order to sell underwear and bras!" And she returned to me and added, "Who in their right mind would want to have an in-depth conversation with a Vogue or GQ cover model? And I may be wrong because I don't speak from experience, but I'd be willing to bet sex with ironically detached people, no matter how beautiful or handsome, isn't very good." She smiled, took a big blue bite, and added, "How's your pie?"

"Dr. Merkin—."

"Don't call me that!"

"Sorry, She Who Runs On The Mountain, have you considered the possibility that… ah…" But I couldn't finish.

"What? That I'm not normal?"

"Yes."

And she beamed. "Of course, I'm not! I'm proudly *not*! The question is, who is sane, and who is mad?" Then she leaned back and gave me the floor. "Your thoughts."

"Well," I said, "today it's getting hard to distinguish between the two."

"But what is madness? Maladjustment? Or perhaps a form of super-sanity where one has an unobstructed view of how accidental and useless life is!" Then she took a heaping mouthful and added, "Your thoughts."

"You forgot absurd."

"Ah! Indeed, I did! Is it safe to assume you're looking for Augie Omega?"

"You've heard of him?" I said.

"Yes. The absurdist author."

"Do you know where I'd find him?"

"Easy, he owns Kafka Deli, just a few miles away. Well, he did own it. It went out of business."

"When?"

"Last night. It blew up."

"What?

"Gas explosion. Didn't you hear all the sirens? Took out half a city block."

"I heard sirens, but I didn't know." I stopped. The air came out of me. "So, Augie Omega is dead?"

"No one knows for sure. They're still sifting through the ashes, trying to identify remains. The last report I heard said there were several people unaccounted for. Maybe one was Mr. Omega. Maybe not."

"So, we may never know who Augie Omega was."

"We do know. He was an absurdist author who owned a deli and liked to smoke with the gas on."

"But his book."

"*The Fifth Door*?"

"You know it?"

"Yes, there's only one copy. It's in the library."

"No. Someone took it. Was it you?"

"No, but I've got a good idea where it is! The bell tower."

"How do you know?"

"I don't. I'm guessing. We're all guessing!" She grabbed my elbow and whispered, "I have new information about the secret bell tower room. Interested? Come close. Can't share," she said as she threw herself against me, pulling my world into her chaos, so close I could smell weed on her breath. "I think I saw someone inside the secret room. The other night, I was lying naked on the quad when I saw a flash of light up there."

"I saw the same flash."

"I think it was Dean Gacy."

"It couldn't have been. He's in a coma."

"He is?"

"He was injured in the theatre fire."

Her face fell, and her Ted Kaczynski eyes zeroed in on me. A glow emanated from her, the last embers of a once great award-winning author and celebrated professor driven mad by modern life. Or maybe it was just the reflection of the soda machines.

"Then whom the devil did we see up there?" she wondered.

"Don't know."

"Here's the scoop. A reliable source informed me that when one dean retires or dies, they pass the key to the secret room to the next dean and the next."

"So, how do I get in?"

"Go to the hospital and get the key from the dean. Good thing he's unconscious."

"Why?"

"It'll be easy to steal!"

"Why don't you do it?"

"I can't go to the hospital."

"Why not?"

"If I were caught there, they'd commit me again."

Ping!

> Dr. Neb,
>
> My SUV is being detailed at VIP Clint's Custom Car Care. Pick it up and bring it to the house. Pronto!
>
> Your Friend,
>
> A.O.

I downed the last gulp of pie and put on my coat. "Dr. Merkin—."

"No!"

"Sorry, She Who Runs On The Mountain, this has been enlightening, but before my next class, I've got to run an errand. I'll just let you go back to yelling at the students."

"I'm not yelling."

"Then what are you doing?"

"Lecturing."

As I left, she stood and pointed at the American flag that hung lifeless over the soda machines and hollered, "Have you ever wondered why there's an American flag in the food court? Why here, of all places? I'll tell you why! Because the less a government does for the people, the more patriotism it demands!"

Ping!

> Dear faculty,
>
> The Student Learning Center has new tips on how to treat students:
>
> 1. <u>Greet The Customer</u>: "Welcome to Burger King, where you rule! My name is ______________. Would you like to try our Whopper with Cheese or a fully loaded Croissan'wich combo today?"
>
> 2. <u>During The Order</u>: Ask them, "Would you like that to be large?" Finish every order by asking, "Can I interest you in two chocolate chip cookies for only one dollar?"
>
> 3. <u>Send The Customer Off</u>: When handing the customer their food, tell them, "You Rule," after they get their food and before they leave.
>
> Many Thanks,
>
> Kenny Aronstein
> Student Learning Vice Officer

Ping!

> Dear faculty,
>
> So sorry. Please disregard the previous email. I sent you the wrong draft in error.
>
> Here is the correct one:

1. <u>Greet The Student</u>: "Welcome to class. My name is ________________. Would you like a copy of today's PowerPoint?

2. <u>During The Class</u>: Be sure to ask them, "Do you understand the lecture? How can I improve my teaching to accommodate your learning style?" Finish every lecture by asking, "Can I interest you in a copy of my personal notes?"

3. <u>Send The Student Off</u>: When handing the students their test, include an encouraging comment like, "Well done," or "You rule" before they leave.

And always remember our motto: Retention Retention Retention!

Kenny Aronstein
Student Learning Vice Officer

"Where do I know you from?" said the pit mechanic in a vocal fry as he walked up, wiping his fingers with an oily rag dirtier than his hands. He had a flat, turned-up nose, bulging eyes, and a large belly.

"You repaired my BMW convertible."

"Oh, right. The philosophy professor. You're here for A.O.'s Mercedes?"

"Yes."

He led me to the corner of the garage, where the black SUV with tinted windows sat. The same car I'd first met the president in. "Got the smoke and pee smell out to where even A.O. won't smell it," he said as he tossed me the key fob and walked away. But he stopped, leaned back, and took a good long look at me before he added, "A.O. is an asshole."

"I know."

"Then why are you friends?"

"Because… That's life."

"Or is it because you're a nobody? Am I right?"

"…Yes."

"The first step to true wisdom is to 'know thyself.'" Then he spit a wad in a cup, slapped a switch on the slimy wall, and the garage door rattled open. Stunned that a pit mechanic could quote Socrates, I got into the SUV and sunk into a world of bleached, silent luxury. As the shop's garage door closed behind me, I stopped, engine idling, and thought about my stupid, flaccid life. Perhaps the first step to true wisdom in this modern world is not to "know thyself" but to ask, "What would Augie Omega do?"

Just then, a side door to the body shop opened, and the mechanic let his junkyard dog out to crap. I watched the spider-walking mutt as he laid a big honker on a sidewalk and went back in. Inspired by Augie, I reached into my backpack, grabbed my copy of Carl Sagan's *Pale Blue Dot*, flipped to the last blank page, ripped it from the binding, got out, and walked toward the dog pile. I glanced around to ensure no one was watching and then enveloped the ick in the paper. Back in the SUV, I thought of rubbing it on the spare tire - that way, his French nose couldn't find the smell. Or better yet, the glove compartment. I reached down to place the time-bomb.

"What the hell are you doing?" I looked in the rearview to find President Boucher in the dark backseat and experienced total organ failure. My lungs collapsed. My heart stopped.

"Lower the window," she ordered. I followed her command. "Toss it." I tossed the poop. "Put the window back up." I did, and then I slowly dared to peek into the mirror. But she wasn't there. She was knocking on the driver's side window. "Open." I opened. "Move over." I climbed over the console to the passenger seat as she dragged her knee replacements up, adjusted her sunglasses, and drove. We said nothing for several blocks before she coolly said, "Can I drop you somewhere?"

"Classroom building," I mumbled, confused by the banality of her question. After several minutes, I got up the courage to ask, "What were you doing back there?"

"You didn't come to the Hilton for our afternoon quickie, so I set a little trap," she said, "Got something you might like," and she slipped a tiny, tarnished tin box from her Gucci, "Open it." Inside, wrapped in tissue, I found the latest addition to her collection, an oxidized pair of angry pliers. "Those are three-hundred-year-old tooth extractors that once belonged to Pierre Fauchard, the father of modern dentistry. The bidding war was fierce, but I won."

"Congrats," was all I could come up with.

She pulled up in a no-parking zone in front of campus, lit a ladylike plastic-tipped cigar, and watched the students laughing and flirting as they crossed the street to class. I waited for whatever horrible fate she had in store for me. After a long hesitation, she sniffed and said, "I like you, Charlie."

"Why?"

"Because you're uncorrupted. You might be the last person who honestly believes ideas and actions can save this foul world. You're a relic, Charlie, a museum piece." On her wrist, she sported a plastic hospital bracelet. She sniffed and looked up at the bell tower. Then she took a sudden breath. It was as if someone had stepped on her soul. A tincture of panic gripped her. "Existence," she said, "has no actual value except in freedom from pain and boredom. Once you understand that, there's nothing to do but sit back and tolerate the joke."

"Take off your sunglasses," I kindly asked. "Please."

She considered me and then tenderly removed them, revealing a circle of black and blue bruises that inked her swollen, bloodshot eye. She had a real shiner.

"What happened?"

"I asked for a divorce," she said as a wisp of a tear gathered. She quickly blotted it with a leftover cocktail napkin.

"Did you call the police on the son of a bitch?" I said.

"President's husband arrested for domestic violence - not a headline the university needs while the State is considering our next year's budget." She looked out at the ivy-covered walls, drifted, and said, "We had a bomb threat called into the faculty senate today, three professors involved in a *ménage à trois* are charging each other with sexual harassment, and the Director of Academic Advising was caught exposing himself to a tour of visiting students from Tokyo." She smirked. "Sometimes I wonder if we'll even make it to Christmas."

My heart went out to her, for I understood she had sacrificed all her high-minded youthful illusions to climb the academic ranks to the safest job there was - for when the sun supernovas, and the oceans vaporize, only two things will survive, cockroaches and university administrators. "I'd like to kiss you," I heard myself say. And I didn't regret it. She looked at me, testing for sarcasm. I offered none.

She plucked a bit of tobacco from her lip and said, "Have at it."

This was not a kiss to save my job but to fence off absurdity from my fretting soul, because, as Sartre and de Beauvoir pointed out, absurdity, like its counterpoint meaning, was subjective. Humans created them, and humans can do away with them. Or perhaps with a kiss, I would finally understand Nietzsche's tragic optimism - a simple idea that permits us to accept life's struggles without delusion, bitterness, or reward. Yet, I also knew my victory would be my defeat, for after our lips parted, my life would stumble on, only now with little room for philosophy. Perhaps the only way to find the sedative of significance is to kiss away all your worries and hopes.

I leaned over and gently placed my lips on the dry gravity of her mouth. I could feel her dentures as she gently kissed back. She was noncommittal. For her, it was just another absurdity added to another absurdity. We parted. She took a puff and blew it out with the words, "Know what your problem is, Charlie?

"I'm an absolute pauper, thoroughly convinced of my utter insignificance?"

"No. You conjure questions, but you don't yet know that the world can never deliver an answer, and until you do, you'll find little rest or happiness." She put on her dark shades. "May I have my tooth extractor back?"

"Oh, sure," I said as I handed over the torture device.

"See you Friday. November 7th."

"What's Friday?"

"You're coming over for dinner, just the two of us. Let's say six."

"Could we perhaps put it off until next week?"

"No, next week will be too late," she said. "Don't worry. My husband is at the Disney Resort & Spa for an Adolescent Psychopharmacology Conference. And do bring some decent flowers this time and, for god's sake, real wine." She handed me a hundred-dollar bill. "This should be a start."

I opened the door and climbed down to the pavement. There, I stood for a moment before saying, "I just want to teach."

"Oh, Charlie, you still can. It's just that your job description is going to change. The university of tomorrow will be smaller. It'll fit on your wrist or in your ear. It won't need bulky buildings or cumbersome libraries. Lectures will be podcasts, labs digital, and papers written and graded using A.I. And all professors, without exception, will be interchangeable."

"And academic freedom?"

"In the future, the only academic freedom professors will know is when they turn in their spring grades and disappear to Cancun for a week." She smiled. I didn't. "That was a joke."

"Was it?"

Disappointed, she said, "Get to class, you'll be late. Whom are you covering today?"

"Schopenhauer."

A slight giggle escaped her as she recalled some far-off undergraduate lecture. "'When the passion of life is extinguished,'" she started slowly but gained confidence as her mind cleared, "'and nothing remains, but its hollow shell, life becomes like a comedy which begins with real actors but ends with robots dressed in actor's clothes.' That's Schopenhauer, is it not?"

"Yes."

She smiled, proud of herself for remembering, then pensively added, "You can't save the world or yourself, Charlie. Once you overcome that delusion, you'll finally find in all this chaos something close to happiness. Not the real thing, but good enough." She stopped, caught by her own words. It was that rare moment when someone knew precisely who they were. It lasted only a heartbeat, and then she quickly cloaked her thoughts and threw me a chuckle. Then she drove off, and I slumped toward class.

Ping!

> Dear Humanities Professors,
>
> It's time to roll up our sleeves for the annual Old Arts and Sciences housecleaning day. We've got significant problems with moldy grout in the bathrooms and rust stains at the bottom of the toilets, so let's plan on an all-day-er.
>
> I'll see all you humanities professors at old A&S this Saturday. Start time is 7am.
>
> Peace Out,
>
> Dr. Jerry Dahmer
> Newly appointed Assistant Dean

"Trigger warnings," I started, "Today's lecture concerns Schopenhauer and contains subjects some may find offensive or troubling - including atheism, pessimism, life without meaning, and non-existence. If you cannot tolerate these, university rules state you are free to leave." Two Mormons walked out, and I started into my well-rehearsed PowerPoint. An hour later, my mind was coasting through the lecture when a flower-tattooed sophomore in the front row put her hand up and said, "Professor? Did you know you're humming to yourself?" The question brought me back to earth. I'd stopped mid-lecture and was just standing there, humming.

"Sorry. Got a lot on my mind," I said as I finally stirred, turned on the lights, and took in the sea of gawking students. Where would my life take me on Friday the seventh? Nurse Cox or President Boucher? The warm jungles of Belize or the cold wilderness of academia?

"If you don't mind," I said, "I'm going to call class early."

"Do you need to go to the Mental Health Solution Center?" a pale young man wearing a camouflaged tactical war vest and jungle boots called out.

"No," I said, "I have to go to the hospital."

17

The nurses made me put on a hospital gown and clear plastic face shield to prevent Dean Gacy's extensive skin grafts from becoming infected. Exhale, my breath bleached the thin synthetic shield, and everything dissolved to a pale blur. Inhale, the plastic cleared, and the red numbers, green letters, and pulsating blue thread of his feeble heartbeat glimmered from the intensive care monitors. Exhale, pale white blur. Inhale, the unconscious dean lay clenched in a bird's nest of bandages, wires, tubes, and drips. His burnt arms and fingers wrapped in splints held up by pullies attached to a hook in the ceiling. It looked like he was reaching up to catch an incoming beach ball.

"He's comatose," said the nurse, "so please keep your visit to less than five minutes."

"Is he going to recover?"

"There's always hope. Were you close?"

"Yes, we loved going to the absurdist theatre," I lied.

The nurse gave me a consoling smile and left. Exhale, pale blur. Inhale, the dean's singed eyebrows, bruised face, and jowl tattoo came into view. He didn't seem like the type to sport a tattoo, especially on the neck, which is the most painful and, thus, the stupidest place to get one. I thought, where else does he have them? A unicorn on his back? Marilyn Manson on his chest? He must've had a wild, unbuttoned youth he now regrets. Then it hit me—that's why he always wore turtlenecks.

Exhale, pale blur, inhale. In the dim light, I tried to focus on his neck tattoo. It had a backward "g" followed by a backward "n," "i," "t," and "i." It looked like some weird cult inscription. Was he a member of the People's Temple or Heaven's Gate? Exhale, pale blur, inhale. I squinted, my brain inverted the letters, and the tattoo coalesced into the words "Waiting For Godot." It was the ink of the playbill permanently seared to his jugular.

"Dean Gacy, it's Charlie Neb here. Can you hear me?" Exhale, pale blur, inhale. The dean's troubled expression never changed. He looked like a pouting newborn, his bluish burnt face cupped by the pillows. I quietly closed the door. Now, all I had to do was go through his things, find the key to the secret bell tower room, and hightail it. But before I did, I couldn't help but take revenge. "Dean Gacy, I know you can't hear me right now, so I just want to say - how many administrators does it take to change a light bulb? More than last year." To my amazement, the dean chuckled, and his crusty eyes cracked. I jumped back and ripped off my shield to make sure I was really seeing it. "Are you conscious?! Or is this some sort of weird coma eyes-open type thing?"

"I'm awake," he murmured, "Where am I?"

"The hospital. I'll call the nurse."

"No." His breathing was fragmented. He swallowed hard and drew a breath from his rigid, cooked lungs. "My briefcase," he said as he inched his head up from the pillow.

"What about it?"

"Find it."

And I searched the ICU and found his leather satchel. "Got it."

"Open it."

I tentatively unzipped. Inside was pepper spray, a pink disposable razor, gum, pens, an even bigger pepper spray, anti-gas tablets, and theatre tickets.

"Find the fuzzy ball," he said. I dug deep into the cluttered darkness and found a single key attached to a pink fluffy ball the size of a baby's fist. The faded heavy-duty key was etched with "DO NOT COPY." Seeing it, he gave me a shaky smile. "It's still there," he said. "Come closer." I leaned in to read his chapped lips. "Give the key to the acting dean," he whispered. "Share it with no one. Promise."

"I promise."

"Say it like you mean it."

"After leaving here, I'll go directly to Acting Dean Popkov and give it to him."

His watery eyes looked hard at the ceiling, and he drew a thin breath. Then his gaze went beyond the sheetrock and insulation into the starless void of an infinite eternity. After a few more labored breaths, he managed, "How different the beginning of our life is to the end." A tear ran from his cheek. "It starts with deluded hopes and sensual enjoyment, while the end is pursued by bodily decay and the odor of death. And the road dividing the two, as far as our well-being and enjoyment of life are concerned, is downhill."

"Ah, Schopenhauer," I said.

"What?" he whispered.

"That's a Schopenhauer quote."

"No. I just made it up."

"Well, then you're subconsciously quoting Schopenhauer."

"But I'm not."

"Or you were inspired by Schopenhauer."

"No, it's original."

"Look, I know what I'm talking about. I once dated a severely depressed German with horrible hair."

"I'm the dean! If I say it's original to me, then it's original!"

"But if I said something I thought was original but was, in fact, Schopenhauer, I'd want someone to point it out."

"What the hell is wrong with you?"

"I might be a bit A.D.D."

"Shut up!" he said. "Just shut the hell up!" His breath became patchy, and he looked up at his burned arms and pondered, "It's all just setup, setup, payoff, know what I mean?"

"Sure, I guess."

"Setup: I went to school for thirty years and put up with loads of worthless academic edu-speak. Setup: For thirty more, I worked my way up the academic ladder. Payoff." The slightest shudder came from his nose, the only part of his face not burned, his eyes rattled and dilated, and he drifted. His last words were, "Who is Augie Omega?"

"Wait," I said, "what about Augie Omega?" Desperate for an answer, I tapped him with my index finger. "Dean Gacy, you can't go to sleep." No response. I gently shook him—still nothing. A gurgle came from his throat, and the blue heart monitor flatlined.

"Holy Shit!"

Red lights flashed, and buzzers wailed as a nurse ran in and shouted, "Step from the room!"

"I can't. He was going to give me the payoff."

"Out! Now!" she said as she propelled my ass into the hall just as a half dozen other nurses and a doctor galloped in, one pushing a defibrillator. From a crack in the door, I peeked in on the choreographed pre-blocked medical drama, complete with standard-issue countdowns, zaps, and firm commands. After a few tense minutes, one by one, the nurses let out a disconsolate breath, and after a protracted silence, the doctor said, "What's the lunch special today?"

"Liver," a nurse answered.

"Damn, I was hoping for bangers and mash."

Ping!

> Campus Wide Scarlet & Brown Alert,
>
> Today, I received the following message from comedian Jackie Diamond.
>
> "I want to unreservedly apologize for the uncalled-for jokes I made during my performance. I'm sorry for the pain I've caused K-Pop fans. I promise I will seek treatment for my struggles with their music. Please call off the social media war. They canceled my HBO special and banned me from The Tonight Show. I need work." Signed Jackie Diamond.
>
> I hope this puts this matter to rest.
>
> Margrett Applewhite, Entertainment Director

As I walked the long corridor of the unconcerned universe holding the pink fuzzy ball and key, I realized no life adds up to a unified whole. Life doesn't have enough structure to make a gift-wrapped Hollywood rom-com or the simplest haiku. We don't ask the meaning behind the shape of the mashed potatoes on our dinner plate, nor should we ask about the meaning of the mash of stuff we call life.

Ping!

> Campus Wide Scarlet & Brown Alert,
>
> Today at noon, we will stage our monthly Active Shooter Preparedness Test. Please remember your options are Run, Rebuff, and Retreat. And if you come face to face with a shooter, remember Safety, Security, and Sanctuary. But let's also never forget the power of just saying "Hello."
>
> Sincerely,
>
> Marsha Margrethe
> Director
> Disaster, Trauma & Stress Management Office
>
> PS: A special thanks to the cheerleading squad for volunteering to play the active shooters this time.

"May I help you?" said the receptionist. She was obviously on her first day because she had the extra-wide eyes of an intern.

"I'd like to commit myself," I said.

"Excuse me?"

"This is the Psychiatric Ward?"

"Yes."

"I'd like to be committed."

I'd managed to walk only a few feet from Dean Gacy's deathbed when I became aware of the pull of gravity, the thickness of the air, and the inadequacy of my legs and lungs. At that dark moment, I found the entrance to the psych ward only a few feet from the hospital's burn unit. And I knew I had to commit myself because I'd lost my sense of humor.

"Do you think you're a threat to yourself or others?"

"Don't think so. But I do have lots of questions. What happens if I go to the bell tower, and it's empty? Or what if the bell tower contains the truth about existence, and I can't handle it? And who is Augie Omega? Is he a real person or just an idea? What happens if I say screw all this, pack up my life, and go to Belize with a woman I hardly know, only to find that Belize is just as crazy as academia, only with beaches?"

"Sir, you're rambling."

"No, I'm having an existential crisis."

"Maybe you should try the Philosophy Department over at the university?"

"I teach there."

"Oh dear," she said, picked up a phone, and pushed a yellow button. "We have another professor who wants to be committed."

Just then, large-and-in-charge entered from the back, holding a stack of color-coded files. "Ask him if he has an appointment!" he barked, his voice bouncing off the file cabinets.

"Do you have an appointment?" the innocent intern asked.

"No."

"Tell him to take a number."

"Please, take a number."

And I took a number and turned to see the latest addition to the hospital, a warehouse-sized waiting room with walls covered with William Wegman's legendary Weimaraner doggy art–a sad lipsticked Weimaraner dressed as a businesswoman, a bored Weimaraner wearing a raincoat, and two bewildered Weimaraners posing as the Little Mermaid and Snow White. The confused mutts looked down on a staging room filled with debt, anxiety, insomnia, irritable bowels, addiction, failed marriages, and all the majestically stewed problems of a flaccid, stupid modern life. I took my place under a baffled Weimaraner wearing a tiara and settled in for a long wait.

Ping!

> Dr. Neb,
>
> I need a piano moved from my house to the garage this weekend. See you at 10 am.
>
> A.O.

I thumb-typed my phone.

> Dear A.O.,
>
> Go to hell.
>
> Charlie Neb

Ping!

> Dr. Neb,
>
> Might I remind you of our agreement? We don't want to get the police involved, do we?
>
> A.O.

> Dear A.O.,
>
> I have photos of you beating your wife. Do we want to get the police involved?
>
> Charlie Neb

That last email was a lie, but it silenced him.

"Ask him if he needs another appointment," said large-and-in-charge.

"Do you need another appointment?" the intern echoed.

And I came out of my email trance to see they were talking to a solemn man with a doleful gaze staring at me or through me. He was standing near the receptionist's desk, but he might as well have been alone in Antarctica. "Mr. Cox, do you need another appointment?" insisted large-and-in-charge as if he were an American tourist trying to make the locals understand English by increasing the volume. The lonely man shook his head, but that little gesture took everything.

"I've got Thursday at three?" offered the intern, but the man couldn't answer.

"Just write it down," said large and in charge.

"Okay, I've got Marcellus Cox at three on Thursday," said the intern.

Marcellus Cox! Nurse Cox's husband! The man whom Augie Omega drove nuts! He sulked out to the hall, and I followed.

"Wait, you said you wanted to be committed," barked large-and-in-charge.

"Feeling better," I said, "The Weimaraners helped."

"You can't leave."

"Watch me."

And he went for the hidden button under the desk, but I made it to the door and ran just before it locked. I tailed Marcellus through the tangled hospital halls, staying close but out of sight. He took a hard right, hard left, and then slipped through a side entrance to the parking lot, where he got into a cherry red BMW convertible. Could it be? I ran out just as he drove away. That's when I saw the Darwin Fish on the trunk. He was driving my ex - my convertible! I ran for my econobox and followed.

18

My senior year in college, I read Suzuki's *Essays in Zen Buddhism* and experienced a mind-blowing moment of spiritual enlightenment. As I closed the thin book, I resolved to quit school and become a monk. I could picture myself living an edifying life filled with daily meditation, essential silence, and calligraphy. The next morning, I dropped out of school and joined a meditative mountain commune where I spent two days arranging flowers and performing tea ceremonies. I just knew that nirvana was right around the corner. But then the commune ran out of food, and the head swami ordered me to take their dilapidated, electric-acid-Kool-Aid school bus into the nearby town and shoplift food from the "capitalist stooges" that owned the local A&P. Before I got there, the bus broke down below a highway billboard advertising a cherry red BMW convertible.

As the steam from the bus's radiator floated up, I gazed at the throttle-open, zip-top advertisement. The macho man behind the wheel of the Beemer was not wasting time with bullshit tea ceremonies and flowers but was living the capitalist's dream of power while driving to the A&P with 400 ponies. The ironically detached model beside him was mindlessly tipsy with the sweet nectar of spring. Neither wore seatbelts. Suddenly, I had an even bigger spiritual enlightenment, for it occurred to me that my handwriting was barely decipherable. How would I ever be any good at calligraphy? Tea is not my cup of tea. And flowers look good pretty much any way you arrange them. And once you achieve nirvana, then what? More calligraphy and flower arranging? Depressed, I abandoned the school bus and hitchhiked back to college.

Ping!

Campus Wide Scarlet & Brown Alert,

We regret to inform you that Dean Gacy has succumbed to his injuries.

To celebrate his long life, the Naming and Labelling Committee has decided that "Reflections of Echoes," the orange I-beam artwork in front of Old Arts & Science, be renamed "The Dean Gacy Memorial."

Have A Great Day,

Acting Dean Bobby Popkov, PhD

"Liberty is meaningless where the right to utter one's thoughts has ceased to exist." – Frederick Douglass

Marcellus left the parking lot with me in distant but hot pursuit. His first stop was an attorney's office. After that, he spent 10 minutes at a gun and ammo store. Then Discount Liquors. His last stop was the Pita Pit drive-through near the highway, the only one that protesters had not attacked. Add it up: attorney, guns and ammo, liquor, and Pita Pit - the answer was obvious. He was going to off himself. Or move to Texas.

As he sped out of town, his driving became so erratic he nearly took out a humanities professor picking up trash. Attacking curves and shifting hard, his speed was tipping 90. My pocket-sized wheels labored to keep pace. I was about to lose him when he veered into a wooded area and up a desolate road. I followed his dust trail to the top of a wooded hill where I came upon my ex-cherry red smashed into a tree, airbags deployed, door open. I stumbled through the steam, smoke, and shattered bark and found Marcellus standing atop a vertical rocky pulpit overlooking a fire-scarred, wide-screened vista. He wore a white flowing shirt, khakis, no socks, belt, or shoes. It was just him, a gentle breeze, and a gun–pointed at his temple.

I know I don't have an excellent track record in such situations, but what choice did I have? From the bottom of the outcropping, I eked out, "Wait!" He turned to me, and I felt all the torment humankind has known. Each of us standing atop a scaffolding, looking out at the skyline of our life, waiting for the trapdoor to trip. But this time, I was better prepared than I was with Felice Wolinski, sophomore communications major, because I'd taken the university's five-part deep-dive stress abatement training webinar and, on my second attempt, scored a 97.8. But in the moment's panic, I couldn't remember any of it. Then I noticed the uneaten Pita at his feet.

"Having a little dinner, are we?" I said, trying to jump-start a conversation. "I like Pita Pit's Hula Teriyaki Bowl."

"Me too," he said.

"I, ah, wish they'd also made it as a pita, not just a bowl."

"Yeah," he said, sniffing back tears. "That'd be a nice option."

"I eat at Pita Pit like twice a week," I said, trying not to stammer.

"I ordered their Chicken Caesar, but they gave me Southwest Steak by mistake. Problem is, I don't eat beef," he whispered. "They screwed up my last meal."

"Well, you know, the employees have been through a lot of late, with their stores being attacked by mobs. Their concentration is probably off." And then the conversation ceased. I thought, keep him talking, say something positive. "You know what I like about Pita Pit? They're hot and quick, which is always, ah, good in today's fast-moving world."

"I don't normally eat there," he said.

"Oh?"

"Yeah, I read on social media they don't have a very good policy regarding Holocaust deniers."

"Well, I think we can forgive them for that. Their business model centers more on falafels and not so much on Nazis." He seemed distracted momentarily, so I took a tentative step.

"Don't come any closer!" he shouted. I stopped. Then he looked to the horizon and mumbled, "You know, it's the little things that pile up. One day, Pita Pit screws up your order, the next, you open your eyes and see with blinding clarity that it's all absurd. For once you look, you can't unlook."

"You didn't, by any chance, happen to get that idea from a production of *Nutcracker*?" I said, but he was too into his little world to hear me.

When I was released from the psych ward, my wife told me she was moving to Belize," he said, choking back tears, "And I thought I don't need a wife. Then I discovered I'd lost my job and thought, who needs a job? Then my soul died, and I thought, what good's a soul? In life, you gotta hedge yourself against the wounds because, in the end, it's all just sour grapes." He drew a deep breath and looked to the sky - at the sublime absurdity of the world. Finding no answer there, he focused his unslept eyes on me. "Sometimes nothingness is better than somethingness."

You're on, I thought. But through the haze and smoke, all I could think was, don't crack a joke, whatever you do, no jokes! Marcellus's finger tugged the trigger. The situation absolutely required a clever, insightful catchphrase that summed up all of life. A concise, inspiring assertion to let him know life was worth living, even though there's plenty of evidence it's just a massive plate of mashed potatoes. Then it hit me. There was a helpful slogan I learned in the deep-dive stress abatement training webinar. What was it? Ah, "Hold on to hope." No, that was the title of one of the porn movies at the sperm bank. I was running out of time. Just as Marcellus was about to pull the trigger, all my synapses coalesced into one brilliant realization. I'd seen Marcellus before. At first, it was just an itch in my brain, but then it sharpened, and it all popped into one translucent ball of recognition.

"You're an actor!" I said.

"So?"

"I've seen you in something."

"Perhaps."

"Were you in the university's mental health training webinar brought to you by Achieve?"

"I was."

"You were good."

"Thank you."

"I thought you really embodied the character of the depressed baseball coach."

"I tried to get into his head," he said. "I'm also in the training webinar on objectification. I played the contractor who makes an inappropriate joke to a woman eating a hotdog and later realizes his mistake. Did you see that one?"

"Yes, you nailed it," I said, even though I hadn't seen it, but this was no time for honesty. Marcellus slowly lowered the gun. If you want to make actors not kill themselves, all you have to say is, "I saw you in (fill in the blank)." I don't know why that's not covered in the university's webinar.

"Being an actor, tough life," I said.

"Oh yeah," he said, "It's full of rejection, and the critics can be downright cruel."

"But in the end, worth it." I smiled, trying to keep it positive. "I wanted to be an actor."

"Oh?"

"Yeah, but," I modestly shrugged, "unlike you, I didn't have the talent."

"I didn't think I did, but I worked hard."

"And became successful." I faked upbeat. "All those years of classes obviously paid off." With the moment's strain broken, I couldn't help myself. I knew what had to be done. "Did you hear the one about the actor who came home one day to find his house burned to the ground?" I said.

"What are you doing?"

"Telling a joke."

"Why?"

"Just hear me out. The actor asks his neighbor what happened. The neighbor says, 'Your agent stopped by, hot-wired your car, drove it through your front door, murdered your entire family, emptied your bank accounts, and set fire to your house.' The actor stands there for a stunned moment, then smiles and says, 'Wow, my agent came to my home!'"

For a fraction of a fraction, he smirked. Comedy is a twinkle of revenge for the subjugated. A moment of comfort for the conflicted. A split second of equilibrium for the wobbly. But then his eyes grew heavy as frustration again gripped him. "All those acting classes, tens of thousands in student loans, and all I do is teach people to answer phones," he said as he took a deep-seated breath. "I am irrelevant."

"But that's not necessarily a negative thing," I said with an optimistic smile, hoping he wasn't going down the rabbit hole again.

"Everything is worse than it was!"

"I wouldn't say that."

"Name one thing that's better today than it was yesterday. One Thing!"

"Ah… Dentistry?"

"We are not citizens of a country. We're residents in an economic system!"

"I agree. Huge multinational conglomerates supervise our every move, but life is still worth living."

"Everything today is large and centralized, faceless and loveless!"

"But not hopeless."

"And the people are controlled by a fetish for commodities!"

"True, but we do need some commodities."

"And our tiny lives are dominated by chronic boredom and prefabricated cooking!"

"But there's still good food out there. Have you tried Pita Pit's Chicken Pesto?"

"We are mere cogs in an economic system!"

"With benefits."

"Not citizens of a compassionate state!"

And I found myself being drawn into his orbit. What the hell was there to be optimistic about in the age of post-happiness? It's all sour grapes. "You're right," I said, "our patriotism is ill spent."

"We affix flags to our pickup trucks!"

"Massive flags for the poor!"

"Minuscule lapel pins for the rich!"

"And no flags for the ultra-rich!"

And our words tossed as our minds joined with connectivity to the point where I couldn't track where his mind ended and mine began. I even lost track of who was saying what, as I'm sure you have.

"It's all just bread and circus!"

"And worry and status!"

"Futile cravings and anxiety!"

"Scarcity and suffering!"

"It's just a meaningless farce!"

"As Confucius said, 'I'm mad as hell, and I'm not going to take it anymore!'"

"Wait," I said, "That's not Confucius."

"Yes, it is."

"No, it's from the movie *Network*, written by Paddy Chayefsky."

"Paddy, who?"

"Chayefsky," I said. "He was an Oscar-winning Hollywood screenwriter."

"Then Mr. Chayefsky was quoting Confucius, who said it 25 centuries ago!"

"Look, I know what I'm talking about because, well, because everyone knows. It's one of the most famous lines in film history."

"No, Paddy Chayefsky is the one who wrote, 'Say hello to my little friend!'"

"No, that's from the movie *Scarface*."

"No, *Scarface* has the line, 'Take your stinking paws off me, you damned dirty ape!'"

"I'm sorry to correct you again, but that's *Planet of the Apes*."

"I have a gun!" Marcellus yelled, "If I say it's Confucius, damnit, it's Confucius!"

"But why would Confucius say that? He was into kindness and sincerity," I said. "This is the problem with the world today. We're not thinking things through logically, we believe any bullshit without questioning where it came from. We're not checking our sources. Not taking the time to write or read footnotes!"

"What the hell is wrong with you?"

"I might be a tad A.D.D."

"I'm about to kill myself! So, if you think about it, logically, this moment is about me!" he said as he re-cocked the gun.

"Okay, calm down," I said. "I'm mistaken. It was Confucius, not Paddy Chayefsky." He took a breath, so I added, "Maybe this isn't the right time to bring this up, but who told you that quote came from Confucius? Was it Augie Omega?"

His cheeks burned as his eyes darkened, and he locked on me with rapturous rage. It took everything he had to punch out a few whispered words, "Did you say Augie Omega?"

"Yeah. I heard he might've died in a gas explosion, but I've got this sneaky feeling he's still out there."

Marcellus drifted for a moment, then said, "I went out for beers with Mr. Omega. He told me about a vacation he once took in...," but he couldn't finish. His breath lurched into rapid, uncontrollable hiccups. He pulled himself together and managed one word, "Wuhan."

"Wuhan? What's a Wuhan?"

"A city in China."

"An odd place to vacation."

"That's what I thought," he said, and his voice went soft. "Mr. Omega told me while he was there, he was having dinner in a market and how he enjoyed the Biānfú."

"What's Biānfú?"

"Bat."

"Holy shit."

"A few days later, he said he was feeling feverish and had trouble breathing, so he flew home with long layovers in Shanghai, Tokyo, London, New York, and Seattle."

"Augie Omega is the one who caused the pandemic?"

"It was him. And I swore if anyone ever mentioned the name Augie Omega again, I would—!" And he raised the gun.

"Please don't! Please, ah, ah, ah. Hold on to hope!"

"Kill them!"

"Kill who?"

"Kill the person who said his name!"

"Do you mean me?"

"Yes!"

And he shot me.

"After food mixes with acid in the stomach, it moves into the duodenum. What is the duodenum, you ask? The duodenum combines bile from the gallbladder and digestive secretions from the pancreas before it moves into the small intestine," the surgeon said. "What's the purpose of the small intestine? The small intestine helps with the absorption of nutrients and minerals. Then, it moves into the ileocecal junction, where the small and large intestines meet. That's where the bullet took up residency."

I'd faded up from my blackout minutes before. All I could make out were the muted faces of the hospital graveyard shift. Above me, from my drug-induced rapture, I could see red numbers, green letters, and a blue thread of my feeble heartbeat's pulsations glowing from the monitors.

"The result was severe damage to the large intestine, so we had no choice but to perform a colostomy," the doctor said. Why do doctors try to talk when you're still in the smudgy time between worlds? Through the fog, my mind rattled off every episode of every medical drama I'd ever watched.

"Don't worry," the nurse said, "changing a colostomy bag is easy. Before you know it, you'll be amazed by how hypernormalized it becomes." They then went into a M*A*S*H-like two-in-the-morning standup routine.

"Hey," said the doctor, "having a colostomy isn't all bad."

"Oh?" said the nurse, playing the straight man.

"It can improve your grammar."

"Really, how so?"

"Because from now on, you'll have to use a semi-colon on a regular basis."

From the gurney, I reached up, grabbed his thin turkey neck, and pulled his shit-for-brains face close to mine while choking his longitudinal pharyngeal muscle. What's the purpose of the longitudinal pharyngeal muscle, you ask? Well, I'm not sure, but I know squeezing it makes breathing difficult. And as the freaked-out nurse hit the panic button and alarms shrieked, I got out, "That's not funny!" And then I withered into the twilight of an intravenous cocktail of Demerol mixed with Propofol and the dull netherworld between being and nothingness.

19

Welcome to the University's 82-part Webinar Series "So You're In A Coma," brought to you by Achieve. Here's a situation you might've encountered. One morning, you're in a simple white cube of a room with a coffeemaker, and you run into your obnoxious joke-telling co-worker Charlie Neb. Tell us about yourself, Charlie.

"Where am I? What's going on?"

Charlie is an Assistant Professor at a podunk "U" who's been brought up on charges because he told an asinine joke that not he nor anyone remembers. He also has a drinking problem, a nose fetish, and dislikes his mother.

"Wait, am I no longer narrating?"

Charlie's the type of man who likes winner-take-all stories. What's the purpose of a winner-take-all-story, you ask? Let's ask three-time Academy Award-winning screenwriter Paddy Chayefsky.

"This is a story where the protagonist sets out against a sea of troubles leading to definite winners and losers," said Mr. Chayefsky.

Who likes winner-take-all stories?

"Men because they've generally been winners. Even if they are losers, like Charlie here, they still relish knowing that at least they're on the winning team."

Mr. Chayefsky, can you give us an example of a *non*-winner-take-all story?

"Yes, an example would be Dr. Neb, who tells jokes on first dates, so he won't have to engage in an honest conversation or reveal the shallowness of his pathetic soul. 'Why can't Stevie Wonder see his friends? Cause he's married.' Charlie actually told that joke on a blind date. When she failed to laugh, did Charlie take the hint? No, he doubled down. 'A family checks into a hotel. The father says to the woman at the front desk, 'I hope the porn is disabled.' The woman says, 'No, it's just regular porn, you sick fuck.' Charlie's date Uber-ed home before the server brought the salads."

Thank you, three-time Academy Award-winning screenwriter Paddy Chayefsky. Check out Paddy's movie *Network* starring Faye Dunaway, William Holden, and Peter Finch - It's freaky good. Mr. Chayefsky, is there anything else you'd like to say before you go?

"Yes, I plagiarized the line, 'I'm mad as hell, and I'm not going to take it anymore.' I should've footnoted that in the movie."

"That confirms it," said Charlie. "I'm in a coma."

Ping!

> Campus Wide Scarlet & Brown Alert,
>
> I'm very sorry for playing the role of a person experiencing homelessness. Given that I was one of the wealthiest people in the world, I had no understanding of the lived experience of such people. I should never have made those movies.
>
> I sincerely apologize.
>
> Charlie Chaplin

Professor Neb, let me take you to a place you remember well. Have you ever noticed the crappier the trailer home, the bigger the American flag out front?

"Oh shit, not my mother's," Charlie said. He looked at the tumbledown home on wheels with the enormous red, white, and blue out front. Charlie knocked several times before the wrinkled woman came to the door with her walker. She wore a floor-length nightgown trimmed with cheap rhinestones and a massive bun of coiled gray held high by an industrial-strength clamp.

"Oh, it's you," his mother said, and Charlie immediately had second thoughts, not because she still had an eight-pack-a-day smoker's cough but because she had the same shag carpet and mid-century-sweat-stained furniture from his childhood. Her 12-foot-wide living room smelled of cancer and cats.

"Mom," Charlie said, "I'm trying to understand why I experience somethingness rather than nothingness?"

"That's easy," she said, "broken condom."

"That's it? That's the reason I have mindfulness?"

"Your father and I were working at the Tyson Food plant. We went into the pork locker during a pee break, and the condom broke. Later, I saw my cat had played with his box of Trojans and that her sharp claws had weakened the condom's structural integrity. And thus you, ya little allergic pantywaist, came into this world with that stupid smile."

Charlie stood there, dumbfounded, "I have consciousness because a cat played with a condom?"

"What did you expect? Some philosophical explanation?" She laughed, drew a death-defying lump of metastasizing smoke into her spit valve, and let it ooze down to her orthopedic slippers. Then she lowered herself into the threadbare indentation in her pea-green recliner covered with crumpled Kleenex and flicked on an ancient Motorola upon which stood a plaster Jesus blessing the davenport with his wounded hands.

"I'm looking for a book my father gave me when I was seven," Charlie said.

"Carl Sagan's *The Pale Blue Dot.*"

"I left it here when you kicked me out. I searched everywhere before I left but couldn't find it."

"That's because I shredded it." She wheezed. "Your childhood will provide no answers. Now get the hell out before I throw you out."

Webinar audience, how should Dr. Neb react? Should he:

1) Develop serious psychological problems that make him tell jokes and then make lame-ass excuses about comedy being protected by freedom of speech.

2) Be forced to submit to brutal public shaming, after which he will be chased into the wilderness by a pitchforked mob of woke academics.

3) Eat at Pita Pit.

4) Jump!

The correct answer? Jump! Night crashed down, the mobile home flew away, and Charlie found himself six stories up, sitting on the narrow ledge of the library window. In front of him shone the stately lights of the campus bell tower.

"Welcome to the age of post-happiness."

"Felice, sophomore communications major?"

"Yes, it's me." She sat beside him wearing her cheerleader uniform and a baseball cap that read "Love Me, I'm dead." She popped marshmallows from a colorful bag and said, "Would you like one? They are mmm mmm good."

Charlie stuck his fingers in, pulled out several gooey white balls, and confessed, "I'm really sorry for that comment I made about your nose."

"I forgive you."

"That's so nice of you."

"I'm not being nice, Charlie. You'll be wearing a colostomy bag for the rest of your life. What goes around comes around."

"Tell me please," Charlie insisted, "you don't believe that."

"Oh, but I do."

"So, because I made a stupid comment about your crooked nose, all the powers of the universe lined up into a massive cause and effect that resulted in me getting a colostomy bag?"

"It's known as the colostomy bag effect."

Ping!

Campus Wide Scarlet & Brown Alert,

I want to apologize for making fun of mutes. What I did was hate speech, well, I was playing a mute, so it wasn't 'speech,' but just the same, I am deeply remorseful. I will attend any sensitivity webinar training you recommend.

Harpo Marx

From above, the local Channel Six news copter drifted in attached to balloons, while below, the marching band played as the cheerleaders danced, and the firefighters inflated a bright flower-bedecked jump cushion topped by a white and black bullseye. But a car blocked their way—a cherry red BMW convertible.

"Charlie, everything in life is reversible," Felice Wolinski, sophomore communications major, said as she playfully dangled her feet off the edge. "An atheist can become devout. A ruthless dictator can find compassion. Even a person who has fully resolved to become a Zen monk can buy a stupid gas guzzler. But two things cannot be reversed. One is the moment you realize you're a loser. For you, that happened when?"

"At the BMW dealership when I bought that stupid car."

"That's right. And the other thing that cannot be reversed is the moment you realize existence is absurd. When did that happen for you, Charlie?"

"When I was seven and my father took me to *Nutcracker*."

"It was Augie Omega who dropped the clump of snow that blinded the ballerina. The world is full of Augie Omegas, so there's only one thing to do."

"Which is?"

"Swan dive."

"But I don't want to."

"Do it! Jump! We don't got all day!" the firefighters and cheerleaders heckled from below. Then Charlie's mother joined in, "Get it over with so I can go home and feed my cats!"

"Charlie, you don't belong here. I don't belong here. No one belongs," said Felice Wolinski, sophomore communications major.

"Then why are we here?"

"The creation has neither morals, manners, nor meaning. It's just there."

"But does God have a sense of humor?"

"For God, there are no absurdities. Thus, God has nothing to laugh at. Thus, God has no sense of humor. Thus, God cannot understand the human predicament. Thus, God cannot understand the creation. Thus, God is imperfect. Thus, God isn't God. Oh Charlie, the world is an ugly mess. So why prolong it? Come on, we'll jump together." And she shook her pom-poms and cheered, "Don't look down! Take a breath! Wipe that frown! And jump to your death!"

"Wait, what's in the bell tower, Charlie said.

"Nothing is in the bell tower, not even bells."

"Then it's all just sour grapes."

"Super sour." And it began snowing marshmallows, both colored minis and white jumbos. Far below, the marching band played Tchaikovsky's *Nutcracker,* and the cheerleaders waltzed. "It will be over in seconds. Freedom. Quiet. Won't it be wonderful to experience the joy of nothingness?"

"Hello, Charlie," said the long-legged beauty sitting in a wheelchair beside him on the ledge. Her white tutu, tights, and tiara tinkled in the helicopter's spot.

"The ballerina!"

"Yes, Charlie. I've come to tell you that we are nothing more than short-term, unseen subatomic particles circling one of those light pins up there. But your biker father was right—there's still beauty in the world."

"Says the woman sitting in a motorized wheelchair," Felice Wolinski, sophomore communications major, scoffed.

"Charlie," the dancer said, "is knowing that the world is absurd doing you any good?"

"Yes. Because it convinces me I exist."

"But it makes your existence extremely unhappy."

"Why are you even talking to her?" sniped Felice Wolinski, sophomore communications major. "You looked, Charlie. Your father told you not to, but you looked."

"But there are ways to unlook," the ballerina said as she offered Charlie a hit of a Havana-sized reefer.

"So, your answer is to get high," mocked Felice Wolinski, sophomore communications major.

"This is medical marijuana, bitch. I fell into an orchestra pit. I'm in continual pain, so lay off!"

"Ladies, let's not fight," Charlie said.

"We're both broken, Charlie, my legs, your childhood." The ballerina smiled, making her sequined eyelids shine like sunlight on a frosty lake. "So, let's laugh before we face the final disappointment." Charlie slowly reached for the reefer. Far below, the grinning firefighters and cheerleaders applauded. Even the marshmallow snowflakes gave Charlie a standing ovation.

"Give me that, you bimbo," shouted Felice Wolinski, sophomore communications major, as she reached out and grabbed the smoking roll.

"Don't use that language with me. I'm a prima ballerina!"

"You're not a ballerina. You're just one of modern life's walking wounded."

"You have no idea what you're talking about!"

"I'm a communications major. I'm an expert at communicating!"

"Then explain to us what the hell a communication major is."

"It's a degree that's designed to teach you effective communication skills that can be applied to, to, to—."

"I rest my case. Even communication majors can't explain it."

"I'll show you some communication!" Felice shouted as she slapped the ballerina, who returned a right hook, which Felice countered with an uppercut while the ballerina launched a karate chop.

"Please stop," Charlie yelled as he tried to separate them on the narrow ledge. Then Felice threw a knockout hook but missed, hitting Charlie's jaw, and he fell.

As he zeroed towards the jump cushion bullseye, Charlie looked over to find Nurse Cox falling beside him. She lay on a cushion of air like a reclining Buddha, wearing a pink bikini with extra-long hip pull-strings and a baseball cap that read, "Go stateless!"

"Nurse Cox?"

"Will you be at the airport on Friday, November 7th at 5pm?"

"I will!"

"Then you're ready to admit that we are precarious and limited creatures who will never stop our relentless stumbling in a world of conflict, confusion, complexity, and ambiguity?"

"Yes!"

"And our only hope of finding happiness is to disable ourselves long enough to get through our days with as few disruptions as possible?"

"Yes! Yes!"

"And that the first step toward a good life is to become aware of the moment and not be distracted by success or anything else."

"Yes! Yes! Yes!"

"And do you promise to stop lusting after BMWs?"

"Couldn't I maybe have a used one?"

"Look out, Charlie!"

Just then, Charlie looked down to see President Boucher sitting in the cherry-red BMW. She looked up, opened her mouth as wide as a whale, and he imploded through her and into the gray earth's protons, electrons, and quarks, where he finally found peace.

"Where am I?" Charlie asked.

"It would be best if you whispered," came a voice from the shadows.

"Am I in hell?"

"Quiet. The guards might hear you."

Charlie opened his eyes. He was lying on a bench in a dark room filled with coffin-like bunk beds packed thin with the barely human forms of the sick and dying. Outside the cracked window, bits of black snow floated past a bare bulb.

"You're in Auschwitz," said a voice from the next bunk.

"What?"

"Shhhhh."

"What the hell am I doing here?"

"You're an intellectual prisoner."

"Who are you?"

"I'm number 45394," said the thin man. "Name's Frankl."

"Frankl? Do you mean Viktor Frankl? The philosopher who survived Auschwitz. When I first met Felice Wolinski, sophomore communication major, I was in the library reading your book."

"I haven't eaten in two days. I'm not sure who I am."

"Well, let me tell you, you wrote an excellent book about the meaning of life!"

"If you say so."

"Now it all makes sense. My coma is obviously trying to tell me that the sweat lodge of academia is a concentration camp. I'm picking up trash on the side of the road and selling out my principles."

"Charlie, University Regulation 259-7 forbids professors from comparing academia to Nazi concentration camps," said Frankl.

"Then why am I here?"

"If I can survive Auschwitz and go on to write an inspirational book about the meaning of life, then you, facing only a fraction of my suffering, can learn to laugh again."

"Did you laugh here in Auschwitz?

"Well, it's not exactly a laugh-fest, but yes, now and then."

"Why?"

"Comedy creates perspective. It allows us to detach ourselves from ourselves and thereby attain the fullest possible control over ourselves and whatever confronts us. Those who cannot laugh are not taking humor seriously."

From the darkness, a weak, suffering voice whispered, "Number 32," and thin snickers cut with tuberculosis and rickets rasped from the shadowy bunks. Frankl, too, gave a faint-hearted laugh that turned into a cough.

"But doesn't comedy make us avoid the truth?" Charlie asked.

"What truth?"

"That God is dead?"

"I wouldn't say God is dead but silent," said Frankl. "If you probe the depth of the sea, you send off sound waves and wait for the echo from the bottom. If God exists, however, he is infinite, and you wait for an echo in vain. The fact that no answer comes back proves your call has reached the addressee, the infinite."

Another exhausted, shattered voice in the darkness whispered, "Number 65." Again, a threadbare giggle that sounded more like a wheeze than a laugh came from the darkness.

"What's going on?" Charlie said.

"We've been here so long we've told every joke there is to tell," said Frankl, "So instead of telling the same jokes over and over, we've numbered them. Saves time and energy."

"I've made a mess of my life," Charlie said.

"Yes," Frankl said, "but every day, every hour, offers you an opportunity to determine whether you will or will not submit to those powers which threatened to rob you of your very self. Are you going to renounce freedom and dignity? Are you going to be a plaything of circumstance? Are you going to be molded into the typical inmate?"

"But I've already screwed it up. It's too late."

"Charlie, always remember this - live as if you were living already for the second time and as if you had acted the first time as wrongly as you are about to act now."

"Number 52," a weak voice called out in the darkness, more faint laughter.

"May I try?" whispered Charlie.

"Be my guest."

And Charlie called out, "Number 87." Silence. Not a single laugh. Nothing. "What happened? Why didn't they laugh?"

"Some people can tell jokes. Some can't."

Thank you, Austrian neurologist, psychiatrist, philosopher, and author Viktor Frankl. Check out Viktor's book *Man's Search for Meaning*. It's freaky good. Mr. Frankl, anything else you care to say?

"Yes. Number 28."

And Charlie gently laughed, even though he had no idea what joke number 28 was. He thought, maybe that's the answer—laugh at life even if you don't get the joke.

Ping!

Campus Wide Scarlet & Brown Alert,

I apologize for everything I ever said.

| Don Rickles

Charlie, it's been a pleasure narrating your coma, but it's time for me to hand the mic back.

"Wait. Can I ask who you are?"

I didn't introduce myself.

"No."

So sorry, I'm Franz Kafka. Check out my novel, *The Trial*. It's freaky good.

"I think he's coming out of his coma," a nurse said.

"How can you tell?" said the other.

"He's laughing."

I felt my body lifting and cold blood warming. I was coming back to the reality of my hospital room. With my half-blind eyes, my body cloaked in the cotton hospital gown and blankets, I became aware of the tubes sticking from my nose and the heartbeat monitors beeping. And I saw the blurred face of the shift nurse.

"You with us, Dr. Neb?" she said.

"Where is the key?" I whispered.

"What key?"

"The key with the pink fuzzy ball attached."

"Don't know what you're talking about."

"It was in my pocket when Cox shot me."

And she checked the possessions bag attached to my footboard and said, "No ball, no key."

"Wait," I said, "what day is it? I gotta be at the airport by Friday, November 7th."

"Well, you've missed your flight. It's Saturday, November eighth."

20

I left the hospital two days later with a prescription for Oxycodone (no refills) and an address for a webinar entitled "You and Your Colostomy Bag" produced by Achieve of New York. Episodes included "What to Do about 'O' Ring Slippage" and "How to Deal with People Who Make Colostomy Bag Jokes." But my favorite was "How to Improve Colostomy Bag Awareness by Nonchalantly Mentioning Your Bag in Everyday Conversation." Suggestions included, "When buying a car, ask the salesperson how airbag deployment might affect your bag," and "How to put people at ease before you get in their swimming pool."

In the webinar, the actor who played the car salesperson also played the lifeguard. Her transition from grossed-out employee to sympathetic, thoughtful advocate was subtle and nuanced. Her face seemed familiar. In the credits, it said her name was Pepper Jo. I looked her up online and found she'd been nominated as best actor in the Webinar Academy Awards held in Branson, Missouri. But other than that, I found nothing. I watched the webinar again and again. I knew we had met but couldn't place her.

I thought about returning to the hilltop where Marcellus had shot me and trying to find the key to the bell tower, but then Frankl's words echoed within me. "Live as if you were living already for the second time and as if you had acted the first time as wrongly as you are about to act now." Maybe, I thought, it would be best if the secret room were never opened. I had been given the opportunity to unsee, and I was determined to take it.

Ping!

Dear Faculty,

Should a student overdose on Fentanyl during your class, please note all lecterns have now been stocked with a generous supply of Naloxone™ Nasal Spray.

Keep them learning!

Sally Sprinkling
Assistant Student Health & Well-Being Officer
Energetic Team Player

"Hypothetical," I started my lecture. "If we live in the age of post-happiness, shouldn't we avoid asking inconvenient questions? Including 'Why are we here?' and 'Does life have an epilogue?' Many unhappy philosophers have asked these questions for thousands of years. And come up with scant answers. But there's one question they've been unable to answer. 'Why is there somethingness rather than nothingness?'" My mind was still foggy from surgery, but I'd run out of mental health and sick days, so I had no choice but to teach. "All these Aristotelians, Platonists, Augustinians, Humanists, Hobbists, Kantians, Darwinians, Sartreans have failed. So, how do we face existence when the very first question we ask of existence doesn't have an answer?"

A youthful student with pigtails in the front put her hand up. She reminded me of my innocent self in my first freshman philosophy class with Dr. Vladimir. And I thought of his words, "On your deathbed, if you've really lived a life of the mind, your last sentence will be a question." My soul lifted. Delighted, I called on her and readied myself for a Socratic dialogue - the true purpose of university education. Not lectures, not labs, but humans asking difficult, unprotected questions.

"About somethingness and nothingness," she said.

"Yes?"

"Are they going to be on the test?"

For a moment, I clearly saw my brief 'flies of summer' future. I'd mouth the same lectures for another twenty-five years, then one day, there'd be a lunchtime party in the commons with a store-bought cake, where colleagues would recall humorous anecdotes about me. Then I'd walk into retirement hoping I'd made a difference, but in the end, I'd leave only a trace of my consciousness in the form of a dissertation that did not change society, predict an eclipse, or improve the structural integrity of buildings in earthquake zones. 101,482 words that someday the library would transfer to deep storage and later misplace.

The End

Well, that would've been the end if the door to the lecture hall hadn't opened, and Acting Dean Popkov confidently marched in with a wide smile. He was too boyish to be a dean. He'd quickly risen through the ranks of academia because of his lightning-fast ability to kiss up and piss down. "So sorry I'm late," he said, but seeing me, he slammed to a stop. "What's going on? Why are you here?"

"That's the question we're considering," I said, "why are we here?"

"No, why are *you* here in this classroom?"

"I'm teaching," I said, somewhat confused.

He glanced at the class, then back at me. "May I have a word with you?" he said as he held the door. It wasn't a question, but a command. I joined him in the hall, where he nervously waited for some students to pass before he asked, "Should I call the Mental Health Solution Center?"

"Why?"

"You're teaching."

"Yes, I know."

"Didn't you get the email?"

"What email?"

"Dr. Neb, you've been suspended without pay until your A.A. hearing."

"Let me guess, by Augie Omega?"

"No. The president of the university."

"She reinstated me."

"Now she's un-reinstated you."

"Why?"

"For not showing up November seventh. President Boucher said you would know what that meant."

"I've been in a coma."

"You should've informed her of that."

"From my coma?"

"Also, the president's husband informed me that the police are looking for you—Something about a break-in. I'm taking your class until a suitable replacement can be found."

"What experience do you have teaching philosophy?"

"I've read a little Ayn Rand. Now, stay here, and I'll get your things," he said as he disappeared into the lecture hall and returned with my backpack and coat. "I'll see you next week at your A.A. hearing, Room 151, *New* A&S. That is, if the police don't catch up with you first." He went back in, and as the door closed, I heard him address the class, "So sorry for the mix-up. Today we're going to play theatre games. So, everyone team up into groups of four."

Ping!

Campus Wide Scarlet & Brown Alert,

It's spirit week, so let's have some hallway hijinks by asking your students to dress up in different daily themes. Here's the schedule:

Monday - Tropical! Beach! Hawaiian!
Tuesday - Twin Day! Grab a friend and match up!
Wednesday - Dress like a professor day!
Thursday - Dress like a Harry Potter character!
Friday - Decades Day! 70s 80s 90s, etc.!

> Prizes will be awarded! Enjoy!
>
> Margrett Applewhite, Entertainment Director
>
> PS It would be nice if the faculty participated this time!

There was nothing left to do but avoid the police, wait for my A.A. hearing, take my antidepressants, worry about "O" ring slippage, forget about the key, Nurse Cox, Augie Omega, my awful life, and try not to overthink as I drove my Uber.

RATE YOUR RIDE

The pessimistic driver rambled on about how we are no more than a "tangle of tendons and teeth" who "take in too many calories and discharge too few." After 15 minutes with him, instead of going to my post-natal essentials class, I asked him to take me back to the bar, where I got more drunk.

RATE YOUR RIDE

He asked me to read his dissertation. 100,000+ words. He had it with him. Very odd.

RATE YOUR RIDE

He talked about injustice, stupidity and having to get his stitches out. TMI!

RATE YOUR RIDE

I take Uber because I want to get somewhere not to attend a Ted Talk on Immanuel Kant's thoughts on the failures of traditional philosophy and metaphysics. Although he did make some good points, and the lecture was informative.

RATE YOUR RIDE

At first, the driver said nothing. He didn't even answer my questions. I thought he was just another anti-social misfit. Then he quoted someone called Montaigne, "I belong nowhere, and everywhere am a stranger." What does that mean? Should I be concerned?

RATE YOUR RIDE

The entire ride, he mumbled the word "Mesothelioma" over and over. I think it was his mantra.

RATE YOUR RIDE

He pontificated about how American universities are filled with "cringing mediocrity, contemptible rascals, arrogant philistines, and stunted adults." Thank you, strange man, you saved me four years and lots of money. I left the car convinced I should not go to college.

OMG! The driver talked about wearing a colostomy bag! I was just trying to get to my weekly ladies' Scrabble meet. I have lost the will to live.

Did someone force him to major in philosophy? No! He had free will and made a choice, knowing full well that no one gives a crap about Plato or Schopen-whomever. When you hit ninety thousand in student debt, a little alarm should go off in your head telling you that the humanities are a gargantuan mistake! Stop complaining and drive.

I'm open-minded. I believe all people have intrinsic value, but this driver was meshuggeneh! I was going to my grandchild's bris, but instead, I had the driver take me to my shrink.

I felt so sorry for the poor driver. He is obviously suffering from PTPHDPSD (Post-Traumatic Ph.D. in Philosophy Stress Disorder). I hope someday he finds meaningful employment with a company with really good mental health insurance.

RATE YOUR RIDE

He yelled at a van full of nuns.

RATE YOUR RIDE

After a long silence, out of the blue, the driver started talking about Nietzsche, whom he said got it wrong, "God is not dead, nor did we kill him. But we did invent him. It's just that we didn't do a very good job." Thankfully I had my meth with me. Never leave home without it.

RATE YOUR RIDE

He muttered about how life is random and momentary and how apathy and despair rule the world. Then, he ranted about the erosion of social solidarity and marshmallows. My children were in the car!

RATE YOUR RIDE

He said he was going to shave his head and become a Buddhist. I had no idea Buddhists wore Crap-Bags. It was surreal! Uber is way cool! Party! Party! Namaste!

After being with this driver for ten minutes, I cannot go on. My mind is numb. "Now I am become Death, the destroyer of worlds." It was my first-time taking Uber!

He talked about how if Plato and Aristotle were alive today, they'd be president and vice president of Nambla. What the hell does that mean?

When I got in, all I said was "Good morning," which started him into a diatribe about existential dread. Do not say "good morning" to this driver!

He talked about how, as a species, we have lost our instincts and also misplaced our traditions and society, so we only have our brains left to rely on. And how this is causing massive loneliness. Then he mumbled a quote from Voltaire, "We shall leave this world as foolish and as wicked as we found it." He's right, but I just don't need to hear about it before my CPA exam.

He liked to blow his horn and give other drivers the finger. He also went out of his way to try and hit a squirrel - He missed.

He spent fifteen minutes raging about how today ideology trumps art and how something called 'Waiting for Go-Dot' was the perfect play because nothing happens, and so no one's challenged. There was also a bunch of stuff about totalitarian regimes suppressing comedy, but I missed most of that because I'd jumped from the car.

He said he was going to an "AA" hearing and was sure he would be fired and never teach again. He said his very existence is unthinkable outside the ranks of academia. I know there's a teacher shortage, but we cannot allow this nut-job back into the classroom.

Uber should only have one question on their employment application. "Did you major in philosophy in college?" If the answer is "yes," then do as most companies do and never hire them.

At first, he went on about how the humanities were dying and how the trillion-dollar student loan bubble will soon burst, but then the conversation drifted to his struggles with "O" ring slippage. I left the car confused and constipated.

He stopped halfway through to yell at a pigeon.

21

New Arts and Sciences was a twenty-first-century technological marvel that included high-arched atriums, floating staircases, and remote-control crash gates that could be deployed in the event of an active shooter.

"Golly jeez, you shaved your head?" my lawyer said as I walked up. "It's perfect! It goes with the whole cancer motif we got going!" I had indeed shaved my head in order to elicit pity from the committee, but as we sat on the womb chairs near the meditation pods outside the A.A. hearing, I had my doubts it would work. "Relax," my lawyer said. "I've worked out a secret deal. You give them a heartfelt apology, they forgive you, and you get your job back with a guarantee of tenure. But there's a catch. You must put an ad in the student paper asking for forgiveness."

"I haven't done that."

"I did it for you while you were on sick leave," he said as he handed me a copy of *The Wild Hog Review*, the once great student paper which, with the demise of the Journalism department, was now reduced to a few wafer-thin pages. I opened it to find, opposite a Pizza Hut two-toppings-for-the-price-of-one ad, my full-page confession with a picture of me in my coma with tubes sticking from my nose. "In it, you beg for forgiveness from the anonymous student who filed the complaint and the whole university population. You also promise to seek weekly help from the self-serve Campus Mental Health Solutions kiosks."

"And the president was okay with this?"

"She's at a conference in Hawaii, although the rumor is she's really getting Psychedelic Assisted Therapy. Won't be back for three weeks."

"That's it? That's all I have to do?"

"Well, there is one more thing. You must promise to drop your mesothelioma lawsuit."

"For tenure, I'd do that."

"And…"

"What?"

"Cough. A lot. Let'em know the meso is kicking in." I let out a gruff mezzo wheeze to prove I could do it on cue. "You've been practicing," he said with an approving eye twinkle. "Oh! Almost forgot. Shall we seal the deal with prayer?" he said as he jerked his head down and went into full devotional mode.

Ping!

> RE: Court Case Number #240AS8938-3
>
> Dear Dr. Neb,
>
> The university's "Motion to Dismiss" your asbestos lawsuit, has been granted with prejudice due to evidentiary issues. Your lawyer failed to file disclosure documents.
>
> Small print legal bullshit. Small legal bullshit. Small print legal bullshit. Small legal bullshit. Small print legal bullshit. Small legal bullshit. Small print legal bullshit. Small legal bullshit. Small print legal bullshit. Small legal bullshit. Small print legal bullshit. Small legal bullshit. Small print legal bullshit. Small legal bullshit. Small print legal bullshit. Small legal bullshit. Small print legal bullshit. Small legal bullshit. Small print legal bullshit. Small legal bullshit. Small print legal bullshit. Small legal bullshit. Small legal bullshit. Small print legal bullshit. Small legal bullshit. Small print legal bullshit. Small legal bullshit. Small legal bullshit. Small print legal bullshit. Small legal bullshit. Small print legal bullshit. Small legal bullshit.
>
> Cordially,
>
> Judge Roger Taney

Frazzled, I interrupted my lawyer's devotion and showed him the email.

"Not true," he said. "I filed everything on time."

"Where?"

"At the courthouse."

"With whom?"

"The guy's name was Augie Omega. Wait, Augie Omega. Holy shit."

You saw that coming. I didn't. Just then, the doors to room 151 opened.

It was zero hour. The meticulous dean's assistant poked her head out and announced with a slight smirk, "Dr. Neb, we're ready." Inside, the Faculty Senate Executive Committee chanted, "Retention, Retention, Retention." She left the door open for us.

"We can still play the meso card," my lawyer insisted.

"How? My case has been thrown out."

"There must be something we can do to ensure you're a victim – Wait! I'm about to be brilliant! What if you mentioned your colostomy bag?"

"Not a bad idea."

"Open your shirt so it shows."

I unbuttoned, revealing the top half of my bag, and said, "Just so happens. I recently attended a webinar about how to nonchalantly bring up my colostomy bag in everyday conversation."

"Gosh darn brilliant," he said with a grin the size of Nebraska and half of Kansas. "Dr. Neb, we're going to win!"

Ping!

> Dear Mr. Neb,
>
> This email informs you that you received the highest ratings of any Uber in your district. Congratulations!
>
> Team Uber
>
> PS Please leave pigeons alone.

As we entered, the room fell silent. Room 151 of new A&S was nothing like old A&S. It had integrated technology, acoustic tiles, and modern indirect lighting. The school's coat of arms dominated the back wall with the university's ivy-laced motto: "Disce, Dequere et Iob Posside" in fraktur font. Below, at a modern conference table on a slightly raised platform, sat Acting Dean Popkov. He attempted a welcoming smile, but his smugness let me know he knew the lawsuit had been dismissed. To his sides sat the older, tight-lipped, tight-sphincter full professors assigned to judge me. None established eye contact.

"Let's get started," the dean said as my lawyer and I sat on hard-backed chairs opposite the conference table. "Faculty Senators, please introduce yourselves."

"Dr. Brinsolaro, chemistry."

"Dr. Charbonnier, computer science."

"Dr. Maris, mathematics."

"Dr. Cayat, structural engineering."

"Dr. Ourrad, information technology."

I leaned over and whispered to my lawyer, "Where are the humanities professors?"

"They're not allowed to attend A.A. hearings," he whispered back.

"Why not?"

"They show too little compassion."

"Madam office assistant," the acting dean said, "please deliver the charges."

"It's alleged," she read from her iPad, enjoying every word, "that Dr. Neb is prone to lengthy classroom digressions and that during one of these verbal excursions, he violated University Regulation #384-1."

I let out a series of minor chipmunk-like coughs followed by a guttural that didn't rise to the level of prose or verse but would've pleased Lee Strasberg. "Dr. Neb," the acting dean said, "are you having some sort of problem?"

"Oh dear," muttered my lawyer just loud enough so everyone could hear, "is your mesothelioma acting up again?"

"I'll be okay," I dramatically said, attempting to clear my throat.

"Are you having side effects because of your last round of chemo? Do you need your nebulizer?" said my lawyer as he took out a grubby inhaler his kid must have used. Chemo and an inhaler, those lies alone justified 200 dollars an hour.

"No, I'll cope," I said with a few cancerous "ahems."

"Then we will continue," said Acting Dean Popkov. "Would you like to make a statement in defense of your indefensible actions?"

"Sorry to interrupt," my lawyer said, "Dr. Neb doesn't want to mention it, but before he speaks, he needs a brief break to change his colostomy bag."

Oh, the looks on the STEM professors' horrified faces, priceless. I could see their moral compass twirling. "You may not know," my lawyer continued with gloating concern, "Dr. Neb was recently a victim of a random act of violence. As a result, he must wear a colostomy bag for the rest of his life. He also has post-traumatic stress disorder." I don't know where that last bit came from - I looked at him as if to say, 'What the hell?' His nod back said, "Play along." I wasn't suffering from PTSD. Sure, I had a handgun in my pocket, but that didn't necessarily mean I had mental issues.

You're probably wondering where the gun came from. I forgot to tell you that part of the story. Please forgive, I've been through a lot. After Marcellus's bullet ricocheted off my rib and lodged in my duodenum, the world didn't fade right away. Instead, he and I stood there staring at each other for a shocking second. Then he started profusely apologizing, "I'm so sorry. If Pita Pit had given me chicken Caesar instead of southwest steak, none of this would've happened!"

"Shit!" I said as I looked down at my bloody intestine peeking from the gash near my belly button.

As I fell to my knees, Marcellus rushed over and held me. "Did you ever get the feeling all our wounds are self-inflicted? There are tsunamis and solar flares and volcanic eruptions, but do you know what I fear most when I get out of bed in the morning? Not the blind randomness of nature, but…?"

"Humans," I painfully whimpered.

"How did you know?"

"Wild guess."

"The French Enlightenment was supposed to bring a logical, manageable order to things," he cried, "but the truth is, human administration is more haphazard than nature, more capricious than any god."

"I'm with you, all the way, but I think I'm dying here!"

"Nature doesn't understand pi or $E=mc^2$. Nor does it understand other human creations like love, justice, or faith. Why? Because nature doesn't understand its nature!"

"Shut up!" I yelled as I grabbed his gun, "Take me to the hospital, or I'll blow your balls off!" At gunpoint, Marcellus agreed to Uber me back to town. As we pulled up to the emergency room, I faded. All I remembered was him running off. Later, I learned he fled the country to escape justice.

The next question you're most likely asking is, why did I bring a gun to the A.A. hearing? Well, moments before, as I sat in the parking lot outside New A&S, a campus cop drove by, and I ducked down to the floorboards to hide. While down there, I saw a lump under the passenger seat floor mat. I thought it must be the ball and key. If it was, it could've been a sign from God telling me to skip the meeting and unlock the bell tower's secret room. But when I pulled up the mat, it wasn't the key, but Cox's 22. I figured that, too, must be a sign from God, so I stuffed it in my pocket.

"Thank you for that important information about your colostomy bag and PTSD," said the acting dean. "Did you know the administration, in partnership with the Campus Mental Health Solutions Center, has launched a new 'courage and candor' directive, inspiring all students, staff, and faculty to be transparent about their personal issues. We want to end stigma and make the students feel at home. Am I right?"

"Yes," said the portly Dr. Brinsolaro of chemistry, "I personally suffer from several issues, including but not limited to obsessive-compulsive disorder."

"I struggle with postpartum depression," said Dr. Charbonnier, the computer science professor, "and borderline personality disorder. I'm also prone to self-injury."

"I suffer from Sleep Arousal Disorder," said Dr. Maris, mathematics, "and nighttime paralysis caused by bouts of depressive anxiety."

"I recently declared bankruptcy," added Dr. Cayat, structural engineering.

"Oh, I forgot, said Brinsolaro of chemistry. "I'm also clinically depressed."

"I'm impotent," Dr. Ourrad of information technology proudly announced.

"Thank you for your honesty," said the acting dean, "Part two of the 'courage and candor' directive will not only place Mental Health Solutions kiosks in every building on campus but will also encourage all professors to list their issues on their syllabuses. In addition, on the first day of class, students will be invited to stand and make public their mental and physical challenges. Dr. Neb, doesn't that make you feel better knowing you're not alone?"

"Sure," I said with a stupid smile, wondering how many of them were also packing.

"Now that we have full disclosure, let's vote," said the acting dean.

"Sorry to interrupt," my lawyer interrupted, "but my client didn't have a chance to make his statement." A chill filled the room.

The disappointed acting dean said, "You may proceed with your statement. You have one minute."

My lawyer handed me the student newspaper confession and beamed with encouragement. I stood, combined a slight cough with a dose of regret, and read the printed apology. "I want to acknowledge the courage it must've taken for this student to come forward and file an anonymous complaint. Because of his, her, or their heroism, I've learned to be a better person–on the inside. I've also been motivated to retake the university's entire webinar series twice. Scoring a perfect 100 both times. Please see below for the attached certificates of completion," and I turned the paper and showed the committee the Achieve diplomas at the bottom of the ad. "I promise that if I'm allowed back in the classroom, I will never again tell a joke. There will be no witticisms, wisecracks, wordplay, not even repartee. Signed Dr. Charlie Neb, Dynamic Team Player."

"Thank you. Sit," said the acting dean.

"Oh," I added, "I also did highway clean up from mile marker 13 to 15, filling over fifty-five forty-gallon bags."

"Duly noted," he said, "Let's vote."

"Wait," my lawyer interrupted, "so we have full disclosure, shouldn't the joke be read into the record?"

I grabbed his sleeve and whispered, "Not a good idea."

"May I have a moment with my client?" he said, huddling up for a private conference. "W.W.L.S.D."

"What the hell does that mean?" I muttered back.

"What Would Luke Skywalker Do?"

"But I don't remember the joke."

"Neither do *they*," he said with a wink. Then he reached into his jacket, pulled out a small note card, faced the inquisition, and read, "Knock knock." A stupid pause. "You know what to do, knock knock."

"Who's there?" said Dr. Brinsolaro, the obsessive-compulsive, clinically depressed chemistry professor.

"Lettuce."

"Lettuce, who?"

"Lettuce in. It's cold out here." Then he confidently announced, "As you can see, no reasonable person would find this joke offensive. Dumb? Yes. Infantile? Totally. A waste of class time. That too. But offensive? We rest our case," he said as he sat down beside me with a big grin.

"Might I remind everyone," said the acting dean, taking charge of the room, "Dr. Neb is not here because he told an *offensive* joke. He's here because he told a joke, period. In today's world, intention is not as important as perception. If someone perceives an attempt at comedy as offensive, that's all that matters. And obviously, someone did. We will now vote."

"Wait!" My lawyer stood and confidently intervened. "We must consider an important question. Are knock-knock jokes comedy?" Oh, that was good, I thought. He then took a dramatic pause. His following words would make or break us. And we waited for his brilliant punch line. And waited. Only a debater of the most remarkable elocutionary talent could hold a pause like this. And then he said, "May I have a word with my client?" and leaned down and murmured, "I got nothing."

"What? You're on a roll," I whispered.

"I know. It was a good start, but I have no payoff."

"You can't leave them hanging."

He turned to the assemblage and said, "My client would like to finish my thought." And he sat. I tentatively stood. Coughed. Delayed. And coughed again.

"Dr. Neb," said the acting dean. "You have the floor for one minute."

"My lawyer's correct," I stumbled through an improvised statement. "Have you ever laughed at a knock-knock joke? Me neither. Knock-knock jokes, like 98% of New Yorker cartoons, aren't funny and thus cannot be considered comedy. And so, I didn't tell a joke, and thus, I'm not guilty."

"You're doing great," my lawyer whispered.

So, I continued gaining confidence, "Back in grade school, I was taught there were five senses: sight, hearing, touch, smell, and taste. But in fact, we have many other senses. For example, during college drinking parties, I became painfully aware of my sense of balance, a sixth sense. But also, there's the sense of time. For me, fourth grade lasted well over a decade, while my twenties sped by in a fortnight. But there is also an eighth, the sense of humor, which is just as crucial to our perception of reality as the other seven."

I had them. Even the acting dean seemed impressed. And I couldn't be sure, but I think a tear came to the eye of Dr. Ourrad, the impotent information technology professor. Then Dr. Charbonnier, the computer science professor with postpartum depression and borderline personality disorder, spoke, "But wouldn't you agree students should feel safe and respected both in and out of our classrooms - that they have the right to go through their day without serious ideological disruptions? Whatever you said, funny or not, it failed to do this."

"The problem with that," I answered, "is if a college environment is too safe, it makes it so the students don't have the antibodies necessary to face new or difficult questions or to consider coexisting truths. This makes the students helpless, hostile, and unable to think for themselves."

"But the students," she said, "are the ones we're here for. They're the customer."

"Are you saying universities are businesses? Because business is about marketing things rather than a marketplace of ideas. You find what the customer wants and sell it to them. In what book does that describe the mission of a university?"

"But you intended to tell a joke, so it doesn't matter if anyone laughed. You were breaking the rules," said Dr. Maris, the mathematics professor who suffered from sleep arousal disorder, nighttime paralysis, and bouts of depressive anxiety.

"Totalitarian regimes are always sensitive to the subversive potential of a good joke," I answered. "They celebrate an author for writing a tragedy but cancel them for comedy."

"But what good is comedy?" asked Dr. Cayat, the bankrupt engineering professor.

"Comedy confronts the inhumanity of the world we've built," I answered. "Comedy makes us laugh at our shortcomings and stupidity. For when we laugh at ourselves, we transcend our postage-stamp-sized identities. When we laugh, we open our minds to routine maintenance. Laughter allows us to change our bulky batteries and embrace a new power source. Which reminds me of a joke."

"Holy shit," my lawyer whispered as he yanked on my sleeve." Please don't."

"Did you hear the one about the two professors walking away from campus to get a cup of coffee?" The dean and professors gasped. "They pass a fish market. The window is piled with glassy-eyed dead fish. And one professor turns to the other and says, 'Oh, that's right, I can't get coffee now. I've got a one o'clock class.'" Some professors snickered. And I couldn't be sure, but I think the dean might've smiled. "That joke summarizes how I feel about what's happening on college campuses. Students today are bored out of their minds because professors are spineless and afraid. Afraid of the administration, unemployment, and, most of all, of making the students think. My esteemed colleagues, we are teaching the next generation to be ironic, detached, and fragile - These are not good learning outcomes."

Sensing he was losing the room, the acting dean interrupted, "I, too, would like to ask a question," he said, and the room fell silent. "Dr. Neb, why were you hired?"

"To teach philosophy."

"That might be true if you were an instructor or grad student, but you're tenure track. This means you were hired to get foundation and government grants, to satisfy the university's shareholders, to take into account the authority of market forces."

The professors nodded in agreement, and I slipped my hand into my pocket and felt the notched steel of the gun's grip. But then I thought, what would they do with my body? Being buried is a downer. And cremation sounds ugly. I read about this outfit in Utah that, for a fee, will dice up your remains, go out in the woods, and use you as tree fertilizer. It'd be kind of cool to be a maple. The only problem is I'd be in Utah.

"To do this," the acting dean continued, "we need every team member to join in the drive towards guaranteed outcomes, synchronous cognitive processing, and retention. We need the students to use the template, heed the rubric, go where Google Maps tells them, and return to the hive for homecoming."

As I placed my index finger on the trigger, I thought, what about American Indian sky burial? But if I did, I'd probably be charged with cultural appropriation, and I was in enough trouble.

"We are creating the future, Dr. Neb, a faster, smoother life that fits comfortably in the palm of our hands. A life where we don't need antibodies because there are no troublesome questions or coexisting truths. A life where we don't need routine maintenance or to change bulky batteries. In short, a life resistant to chipping. But you, by telling jokes, funny or not, circumvent the purpose of education. For when the students laugh, they never again take their alumni newsletter seriously."

"Shut up," a voice came from the overhead speakers. The dean and professors fell into a petrified silence. Then, a buzz as two large wall-mounted acoustic panels powered open, revealing a flat-screen monolith. After a few techno flashes, President Boucher zoomed in wearing a new wig. She looked haggard, in need of a drink. The blurred background obscured her broadcast location.

"Holy crap," I thought out loud.

"Thank you, Dr. Popkov. I'll take it from here," said the president.

"Yes, of course," the dean said, throwing in a little ass-kissing head bow.

President Boucher took a long breath and considered me. She was trying to recognize me without hair. "You shaved your head."

"I—."

"Madam President," my lawyer cut me off, "Dr. Neb is suffering from cancer."

"What type?"

"Mesothelioma."

"Bullshit." Then she turned to me and said, "Charlie, really, why did you shave your head?"

"To make it appear, I had cancer," I said, and my lawyer elbowed me. But I knew the game was up. My only tactic left was honesty.

"But you don't have cancer."

"Not that I know of."

"Strange. I do," she said as she pulled off her wig, revealing her shiny, hair-free head. The professors gasped. The acting dean's mouth dropped. The president gave me a poignant smile. "Charlie, answer me this, what would happen to laughter if we corrected all the world's problems?"

"I guess we wouldn't need it," I said.

"That's right," she said. "Sadly, I'm incapable of imagining such a world. Can you?"

"No."

"Why, Charlie?" Her eyes filled with tears. "Why did you look? In this long suicide called life, what good has it done you to know it's all absurd? How does that make you happy? Wouldn't it be best just to go back to your default factory settings and get on with life with as few disruptions as possible?" At that moment, sitting before the stoic committee, the last of the youthful wonder that had driven me towards love, honor, and hope vanished. All that lingered was the tattered silence of objective reality, devoid of symbolic meaning and teleological purpose. I was, for the first time in my life, wholly undeceived. And I understood the only way to stop being driven to the uttermost edge of despair was to close my eyes and turn off my brain, for living a life of the mind leads only to chaos.

"It's done me no good whatsoever," I said.

"So why expose the students to your disorder?"

"Because it's my job to make them think about shit."

She smiled and said, "Still trying to be funny." But then she shook her head and added, "Oh, you poor darling, you just don't get it, do you?"

"Get what?"

"You, Charlie, are the antagonist in this story." My vision tunneled. The panel of pejorative professors grew dull. I was alone with just her. Then she sighed as if we were lovers and delivered the news. "Because you, like all good humanities professors, are caught in the great schism between the chaos of real life and the unity of the artificial arts. That's what the humanities are—humans forging chaos into unity. But that unity is an illusion, a wish. And in your heart, you know it. As a result, the only possible outcome is anxiety. That's why the humanities are dying because who needs more anxiety in the age of post-happiness? As Augie Omega said, 'If you step from the cave into the light, you'll know that there are no saviors, no salvation and that every unifying philosophy you come up with is equally wrong. And that will never change, no matter how hard you wish.'"

The blank space above is intentional, for there was nothing to say. She was right. All my teaching did was expose the students to my hopeless search for meaning. I was the villain who opened the protagonist's eyes to a world filled with confusion, complexity, and ambiguity for no reason but the vanity of dragging them down to my absurd level, where catharsis was not an option.

"You're humming to yourself again," she said.

"Let me put an end to that." I pulled out Cox's gun, put it against my temple, and pulled the trigger.

The End

Well, that, too, would've been the end if there had been bullets in the gun. Later, I heard that in the middle of the chaos that followed, Acting Dean Popkov needlessly deployed the active shooter crash gates, but afterward no one knew how to raise them, so the administration was forced to work out of rented trailers for the next month.

Ping!

Campus Wide Scarlet & Brown Alert,

The university has permanently banned Professor Neb from campus. If you see him, call the police immediately.

Have A Great Day,

Acting Dean Bobby Popkov, PhD

"Everything negative—pressure, challenges—is all an opportunity for me to rise." – Kobe Bryant

22

Behind the barred windows of the Basel Mental Health Hospital, I spent my pajama days watching webinars in the TV room. My favorite was "An Emotional Toolbox for Combating Negative Thoughts," which starred Pepper Jo. I loved her multi-dimensional portrayal of the concerned psychiatrist who helps the sadistic stay-at-home parent with no sense of self-worth achieve inner peace. I watched it a dozen times but still couldn't place her.

After a week of constant monitoring and undergoing multiple evaluations, they brought me before the chief psychiatrist to assess if I posed a threat to society. She greeted me with a warm smile and sympathetic eyes and asked about my childhood and dissertation. Then she said, "Prove to me you're ready for the real world." So, I told her a joke. "Did you hear the one about the two psychiatrists - they could be any race, religion, ethnicity, physicality, or sexual orientation - who were taking public transportation back into the city after Thanksgiving? One turns to the other and says, 'I made a terrible Freudian slip at my mother's house. I meant to say, "Would you please pass the *hot cross buns*?" But instead, I said, "'You ruined my life, you bitch.'"

She chuckled but added, "You're making progress, but I think we should keep you in for at least another week." As the guard came to escort me back to my simple white room, she said, "When you do get out, you should go see this hot new comedian playing at the Pits of Hell Comedy Club. His name is Augie Omega." An hour later, as alarms blared, I scaled the hospital's fence, and escaped.

Faded caricatures of Richard Pryor humping Phyllis Diller and Joan Rivers goosing Lenny Bruce adorned the gray walls of the Pits of Hell Comedy Club. On the smoky stage, lit by only a few low-hanging barn door lights, stood a class clown wearing high-topped tennis shoes and spiked hair. Beside him, a mic, a beer, and a three-legged stool. What other profession requires so few props? In the darkness, an audience of working-class workaholics clung to the hope that cocktails and comedy might make them forget their lesser lives.

"Did you hear the one about the Jewish boys sharing a hospital room before their operations?" The comic riffed with perfect Borscht-Belt timing. "'What're you in for?' one says to the other. 'Tonsillectomy.' 'Oh, no worries. It hurts a little, but they give you lots of ice cream.' 'What are you in for?' 'Circumcision.' 'Oh God no,' said the other, 'I had that when I was eight days old, and I didn't walk for a year!'"

Everyone in the hole-in-the-wall that smelled of booze and fermented drain gunk roared—everyone except a righteous drunk near the front. "I'm offended by that!" she yelled.

"What?" the comedian said, placing a hand to his forehead to see under the glare of the stage lights.

"How dare you make fun of circumcision!"

"Lady, it's just a joke."

"Tens of thousands of women are circumcised each year against their will!"

"My joke was about male circumcision. If you haven't noticed, men are a little different down there. But looking at you, lady, I'd guess you didn't know that."

With a nervous chuckle from the audience, the woman doubled down, "You're normalizing violence! You're a terrorist!"

"I'm a comedian. I tell jokes. Now and then, one bombs but that's as close as I come to being a terrorist."

"Circumcision is never funny!" she said as she pitched the remains of her Piña Colada on the comedian's groin. Then she grabbed her coat and complicit boyfriend and, to a chorus of hisses, ushered him through the tightly knit tables.

"I'll send my cleaning bill to your room in the nuthouse!" the comedian hollered.

She flipped him off and slammed the door. Her protest worked, for after she left, the comic's timing was tainted. Thrown off, he fumbled for his next gag before giving up and saying, "All it takes today is for one twit to object, and society goes stupid." Not appreciating the scorn, some in the crowd booed. But the comedian wasn't finished. "Keep this bullshit up, and stages like this will soon be turned over to jazz soloists, poetry slams, and open mic readings of people recalling their best prairie home Christmas," he mocked. "Why? 'Cause that shit's safe!" More boos, but he continued, "Like modern abstract art, know why there's so much of it today? Because no one gets it, so no one can be insulted. Unlike monuments and statues, the city council never has to tear down that ugly steel I-beam piece of shit because some closed-minded-new-age-puritan-cultural-warrior-asswipe had her feelings hurt - boohoo!"

"Go home and have sex with your ugly mother," a drunk yelled from the audience.

"I quit!" the comedian hollered as he flipped off the audience and left the stage to a chorus of jeers and heckles.

"Let's have a big round of applause for Jackie Diamond," the emcee said as he stumbled out on stage, trying to cover for the suddenly departed comedian. Some of the inebriates politely clapped, but most booed.

"Why are you wearing a bathrobe and pajamas?" said the bored bohemian barkeep.

"I'm Buddhist," I lied.

"Really? That's why you shaved your head?"

"Yeah, I'm dedicated to a life of poverty and calligraphy."

"Awesome," she said as she pitched a wasted beer bottle into a trash barrel with such force she must have thought the bar was a product-testing center. "Can I get a cocktail for a holy man?"

"I have no money."

"On the house," she said, planting a watery rum and Coke before me.

"And now, ladies and gentlemen, the act you've been waiting for! Strap yourselves in, turn off your moral outrage, and welcome to our stage the funnyman who's taken comedy to an all-new level! Straight from long runs in Orlando, El Paso, and Sandy Hook. Give it up for Augie Omega!"

Every part of me, even my fingernails, went into hyper-awareness. A round of claps and hoots as Augie jumped onto the stage. He looked like the illegitimate son of Truman Capote. His chubby frame, bald head, and ill-fitting sports jacket should've made him a putz, but a heavy dose of cocky confidence zeroed them out. He was that whiz kid, the smart aleck with the puckish face and Buddy Holly glasses that everyone in high school wanted to slap. He washed down a swig of beer, adjusted the mic to his shortness, cleared his scratchy throat, and raised one prickly eyebrow, triggering giggles.

"Go for it!" some plastered businessman shouted.

Augie raised the other brow. More giggles. Only someone who knew their opening gag was the funniest joke ever could have the audacity to make the drunk masses wait this long. "Say something funny! Say something funny!" The chant grew as the audience pounded their tables. "Say something funny!" Augie raised a finger. The audience fell silent. Then he leaned in and placed his prickly lips so close to the mic he must've tasted the previous comedian's beer and said with a Harvey Fierstein helium voice, "Did ya hear the one about Mother Teresa?" The audience went wild. And I thought, here goes, this's what life's about - the damn payoff. The death wish, what Freud called "dying in one's own fashion," is only an attempt to end with a well-timed punch.

"Her holiness was on a mission helping poor people in Tanzania," Augie quipped. "After she handed out a bunch of breadcrumbs and prayers, a gaggle of nuns came to the tiny airport to see her off. Then, roaring down the runway, Mother Teresa's prop plane unexpectedly veered, crashed into the crowd, and decapitated a shit load of nuns. This is a true story - look it up. What's black and white and red all over? Nuns being decapitated by Mother Teresa's plane."

I couldn't be sure, but I think I heard a drummer's ba-dum-bum and a rim shot far off in the wings. Then, a curdled silence. The room was so dead I could hear the ice melting in their drinks. Beside me, the bohemian barkeep whispered, "Unreal," as she took a hit of rum straight from the bottle.

"Thank you, thank you very much," Augie said. "Hey, did ya hear about father of the year? The legislature of Ohio voted this guy the number one dad in the state. A few weeks after he got his major award, he decided to surprise his son at homecoming - his son was the high school's all-star quarterback. So, get this, father of the year took skydiving lessons. He was going to jump right before kickoff, fly in, land on the 50-yard line, and, to the crowd's cheers, deliver the game ball to his son."

"Oh god, no," someone whispered in the front row.

"Don't get ahead of me!" Augie snickered. "Ah hell, fuck it, you know the punch line. That's right, father of the year's parachute failed to open. And he fell to his death, crippling several members of the coaching squad. I know what you're thinking - did the home team win?"

Again, ba-dum-bum, rim shot. Zero laughs. The audience was now in a neuro-linguistic stupor. Unable to make their diaphragms function. They couldn't even boo, let alone walk out. For a second, I thought I might be in the presence of some tiny evil deity. Then I remembered Voltaire's quote, "God is a comedian playing to an audience that's too afraid to laugh."

"What killed a million birds, hundreds of thousands of turtles, tens of thousands of pelicans, and over a thousand dolphins? Deepwater Horizon!" Ba-dum-bum, rim shot. "Thank you! Thank you very much!" And Augie continued telling "jokes" about fracking protesters being crushed by falling windmills, mass casualty shootings at peace rallies, and global warming ending all life on earth. Not one "joke" got the slightest chuckle from the stupefied gathering. And then he, like all good comedians, finished with his best bit.

"Did you hear the one about the nearest star to our sun? It's 4.24 light years away. This means if we humans wanted to visit, using our current or any foreseeable technology, it'd take about 19,000 years for us to get there. That's over four hundred generations. Can you imagine if you were the two hundredth generation stuck on that tiny spacecraft? All you or your parents, or your parent's parent's parents, had ever known was life on a small craft traveling through endless space. Know what would happen to the people inside? They'd forget the reason for their trip. Then they'd go mad. And don't give me that bullshit about humans being resilient. We can't tolerate a two-year pandemic without going ape shit. How the hell would we make it through 19,000 years of solitude?" he shouted. Then he pulled back and whispered, "The truth. We're alone and have forgotten our mission. So, what's left to do but trash the place!" Ba-dum-bum, rim shot. "Thank you! Thank you very much!" he said as he kicked over the stool, smashed the mic, and walked off to a dead hush.

"Let's have a giant round of applause for Augie Omega!" the emcee shouted. Silence. The house lights faded up, and the anesthetized audience sat for a full three minutes before slowly putting on their coats and filing out. They didn't even finish their drinks. Stunned, the bohemian barkeep grabbed my rum and Coke and used it to wash down a Fluvoxamine.

Moments later, I shivered in the dark, frosty alley behind the club near the steel stairs leading to the stage door. Inside, I could hear the comics cracking jokes and congratulating each other on "killing it." Then the graffitied door squeaked open, and out came Augie. He looked even shorter than he had on stage. He couldn't have been more than five foot - more like four foot twelve. "Night, everyone," he said with his abrasive crackerjack voice. I thought he'd used it on stage for comic effect, but he really spoke that way. Close up, he was just another jaded comedian on the road so long he couldn't find home. He turned his collar up against the evening chill and flicked a cig that sparked into the gutter. As he clucked down the stairs, his eyes locked on me for a flash, but straightaway dismissed me as just another jammies-wearing alleyway drunk.

"What the hell is wrong with you?" I said as he passed.

"You talkin' to me?"

"Yeah. What you did in there wasn't funny."

"I heard people laughing."

"No, they didn't. No one laughed."

"We agree to disagree. Goodnight."

"All you did is bring up a bunch of hopeless, tragic bullshit."

"It's known as observational humor," he lectured me. "It was made famous by George Carlin and Jerry Seinfeld."

"But they were funny. I mean, at least Carlin was. You're not."

He stopped and considered me as he might a heckler. Then, he smiled a grimace as he took up the challenge, "Are you saying paraplegic veterans in Texas dying during a veteran's day parade when their float is hit by a speeding freight train isn't funny?"

"I'm saying *none* of it was. I'm surprised you didn't bring up the Armenian Holocaust."

"Ooooo, gooood," he grinned, whipped out a fifty-dollar bill, and handed it to me.

"What's this?"

"I'm buying your joke. The Armenian Holocaust is the best one I've heard since Chernobyl—comic gold. If you come up with more gems like that, let me know," he said as he turned and walked dead center down the dim, dripping alley clogged with derelict dumpsters.

"Did you once work at a cryobank?" I called after.

He turned and smirked like an impish cream-fed cat. "So?" he said.

"You caused a lot of parents a whole bunch of pain. Do you realize how distressing it is for Republican parents to give birth to Democratic socialist children?"

"Sperm with two tails, that, I must say, was one of my better gags," and he beamed and remembered his triumph.

"And what about HolyHub Publishing?"

"I made a few improvements to their Bible, so what?"

"Have you ever been to Wuhan, China?"

"Played a gig there once."

"You also burned down a theatre and caused a massive gas explosion."

"Your point?"

"And was it you who dropped an immense clump of fake snow on a ballerina, causing her to fall into an orchestra pit?"

"What's this, a list of my greatest hits?" he said, giving me a puckish grin.

"What are you, the Devil?" I don't know what made me say it. I didn't and don't believe in a devil or hell. He gripped me with his thorny eyes. My breath teetered. My veins went brittle.

"There is no Devil," he grinned.

"Then what are you, God?"

"Doesn't that tell you something? You couldn't tell the difference." And he jumped up on an overturned trash can under a fading, flickering streetlight, threw his arms out, and announced to an empty universe, "Earthquakes, volcanoes, hurricanes, wildfires, heatwaves, droughts, blizzards, cyclones, tsunamis, and more viruses than there are stars in the universe! Tally it up! If you're honest with yourself, really honest, what's the one thing you know to be true about me?"

"You don't give a shit."

"Not only that, but I'm incapable of giving a shit."

"At the very least, you could add a modicum of optimism to your routine."

"Optimism?" Augie snickered, then he caught my eyes and added, "Want to hear the funniest joke ever?"

"Sure," I said, trying to hold my own.

"There was once this pale blue dot called Earth, the only place in the vast universe with viruses," he sneered. "All the other life forms living in all those other galaxies out there, and there are billions and billions, lived long, happy lives, but they had no protection against viruses, so they were forced to quarantine the earth. Oh, sometimes they'd send in a UFO to anally probe someone from Mississippi, but they knew the Earthlings could never be invited to their happy, star-filled party! Not knowing they were untouchable and disappointed with their small, fragile lives, these Earthlings sought imagined victories through sports, fictional romance on the Hallmark Channel, and pretend meaning in politics as they piled one 'ism' atop another—realism, romanticism, surrealism. Then, one day, they came to the end of the line, the last God standing, Absurdism!"

"Is there a punch line?" I derisively doubted.

"Yes!" He jumped from the trashcan and pushed me against the gritty comedy shop's bricks. My knees buckled, bringing us face to face. He put his puny mug so close I could smell the gin and nicotine on his breath. In the alley's darkness, he had no pupils, no emotion. "What these humans didn't know was that their ability to imagine God was far greater than any real God. Their ability to imagine love greater than the human emotion called love. Even their ability to imagine happiness was far bigger than their actual ability to experience happiness. And thus, they were condemned to live forever in the age of post-happiness. Ba-dum-bum." His lips curled into a sarcastic grin. "Now, if you'll excuse me, I've got another gig to get to."

"Where?"

"Why do you care?"

"I want to avoid the place."

He laughed. "You can't avoid me."

"What are you going to do?"

He stopped, pondered me for a moment, then lit a new cig and took a long drag before he said, "Do you know who André Breton is?"

"Yes."

"You do? How would you know that name?"

"I'm a philosophy professor."

He chuckled, and it turned into a cough. Then he said, "So tell me, Mr. Philosophe, who was he?"

"Absurdist writer, poet, he wrote the surrealist manifesto."

"And what did he say was the most effective surreal action a person could take?"

I paused as I tried to remember the obscure document I hadn't read since grad school, but then, in a flash, the quote came to me. "He said the most effective surrealist action would be to start shooting blindly in the streets."

"If I were you," Augie grinned, "I'd avoid campus tonight." He turned and walked, and I saw it, poking from his back pocket, the dean's fuzzy pink ball.

"Wait," I said, "that's the key to the room in the bell tower."

He looked back with a smirk, playfully held up the dangling copper key, and said, "Want it? You can't have it."

"Where did you find it?"

"On a hill near a crashed BMW." He giggled. It turned into a childish laugh of complete victory, which I silenced with a slug. I'd never punched anyone in all my years, but my first was a winner. I heard his jaw crack as he went down. From the mud, he huffed, choked, and spit blood. Then he smiled and said, "Once you look, you can't unlook."

I grabbed the key and ran.

23

A half-hour later, I was back on campus, mingling with the drunken hoards celebrating that night's football victory as they streamed from the majestic lights of the stadium to the dark steps of Old Arts and Sciences. It was the annual post-game Thanksgiving Turkey Decapitation. This drunken Mardi Gras-like party started a hundred years earlier when the Varsity Club guillotined a terrified turkey while singing the school's alma mater. Today, they celebrated by chopping the head off a ten-foot papier mâché turkey, but the event was no less graphic.

"What the hell?" someone said in the crowd, and I turned to see Dean Popkov. "You're banned from campus!" He, like the crowd, was plastered. He hid his fifth of whiskey and shouted, "You're in big trouble, mister, big-big trouble!" Then he fumbled for his cell and dialed. "I need the police at old A&S, stat!"

To throw him off, I zigged within the swarming crowds and switch-backed through the ranks of the marching band. In the stampede of humanity, I found "The Dean Gacy Memorial," climbed through the steel I-beams and into the arms of Augie Omega. His nose blackened with blood, he barked, "Give me the key, asshole!" I shoved him into a gang of drunken, shirtless, body-painted frat bros and ran past giggling cheerleaders pouring fists of tomato-red confetti into the hinged neck of the cartoonish gobbler. Then I forced my way to the front doors of Old A&S. There I looked back. Augie was gone, but Popkov and two cops were closing fast.

Inside, I skated the marble floor and mounted the grand staircase towards the bell tower. "Stop!" a shout came from the campus cops one story below. "That's an order!" Legs pumping, I huffed my way up. On each landing, the law narrowed the gap. On the fifth floor, a cop lunged for the hem of my bathrobe, yanking me back. As he fell, I slipped the sleeves of my bathrobe, sprung for the door, and wiggled the key into the rusty hole—it fit. With a fierce thrust, the old hinges gave. I rushed inside and locked the door. "Open this door," the cop's muffled yell came from the hall. They pounded, shaking the frame. My frenzied breath stagnated, and I grappled the dark wall for a switch. With a dull click, the decrepit fluorescent tubes blinked to life. I turned to find a vaulted chamber that smelled of dead leaves. Its cracked walls layered with peeling, protestant-gray paint, the windows stained with dust and etched with cobwebs. Above, cold air fell from the tall tinder beams of the bell tower.

Out of breath, Popkov yelled, "Charlie, unlock this door! Now! Before it's too late!"

I clicked another switch, and a buzzing second row of dingy neons flickered, revealing dozens upon dozens of army-green filing cabinets lined up hip-to-hip and covered with hardened pigeon poop. Five stories below, the merrymakers shouted, "Kill the turkey! Kill the turkey!"

"Plato, Aristotle, Confucius, Voltaire, Descartes, Simone de Beauvoir," Popkov drunkenly bellowed from behind the door, "what good are they? Can they get you out of this mess? No. Because they got you into this mess!"

I approached one of the decrepit cabinets. The peeling yellow label above the handle read "1886." That was the year the university was founded. The drawer below read, "1887." The dates went through the many years to the present. As the police battered the door, my thumb pressed a random latch. The drawer stuck. Nobody had opened it in decades. I yanked. It gave.

"Kill the turkey! Kill the turkey!"

Each manila file in the drawer was carefully labeled with a professor's name—Dr. James Night, Dr. Evelia Salt, Dr. Chuck Conesko, etc. I drew out one forgotten file and peeled it open. Inside was a single sheet of yellowed onion paper that read: "Dr. Albert Jones (1886): My GOALS (Goal Oriented Attainment List for Success) for the coming academic year are:

➢ To deploy overarching and pivotal inquiry
➢ To innovate meaningful initiatives

> ➤ To enhance participation structures
> ➤ To align my meaning-centered objectives

I yanked another paper-filled drawer and opened a file that read, Dr. Lianna Lee (1955): My GOALS for the coming academic year are:

> ➤ To motivate thematic strategic change
> ➤ To triangulate the hygiene of thought
> ➤ To develop a regrowth mindset
> ➤ To innovate and leverage my learning-focused inquiry

My breathing lurched as I crashed open another drawer and another file. Dr. Peter Lutz (2024): My GOALS for the coming academic year are:

> ➤ To be responsible, centered & input-based
> ➤ To strategize and enrich my site-based action units
> ➤ To update my conclusion-based engagement teaching
> ➤ To create a holistic, dynamic, intuitive setting

Angered, I slammed the drawer so hard the cabinet pitched, its files scattered to the floor. Then I sank to my knees. I'd found the source, the motherload, the great through line of history.

"We talk of transcendence," the drunken Popkov bitterly called from behind the door, "that moment when we peeked past the boundaries of life and realized we might be participating in an immensity greater than ourselves. Well, Charlie, now you know, there's also absurd transcendence when you realize it's just one big meaningless joke!"

And it occurred to me that Augie Omega was more than one person. He was the French and Polish townsfolk who delivered their Jewish neighbors to the Nazis. He was the corrupt cops who put their knees on black men's necks. He was all those people who created the university's mosh pit where one absurd calamity randomly slammed into another. Kierkegaard wrote, "Our age reminds one very much of the disintegration of the Greek state. Everything continues, and yet there is no one who believes in it. The invisible spiritual bond that gives it validity has vanished, and thus the whole age is simultaneously comic and tragic: tragic because it's perishing, comic because it continues."

Then I saw the sniper's nest.

At first, it was only a shadow within a shadow, then a dark spark of tinsel. I refocused, the periphery of my vision contracted, and the telescopic scope mounted atop the AK-47 became an active blur. The barrel pushed out a broken window. The tripod nested on a cluster of ammunition boxes.

"Kill the turkey! Kill the turkey!"

Then, into the hot spot of my brain came the soft outline of a person standing in frozen silence beside the gun. He was as shocked to see me as I was him. Just a boy, perhaps nineteen. He had pale skin and straight, dull hair that fell over his soft, sleepless eyes. Dressed in black, his slender body blended perfectly with the rough-hewn rafters of the bell tower. We stood blinking at each other, not saying a word, while outside, the police hammered the door.

"I, ah, was just getting some files," I said, trying to be nonchalant. "I'll be going."

The boy picked up a black pistol and muttered, "I'm going to blow your head off!"

Scared shitless, I managed to say, "I've already been shot once this month. I'd rather you not."

"Do you realize the pain and suffering you've caused? But your reign of terror is over!"

"I'm sorry."

"That's all you have to say?!"

"I'll never tell another joke, I promise."

"What the hell are you talking about?" he said.

"The same thing you are - I caused people pain because I told a joke in class."

"No, I'm talking about 9-11, asshole. I'm talking about climate change and all the other bullshit that's led to the age of post-happiness!"

"What?"

"Aren't you Augie Omega?" he said.

"No, I'm Charlie Neb."

"Who?"

"I'm a philosophy professor. Or was."

And the young man's brain short-circuited momentarily as he tried to add it up. "Isn't' this your sniper's nest?" he said.

"I thought it was yours."

"No. Wait, hold on, I know you. I took a class from you - Existentialism 101. You're the funny professor."

"Thank you," I said.

"Kill the turkey! Kill the turkey!"

Confused, he asked, "Why are you wearing pajamas?"

"I escaped from a mental hospital. I'm trying to stop Augie Omega."

"So am I," he said. "But why are the police after you?"

"Kind of a long story. It all started with Felice Wolinski."

"Sophomore communications major," he said as he lowered the gun. "She was driven mad by Augie Omega."

"What about you?" I asked. "How long have you been looking for him?"

"Since my father died in Kabul."

"Afghanistan?"

"He was part of the final evacuation. Got himself blown up on the last day," and his mind coasted to a distant memory, "I sang at his funeral."

"What do you sing?" I said, trying to lighten the moment.

"I'm a tenor, used to solo in my church choir."

"Me too," I said.

"The last time I sang was at his funeral." His voice cracked as a tear clutched the corner of his eye. "After the service, I told my mother I wanted to see him one last time. She told me not to, but I opened the casket anyway. I looked. And once you look. ..."

"You can't unlook," I said, and for a moment, it was as if we'd exchanged a secret password. Outside, the police fell silent. I could hear muffled bursts from their garbled radios. They were plotting something. Below, the cheerleaders led the bellowing crowd, "Kill the turkey! Kill the turkey!"

"How did you get up here?" I whispered. "There's only one key."

"I've been trying to get in here since I was a freshman. I even took a hammer and crowbar to the door, but no luck. Then tonight, I was sitting on the toilet in the men's john two stories down, and I looked up and saw the air vent," he pointed at a round hole in the floor so small only someone with his youthful slimness could slip through. "And I climbed up. It was hell getting the grate off."

"Kill the turkey! Kill the turkey!"

Then I saw, in the young man's hand, the book. "Is that *The Fifth Door*?" I said.

"Yes."

"You stole it from the library?"

"Yes. Have you read it?"

"No. What does it say? Does it give the answer?"

"To what?"

"To the absurdity of modern life?"

"No," he said. "It's impossible to read. It makes no sense."

"May I?"

"Sure," he said, and he tossed it to me. It was a paperback, about an inch and a half thick. On the black cover, the title and "Written by Augie Omega" appeared in blood-red letters. The first few pages contained random, senseless Dadaist lines, dots, and a circle. No text. No meaning. The young man sank to his knees and cried. "It's hopeless," he whispered. His tears clung to his cheeks like tiny, suffering butterflies.

"We did a good thing tonight," I tried to comfort. "We stopped a mass shooting."

He shook his head. "There'll be more." He drifted and took a death-rattle-like breath. "Augie Omega got it right," he said. "It's all a pointless farce, so maybe we should embrace chaos. Just start piling one absurdity on another until it all goes bust." He sniffed back a tear, his breath softened, and added, "We are just an evolutionary mistake that's no longer in sequence with nature because we ask questions not even the creator of the universe thought to ask." I knelt beside him as he wept. "So how do you find an answer," he said, "when modern life is filled with Augie Omegas?"

And there you have it. How do we find meaning when, for the first time in human history, our demise, not just as individuals or countries but as a species, has clear definable features? Do we attach ourselves to any comfortable narrative that allows us to close our eyes to reality? Do we commit mini-suicide by binging meaningless Hollywood crap? Do we safeguard our last bit of intellect by fleeing to the jungles? Do we party as the ship goes down? Or, as we watch the world crumble, do we write cloistered dissertations and obscure academic papers that might as well be shredded after writing, for no one will read them, and they will change nothing?

"I also escaped from a mental hospital tonight," the boy said. "While I was there, the doctors allowed me one personal possession. I chose *The Fifth Door*. I thought if I could figure it out, I'd get well. When the doctors tried to take it, I ran."

"Kill The Turkey! Kill The Turkey!" the cries grew in intensity.

"I was also allowed only one personal item," I said. "I took a bible."

"Oh god no, you're not going to witness to me."

"No, not that bible, a one-of-a-kind manuscript I stole from a church."

"You stole a Bible?"

"Yes, but this one is different. Instead of being filled with dogma and miracles, it's filled with very human ideas. Some terrible, most completely useless, but bits and pieces were inspiring. In it, I found this quote, 'Since all the alternatives are absurd, let's choose the noblest.'"

"Wait," the boy said, "I read that in my English class. That's the French novelist Gustave Flaubert."

"That's right," I said. "Those words are more sacred to me than anything I've ever found in a holy book. If our existence is just an absurd tale of scarcity, misery, and exploitation, shouldn't we at least try to be noble?"

"So, we're noble, and then we die," his voice shuddered with resignation.

"Yes. But then I folded the page and found this quote, 'Death is but a single night.'"

"Who?"

"Aristotle. And it occurred to me that the billion-year sleep I woke from when I joined this chaos feels precisely the same as the few hours I got last night. And I'm sure it'll be the same as the billion-year sleep to which I'll return."

"A single night," he muttered to himself, but then he added, "I can't, I can't live unless I can draw some binding meaning from the universe."

"Kill The Turkey! Kill The Turkey!"

"In this same rewritten bible, I found the answer. 'The meaning of life differs from person to person, day to day. Even hour to hour. What matters, therefore, is not the meaning of life in general but rather the specific meaning of a person's life at a given moment.'"

"Who said that?"

"Viktor Frankl."

"Don't know that name."

"He was a philosopher who survived the Holocaust."

"Kill The Turkey! Kill The Turkey!"

"So, we don't look to the universe or the God of nature for meaning," he said.

"That's right. For us, meaning comes into focus only day to day and hour to hour. This is what all the world religions and most philosophers never understood—you can't extract meaning from vastness."

"In other words," he said as he wiped his tears, "Size matters." I smiled at his little joke, and we shared a slight moment of laughing acceptance. Then, I opened the book. Instantly, it became clear.

"Wait," I said, "it's a flip book."

"A what?"

"A book that's like an animated cartoon. You're supposed to flip quickly through the pages in rapid succession. Then it'll make sense." Using my thumb, I spun the frames of the pages and showed him as the dots, lines, and circles animated. The circle became a woman's face, the sticks her body. She was a ballerina. The random dots were now swirling snow. She performed a picture-perfect tippytoe arabesque, jumped up, and fell back to earth into an open sewer, where she died. The end.

"What does it mean?" the young man said.

"It means life is horrible and painful and filled with Augie Omegas, but if we're going to survive on this spaceship hundreds of generations away from the answer, we must make ourselves at home and enjoy a good laugh. I have no doubt that other animals feel pain, joy, love, frustration, and loneliness, but because they never think of dancing on a field of fake snow, they don't understand the pain of comedy."

"Laughing at absurdity is the fifth door," he said.

"Yes."

"The ballerina fell in a hole," he chuckled. And I joined him.

C.S. Lewis wrote that we humans are different. We "propound mathematical theorems in beleaguered cities, conduct metaphysical arguments in condemned cells, make jokes on scaffolds, discuss the last new poem while advancing to the walls of Quebec, and comb their hair at Thermopylae. This is not panache. It's our nature." To which I add, we also laugh when a ballerina falls.

Just then, the crowd below erupted with cheers and laughter as they decapitated the papier mâché turkey. "Hello, can you hear me?" came a voice behind the door. "My name is Lieutenant Joe Patroni. I am a C.I.O., a trained Crisis Incident Officer. My certification number is 49250489. Charlie, are you there?"

"Go away," I shouted.

"The newly appointed Dean of Loneliness is here. Also, Dr. Jerry Loudie from the Mental Health Solutions Center."

"We want to help you, Charlie," Loudie pleaded. "I even unlocked the puppy play date room. How about if we all go there for a little cuddle time?" And I giggled. So did the boy. It grew into the joyous cries of a cackling guffaw as we laughed through our tears.

"Are you laughing at us?" Popkov shouted. "Use the damn battering ram!"

"You've gotta get out of here," I whispered to the boy.

"What about you?"

"I'll never fit."

Bang! The battering ram hit the steel door, filling the room with dust and splitters.

"What'll happen to you?"

"I'm a professor. They can't make my life any worse than they already have. Go, be a college kid, enjoy the parties, study a lot, and each day and each hour, find purpose and meaning by choosing something noble. And when it all goes to hell?"

"Laugh," he said.

"Loud and often."

And I helped him as he wriggled his thin frame into the airshaft. Bang! The doorframe cracked. Light cut in from the gash. The boy gave me one last consoling smile and shimmied into darkness. I reattached the grate and tightened the bolts, just as, Bang! With an enormous moan, the massive door came off its hinges and slammed to the floor. "Hands up!" the SWAT team hollered as they stormed in, guns drawn. With half a dozen barrels pointed at my heart, I raised my hands. Then from the hall, cocky and backlit, entered Popkov. He suspiciously looked around and said, "Who were you laughing with?"

"No one. It must've been the echo from the tower," I said. And he looked up into the dark chasm. Then his eyes fell to my hands.

"Where did you get that book?"

I'd forgotten I was still holding Augie Omega's volume. "Stole it from the library."

"That's university property! You're in big trouble." He stopped and saw the AK-47 and sniper's nest. Staggered, his eyes returned to me. "I ought to punch your guts out."

"I'd advise against it," I said.

"Oh yeah?" Dean Popkov said as the cops held me and he socked my stomach so hard my bag exploded, launching a massive shitstorm through my pajamas and into his shocked, open mouth. Gasping, we both dropped. The officers slammed my face to the floor and threw in a few extra kicks and punches as they hog-tied me. Then, from below, as I lay flat on my busted belly, my wrists and ankles handcuffed, came the sweet melody of the mob singing the alma mater.

> *Oh, yonder days*
> *We think of you*
> *We wish we could stay*
> *But as we sing and remember anew*
> *All those yonder days*
> *When we were young and true*

I swore I heard, floating above the dark, drunken throngs, the clear, bright voice of a tenor.

24

The sun, made bittersweet by the summer wildfires, was falling off the edge of the orange sky as I hiked up the burnt, scuff-marked hill where Marcellus had tried to off himself. Far off, a tanker plane bombed a nearby peak with pink fire retardant as I took in the wideness of Kafka's clown carnival and the sublime arc of Carl Sagan's pale blue dot, now gray with smoke.

Thanks to the prayerful Star Wars-inspired work of the Copeland, Osteen, and Swaggart law firm, the police were forced to admit that the fingerprints found on the AK-47 and pistol were not mine, nor could they identify them. Nor could they trace the arsenal to me, or anyone named Augie Omega. So, the grand jury did not indict.

At the peak, as I stood on the narrow ledge of sanity, the sheer clouds cracked open as if on cue, and the sun's spotlight fell upon me. It was time to answer the ultimate question: "Is there a joke so funny even God would laugh?" Nietzsche said he could only believe in a God who danced. Well, I could only believe in a God who laughed. So, once again Sisyphus climbed the hill. Only this time, I left behind my rock and instead took a mic, a beer, and a three-legged stool. At the pulpit of the hazy hilltop stage, I started my standup routine.

"Ladies and Gentlemen, and Zeus or whatever divinity might be listening in," I called out to the emptiness, "straight from gigs as a philosophy professor, a sperm donor, and an Uber driver, put your hands together and welcome to our comedy stage the one, the only, Charlie Neb!" And blinded by the setting sun, I began telling jokes. My routine was full of witticisms and one-liners. It included comedy that was anecdotal, observational, and situational. There were puns, slapstick, and even a few

"How many does it take to screw in a light bulb?" jokes. I stole from George Carlin's "Seven Words You Can't Say on TV," Abbott & Costello's "Who's on First," and Norm McDonald's "A moth walks into a Podiatrist's office." I lifted bits from Richard Pryor, Phyllis Diller, Lenny Bruce, Joan Rivers, Wanda Sykes, Chris Rock, Bob Newhart, Bill Hicks, Jonathan Winters, Janeane Garofalo, Jack Benny, and even Gallagher.

When it was over - I died. I mean, I bombed. More than anything, I wanted to hear a heavenly chuckle or see a cloud-cracking smile. Hell, I would've been happy with just canned laughter, but there were only crickets. When a joke misfires, we blame the audience. But, in fact, what a failed joke proves is that you and your audience have little in common. And that's true of God, too. Voltaire said, "God is a comedian playing to an audience that's too afraid to laugh." It would be more accurate to say, "Humans are comedians playing to a God that doesn't know how to laugh." Tough audience.

Like a good boxer, the universe is constantly moving, so we try to trick it into standing still so we can land a good punch line. This is why we created philosophy - it's an attempt to trick the dim-witted universe into pausing. When we create art, make a scientific discovery, or metaphysicalize the universe through philosophy, we're no different than a young mother who places her daughter against a colorful door frame on a bright Saturday morning and pencil marks the child's height. The artist, scientist, philosopher, and mother are all trying to stop the ticking time bomb that is the universe. They're saying that today, at this fleeting moment, it's an unalterable fact that our child is two feet tall. A given that five hundred years ago, Leonardo saw an Italian noblewoman smile. A truth that penicillin stops bacteria. And that a particular philosophical insight helped us find meaning on this day and this hour. But we all know, in the next moment, the noblewoman's smile faded, the bacteria grew resistant, the philosophical teaching grew stale, and the lines drawn on the colorful door frame were painted over by the next owner. This was why I desired tenure–to make everything stand still long enough so that the entire universe would be within my insignificant reach, and I would be allowed to transcend the spirit of gravity. But now I knew no matter how great our transcendence, we, like a ballerina, will reach our apex, after which nature will always, always, always win. Like Sisyphus, the dancer goes up. The dancer comes down.

As I stood in the cooling ash, the glorious Technicolor spotlight drooped into the plumb-line of the horizon, and I looked up at the first cold stars of the evening. So, I unrolled my story from back to front, and it occurred to me that my life had improved because I no longer lived five minutes from chaos, more like fifteen. So, I took a grand bow and, for a moment, experienced true Sartrean existentialism, that dreadful freedom most avoid. Then I retraced my steps back down the hill to my econobox and drove over to Faith Light, where I left the misquoting bible on the church's steps, like an orphan. Beside it, I placed an anonymous apology.

I know the narrow sequence of events in a proper story should end a few pages after the climax and that catharsis is supposed to capture some semblance of order in all this chaos. But life has no narrative, and the most significant catharsis ever written is short-lived. So please take a moment to join me for a cathartic laugh as I clear out my "edu" inbox for the last time:

> Campus Wide Scarlet & Brown Alert,
>
> I'm thrilled to announce that the K-Pop band GENDERREVEAL! has agreed to perform at commencement. They will be singing their worldwide hit "Bounce Rum Pum."
>
> Margrett Applewhite, Entertainment Director

> Campus Wide Scarlet & Brown Alert,
>
> It is with deep sadness I announce that President Boucher passed away last night of lung cancer.
>
> To celebrate her life, "The Dean Gacy Memorial" will be renamed "The President Boucher Memorial."

In addition, there will be a moment of silence today at noon in the lobby of the Bank of America Business Building.

Have A Great Day,

Dean Popkov, PhD

"The future belongs to those who prepare for it today." - Malcolm X

PS After the incident that occurred during Dean Gacy's candle-lighting ceremony, no candles (or Bunsen burners) will be allowed at this event.

Dear Faculty,

Thanks to a grant from one of our (un)recognized donors, we now have the funds to build an outdoor set that looks exactly like the theatre's burnt-out wreck(age). And yes, it's OSHA-approved.

Our modern dance production of Strindberg's (sur)realistic *A Dream Play* is a go! Tickets are on sale!

Sending Good Vibes,

Dr. Skippy
Theatre and Dance
Director of the Brechtian Institute
Vice Chair of the Worldwide Strindberg Foundation
Co-Chair of the Ionesco Center for Advanced Study

Dear Charlie,

I'm writing from a small public library in Jalacte in Belize. My husband has joined me. He wants you to know he's very sorry for shooting you.

Two days after he arrived, he was kidnapped by the People's National Liberation Front, a guerrilla army in nearby Guatemala. Would you be so kind as to start a GoFundMe campaign to help me raise his ransom?

Must go, they're watching me.

Nurse Cox

Dear Colleagues,

A twenty-five-year-old video has been uncovered in which former President Boucher is seen allowing her children to dress up as Tom Cruise and Rain Man for Halloween.

As a result, the Public Art Committee has decided that <u>all</u> orange I-beam artworks will be removed from campus immediately.

Have A Great Day,

Dean Popkov, PhD

"All kids need is a little help, a little hope and somebody who believes in them." – Magic Johnson

Dear Faculty,

Please be advised seven football team members and all of the Sweet-16 Halftime High-Stepper Dance Team have tested positive for the Omega variant. They will be in quarantine for the next three weeks.

Want to be a hero? Sign up to tutor the infected members of the football team. Sorry, all tutoring slots for the Sweet-16 High-Steppers have been taken.

Go Fighting Frogs, Go!
Nancy Herzing, RN
Campus Health Center

Campus Wide Scarlet & Brown Alert

Dear President Sternberg,

After attending a Cato Institute think tank, I have devised a plan to eliminate the Humanities. It's best to force them into failure mode slowly, so no one will notice. We can do this by:

➢ Cut state budgets, thus forcing all departments to survive on student-generated fees. STEM will bring in lots of money, humanities very little.

➢ As humanities budgets shrink, replace tenured professors with easy-to-hire-easier-to-fire adjuncts who, lacking job security, will be incapable of disobedience.

➢ Distract professors by requiring them to write impact statements justifying their existence. The key is to require multiple drafts, wasting as much of their time as possible.

➢ Once the last tenured professor quits, quietly eliminate humanities programs because they are not "meeting expectations based on cost-benefit analysis."

Congratulations on becoming president,

Dean Popkov, PhD

"Have no fear of perfection - you'll never reach it." —
Salvador Dali

Campus Wide Scarlet & Brown Alert,

Please disregard the previous email. It was sent to you in
error.

Regards,

Sally Blankenship
Office Assistant to Dean Popkov

Dear Dr. Neb,

For the upcoming fall university recruitment brochure, we
highlight the many diverse people on campus, including
differently-abled students and faculty.

I was told you have a colostomy bag. Would you be willing
to be part of the brochure?

Sincerely,

Joe Threadneedle
Chancellor of the Office of
Learning Diversity and Inclusive Planning

Campus Wide Scarlet & Brown Alert,

The administration is happy to announce that the comedian Shannon Shandell will be coming to campus. She will perform her safe comedy routine about the difference between loafers and shoes with laces.

Friday at 8pm at the AT&T Lecture Hall. Tickets are free.

Have A Really Great Day,

Margrett Applewhite, Entertainment Director

PS Faculty do not get free tickets.

Dear President Sternberg,
In the new existentialism that defines modern universities (and our pro-business modus operandi), all professors must take responsibility and suffer the consequences of their actions <u>and the actions of others</u>.

For example, the learning outcomes we require the professors to write do not consider what drugs the student is taking, whether the student has serious psychological problems, or even if the student has enough to eat. But we should still hold the professor and not the student accountable if the learning goals go unmet.

This new existentialism leaves professors isolated and powerless, yet fully responsible for everything. We must ensure professors have no one to blame but themselves.

Dean Popkov, PhD

"Some beautiful paths can't be discovered without being lost."
– Erol Ozan

Dear Faculty,

Please disregard the previous email. It was sent out on the faculty server in error.

Have A Great Day,

Dean Popkov, PhD

"All the great things are simple, and many can be expressed in a single word: freedom, justice, honor, duty, mercy, hope."
– Winston Churchill

Dear Faculty,

So that the University can achieve greater effectiveness and success, the Board of Trustees has approved a reorganization of academic units.

The following departments have been deemed not useful in generating practical skills that the world actually needs. Thus, they will be purged to make room for more vocational-directed majors:

1. Geography
2. Music
3. Dance
4. Theatre
5. Classical Languages
6. Indigenous Studies
7. African-American Studies
8. Women's Studies
9. Gender Studies

10. Philosophy

Think of this as an opportunity,

Chairperson John Sullivan
Board of Trustees
CEO Pan-American Energy Group

Dear Faculty,

From now on, we will replace the word "Tenure" with the word "Residence." And "Professor" with "Student Fulfillment Facilitator."

Sincerely,

President Sternberg

Campus Wide Red Alert,

It's reported that Dr. Jerry Loudie has taken hostages and barricaded himself in the Mental Health Solutions Center's puppy play date room.

All students are to go to their safe space, but not the puppy play date room.

This is not a drill.

Be well,

Janet Cassette
Assistant Campus Mental Health Engagement Officer
Mental Health Solutions Center

Dear Faculty,

I'm delighted to announce that, thanks to a large corporate donation by Pita Pit, we can begin construction on an even newer New A&S administration building. Construction will start next fall!

Faculty parking lots A, B, C & D will be closed next year and the year after. Please explore alternative parking opportunities.

Sincerely,

President Sternberg

Mr. Neb,

Our bill is attached.

Thank you,

May "The Force" be with you,

The Law Firm of Copeland, Osteen, and Swaggart

Dr. Neb,

I hear your contract has been terminated, but I'm happy to present you with a new opportunity. Because of your high teaching RAP ratings, we would happily consider your application to become part of the university's adjunct lecture pool.

Are you interested in this unique, promising opportunity?

Jimmy Dean Baker, Ph.D.
Part-Time Lecture Pool Coordinator

PS Please include in your application proof that a qualified mental health authority has cleared you to work with students.

PPS In addition, a full background check would be required.

Campus Wide Scarlet & Brown Alert,

I am saddened to report that creative writing professor Dr. Flaneur was struck and killed just outside town near mile marker 14.

During his life, he published three books of Haikus and was known for his attention to detail regarding roadside beautification and similes.

He will be missed.

Dr. Ember Decker
The Department of Diverse Languages and Literature
(Formerly the Department of English)

Dear Mr. Neb,

Your email account will be suspended at noon today.

Live Long and Prosper,

Aileen Warners
I.T. consultant

Dear Dr. Neb,

In her last will and testament, President Boucher left you her collection of vintage dental instruments. Any time you'd like to stop by the office, you can pick them up.

Respectfully,

Martha Somerman, Esq.

PS It is a sizeable collection. You might need a van.

With over a thousand Buffalo Wild Wings located worldwide, I decided to let my GPS be my idiot narrator until I was travel sore or my coupons ran out. The road ahead was a new calendar with not a single day crossed out and my life a maze of choices. Once again, I was at the beginning, but things would be different. For this time, as the philosopher Descartes said, I would roam the world trying to be a spectator rather than an actor in all the comedies played out there. Once you look, you may not be able to unlook, but you can lead a happy life amid madness. This becomes possible when you pitch your expectations so low that any unexpected kindness or courtesy that falls upon you is a beautiful exception.

25

It just so happens I did have talent as an actor because, after I became a five-time Jeopardy champion and used my winnings to pay off my student loans, I found regular employment at the webinar maker Achieve. My first role was playing a patient in a melodramatic mesothelioma doctor's office scene. I got the part because the director said my cough was realistic. Later, I'd star in several others. Perhaps you've seen me in the 12-part "How Your Employees Answer the Phone can Make or Break Your Company" webinar. I also played Estragon in an Off-Off Broadway production of *Waiting for Go-Dot*. A review in the Bronx News said of my performance that only an actor of "exceptional communication skills could prove human-to-human communication was not only futile, but totally impossible." I took it as a compliment.

The following December, I was at the corporate headquarters of Achieve on West 72nd in New York. Before going in, I stopped to mail a postcard to my father even though I hadn't heard from him in decades:

> To Charlie Neb Senior,
> Harley-Davidson Homecoming Rally
> General Delivery
> Milwaukee, Wisconsin
>
> Is it solipsistic in here, or is it just me?
>
> Little Charlie

I was about to drop it in the mailbox when a thunderous Easy Rider chopper with a black POW flag pulled up. The gray-haired biker had skull tattoos, corrugated skin, and a horseshoe mustache. I stared, trying to add his features to my distant memories. It was possible. It might be my father. I walked toward him and stopped. He looked up, caught my eyes, and said, "What the hell are you looking at, boy?"

It wasn't him. I apologized, turned, and walked straight into Pepper Jo, the webinar actor. She was about fifteen years older than me, thin and striking. She had long legs and woeful eyes. I introduced myself and congratulated her on her webinar Academy Award. She accepted the compliment, and we had a generous conversation about Branson, Missouri. Then I got up the nerve to ask her if she'd like to get a cup of coffee. She was delighted. We walked through the snowflakes to Strawberry Fields, where I bought us hot brew from a street cart. Then we sat on a bench under a leafless winter tree right from the set of *Waiting for Godot.* I talked about my post-academic life. She about how she was once a ballerina and how her career ended when she fell into an orchestra pit. She was genuinely touched that her story had such an effect on me. But I didn't tell her I was there.

"That night," she said as she looked up at the gentle snowfall, "I learned philosophy was born when the first human laughed at the absurdity of our situation." Then she showed me a picture of her child, her little "Bean." "He laughs all the time," she said. "I swear he was born laughing. It was as if the universe told him the funniest joke ever just before he came out."

"You're married," I said, disappointed.

"No, I was artificially inseminated."

The blank space above is intentional. You know why. I did make numerous donations. There's always a one-in-a-billion.

"You okay?" Pepper Jo said as she tried to read my dazed look.

"Sure."

We were just two people on a snowy afternoon who had no one to check on us. No one to call if we needed help. No one to tell our problems. No one to give us a second thought. But other than that, we had little in common. She liked pedigreed cats. I loved mixed-up mutts. She wanted to leave the city. I talked about my love of the city. She believed in God a little bit. I still had doubts. She was a moderate Republican who drove a gas-electric. I was a Democratic-Socialist who liked gas-guzzling BMWs. She smoked. I coughed.

After an hour, the cadence of the conversation idled, and she said she had to pick up "Bean" from the sitter. So, we walked to the underground bunker of the West 79th Street station and lingered under a massive peeling advertisement for the "Augie Omega Show–On the Fox Radio Network." As we waited for our trains, I caught Pepper Jo looking at me as if she knew me from another life. She grinned and said, "Why do you hum to yourself?"

"I'm just trying to fill the void," I said.

"Me too." Then she added, "I like your hair."

"It used to be shorter. I've let it grow."

"It's nice."

"And you have a wonderful nose."

"Thank you." She shyly laughed, not used to a compliment.

That might've been the beginning of something, but just then, my train arrived, so we said our goodbyes. But as the doors closed, the express lost power, and she and I were forced to look at each other through the gang-scratched window of the subway car. From the platform, she gave a polite smile and waved. From inside the car, I the same.

Then she reached into her bag, pulled out a book, and pretended to read. It was Carl Sagan's *The Pale Blue Dot*. I quickly reached into my knapsack, took out my copy, knocked on the window, and pressed it against the glass. She beamed, and we shared a faint trace that sometimes jumps the gap between humans. We stood where millions of others had - asked the same questions, held the same hopes. And the universe gave us the same silent treatment.

For a moment, I wished for the doors to open and the conductor to announce the train was out of service. Who knows where life would've taken us if it did? Maybe she'd learn to like dogs. And me cats. Maybe she'd give up smoking. Perhaps I'd find someone to laugh with. But, just then, the train yanked as its motors powered, and I watched a slow trucking shot of the platform as she disappeared into the crowd.

But that's not what happened - as I stood on the train looking at Pepper Jo holding her copy of *The Pale Blue Dot*, I remembered Viktor Frankl's philosophy, "Live as if you were living already for the second time and as if you had acted the first time as wrongly as you are about to act now." I grabbed the emergency cord, stopped the train, forced the doors open, and confessed to her about my gunshot wound, colostomy bag, breathing problems, and that I was there that night. I was the kid in the World War One German helmet looking down from the railing. And she smiled, laughed, and opened up about her fractured hip, broken pelvis, sprained ligaments, shattered lumbar vertebrae, damaged medulla, faltering kidneys, displaced intestines, internal bruises, ruptured spleen, and sinus headaches. And I asked her out, and she said, "Yes." And we had a great date because we went dancing. Leap right. Jump. Wave. Run. Jump. Crouch. Kick. Leap left. Afterward, we found a quiet restaurant and lingered over a dinner of organic red wine, pasta, shiitake mushrooms, and for dessert - comedy. We laughed so hard she got hiccups.

Later, in her apartment, as "Bean" slept, we lay in bed under her poster of Schopenhauer.

"Love... interrupts at every hour the most
serious occupations, and sometimes
perplexes for a while even the greatest
minds... It knows how to slip its love-notes
and ringlets even into ministerial portfolios
and philosophical manuscripts..."
                    – Schopenhauer

I shawled a wool blanket over us, and we held each other against the blue-black oblivion of the universe. And as we looked up at the confetti of saltshaker snowflakes that peppered her skylight, I told her about Pioneer 10 zooming towards the star Aldebaran and how it'd make it there in two million years–a single night.

Albert Camus asked if Sisyphus was happy. But we must ask a far more critical question: Is Sisyphus laughing?

The End

Charlie Neb's Obituary

Charlie Neb was the first person to live to the age of 200. He married 7 times and outlived 6 of his wives. He had 14 careers during his long life, including philosophy professor, sperm donor, Uber driver, webinar actor, lawyer, scientist, and astronomer. At 134 years old, he became a standup comedian. He had 8 college degrees, including 4 PhDs in philosophy, theology, and biology. He finished his Ph.D. in mathematics when he was 197.

At different points in his life, he had been a Catholic, a Muslim, a Hindu, a Buddhist, a Rastafarian, and a vegan. He became a Swami at the age of 154 and a BMW auto mechanic at 165. During his life, he was a Republican, a Democrat, a socialist, and a small 'm' Marxist.

Because of his extraordinarily long life, various celebrity newscasts often interviewed him. The questions he was asked the most were, "What is the secret to longevity?" and "What is the meaning of life?" To the first, he said, "I've lived so long because I stopped asking about the meaning of life when I was 144." To the second, he said, "The meaning of life is that it has no long-term meaning."

In his last interview just hours before his death, the last thing he said was the question, "What the hell was that about?"

About the Author

William Missouri Downs has written for the NBC sitcoms *My Two Dads, Fresh Prince of Bel-Air,* and *Amen.* Also, a playwright, he's had hundreds of productions of his plays from the Kennedy Center to the San Diego Rep and has won 2 rolling premieres from the National New Play Network. He's twice been a finalist at the Eugene O'Neill. His plays have entertained audiences in Spain, Canada, South Africa, Russia, Singapore, Switzerland, Austria, Israel, India, UAE, Australia, South Korea, and the USA. He's published over a dozen plays with Concord, Playscripts, Heuer, TRW, and Next Stage Press. In addition, he's written several popular textbooks, including *The Art of Theatre, Screenplay Writing The Picture,* and *Naked Playwriting.*

Note from William Missouri Downs

Word-of-mouth is crucial for any author to succeed. If you enjoyed *Five Minutes from Chaos*, please leave a review online—anywhere you are able. Even if it's just a sentence or two. It would make all the difference and would be very much appreciated.

Thanks!
William Missouri Downs

We hope you enjoyed reading this title from:

www.blackrosewriting.com

Subscribe to our mailing list – *The Rosevine* – and receive **FREE** books, daily deals, and stay current with news about upcoming releases and our hottest authors.
Scan the QR code below to sign up.

Already a subscriber? Please accept a sincere thank you for being a fan of Black Rose Writing authors.

View other Black Rose Writing titles at www.blackrosewriting.com/books and use promo code **PRINT** to receive a **20% discount** when purchasing.